Someone with powerful halogen headlights had pulled out of one of the development's access roads and zoomed right up to my back bumper.

Idiot, I thought. At the stop sign for the state road, I expected the cowboy behind me to pull out around my car, but the lights remained planted blindingly in my mirrors. I wheeled onto the state road and hit the limit. The lights never wavered, and when the oncoming lane was clear and I slowed down to let Mr. Impatient pass, it turned out that he was content to wait.

I made a quick right without signaling. The squeal of his brakes rushed in with the night air, and I was again dazzled by reflected headlights. I had no doubt that I was being followed, probably with felonious intent.

★

Previously published Worldwide Mystery titles by
JANICE LAW

BACKFIRE
A SAFE PLACE TO DIE
TIME LAPSE

JANICE LAW

CROSS-CHECK

WORLDWIDE.

TORONTO • NEW YORK • LONDON
AMSTERDAM • PARIS • SYDNEY • HAMBURG
STOCKHOLM • ATHENS • TOKYO • MILAN
MADRID • WARSAW • BUDAPEST • AUCKLAND

CROSS-CHECK

A Worldwide Mystery/November 1998

First published by St. Martin's Press, Incorporated.

ISBN 0-373-26291-4

Printed in U.S.A.

For Jerry, with love and thanks

ONE

"NOW SOME CRUNCHES," the smooth-voiced physio said. She'd already explained the benefits of this maneuver: we were strengthening my abdominals in order to take some of the strain off my back. That's what we were doing in theory. In practice, she was standing around with her clipboard looking like an ad for a health salon, while I was flat on the blue exercise mat subjecting my anatomy to a series of peculiar and painful maneuvers.

Every time I lifted my shoulders, I caught glimpses of my fellow martyrs: the arthritis and carpal tunnel syndromes squeezing rubber balls and bravely making small talk with the trainers; less fortunate back cases sprawled over immense rubber balls, trying to get their balance straightened out; the arm and shoulder sufferers strung up on pulleys and weights like so many medieval saints, and, out of sight but audible in the rumble of gears and flywheels, the fools of sports toiling to rebuild their shattered knees with the exercise bicycles and treadmills.

There was no denying that I was in bad company, and I was very conscious of the unfairness of it all. Despite having assiduously avoided unnecessary exercise, I'd been brought to the same pass as these fanatical pursuers of health and fitness.

"You're not doing any heavy lifting, are you?" The physio was all sweetness and light, because, for once, I was on time and on task.

"Not so much as a ream of paper," I said. In truth,

anything much heavier had been genuine pain since the
day I unwisely detained a fellow several decades my
junior. He was set on leaving an office where Executive
Security had been investigating the theft of computer
parts. We broke the case and recovered a small fortune
in Pentium chips, but I'd torn a muscle in the process,
and, as my physio repeated ad nauseam, I had to improve my general level of fitness to promote healing.

That's why I was lying in a public place, waving my
legs in the air, performing the so-called dead bug. I could
have pointed out that *dead* bugs don't wave their legs
and that *dying* bugs, which is what I felt like, were apt
to be less vigorous than my cheerful tormentor required.

"Much better," she said, checking her watch. "Much
better. Another week or so and you'll be outa here."

The promised land! I breathed in the pervasive odor
of sweat, liniment, and chlorine with something ap-
proaching good cheer.

"Of course, maintenance is important."

You can see how I've come up in the world, like a
car or some other important, temperamental, and expensive piece of equipment, I now need to be "maintained." It appeared, in fact, that a repertory of dreary
exercises was to be my permanent fate.

I complained loudly and pretty steadily about this, but
neither my husband, Harry, nor my staff at Executive
Security was sympathetic. Harry suggested I start leaving the legwork to Mike Garrett, our other senior investigator. When I wasn't enthusiastic about that idea, he
bought me a nifty exercise mat and a terrifying contrap-
tion that mimics cross-country skiing minus the plea-
sures of either skiing or the country. The office staff
presented me with an extra-large-size podium so that I
could work standing up. With my notebook computer

glowing on top, the whole effect was Star Trek bridge, but comfortable.

I conceded "comfortable," especially whenever I had to work at one of the other screens, like Baby's, where, fresh from the physical therapist's, I watched a waterfall of names and figures. The blue and green tide of companies and land developments formed an interlocking corporate entity as intricate as a living organism. On the screen, Wilborne Futurity looked like orderly runnels of wealth: a testimony to human ingenuity and energy. Offscreen, those same figures translated into delayed retirements, lost tuitions, foreclosed mortgages; a legacy of withered hopes and abandoned dreams.

Baby turned, a quizzical look on her sharp, pretty face. I set the file down on her desk, took another look at the screen, and said, "He's a crook."

"Probably," she agreed. Baby, aka June Quigley, vice president and second-in-command, takes an almost aesthetic pleasure in fraud. Laying out the bones and interconnections of a company absolutely makes her day, particularly when she can bring hidden connections to light.

"Beautiful," I said, tapping one particularly suggestive set of figures.

She smiled and brushed a lock of hair out of her eyes. Today's coiffeur was a particularly fetching auburn shade. Success has suited Baby very nicely. She's ditched the gum and the tight skirts and grown up into power suits and expensive hairdos for which her clear, analytical mind is the best possible fashion accessory.

I put a bundle of letters forwarded from a local NEA branch on her desk. They were all from elderly teachers who had lost their savings in a Wilborne Futurity retirement scheme. "I think this is our best shot at him," I said.

"He's up to his eyes," Baby said, "but proving fraud will be a bitch. He's got lawyers to die for, too."

"I spoke to Boldoni this morning. The teachers association has given us the go-ahead. They want this guy, and they're willing to pay to nail him."

"In that case," said Baby, patting the computer, "we'll get him sooner or later." She settled herself into her console chair and began tapping away with the enthusiasm of a hound on the scent. Baby's thoroughly modern; monitors don't make her eyes burn, and sitting in her ergonomically correct chair doesn't set her back aching. While admitting the utility of the computer, I'm less enthusiastic, and after another hour of working over her shoulder, sorting through files and databases, my well-maintained back was starting to protest. I wasn't at all sorry when Skipper looked in and said, "Anna, can I see you for a minute?"

He sounded nervous and a little unsure of himself— an almost unheard-of mood. Skipper came to us from the Eagles, after he blew out his left knee in a late-season game. Self-assurance is a top quarterback's stock-in-trade, and Skipper converted his to an immediate success with Executive Security. He has outstanding administrative ability, and his knack for organizing big events and placating big names has expanded our business, especially within the black community.

Rappers and rockers and all the princes and princesses of athletics love Skipper, who's brought in enough low-risk, high-profit business to start out for himself several times over. To be perfectly honest, Skipper and Baby together could run a very tight and profitable ship— tighter and more profitable than my version of Executive

Security will ever be—and recently I've found myself
letting the two of them take on more and more responsibility. In some ways, I'm becoming a casualty of my—
and their—success. The business rolls along, generating
nice incomes for all concerned; I'm able to take time off
when Harry does a lecture somewhere or when he has a
show of his prints out of town. Everything is solid and
profitable and well organized—and just a little bit boring.

"Problem," said Skipper as I followed him into his
office. Skipper alternates sportspeak with clipped busi-
nesseze.

"Not more decorating decisions?" I asked. The last
time Skipper needed my advice was when he was doing
up his office in the Eagles' green and silver color
scheme. The results cost a small fortune but were genuinely impressive: a big green marble slab for a desk
and a subtle white-and-silver patterned rug. To my less
demanding eye, the office was perfect already.

"No, no," he said, looking harried.

When do quarterbacks ever look harried? Perhaps his
wife was pregnant—Melinda had had a very difficult
delivery last time....

"I've gotten myself in a bind," he said, closing the
door. "You know Jurgen Parkes—T-Rex?"

"Pardon?"

"The hockey player. Top centerman the last two
years. Six feet three—looks like a boxcar on skates. Everybody's all-everything."

"Oh, right," I said, as dim memories of Hockey Night
in Canada and MSG Cable Sports flickered across the
neurons. My husband has a yearly love affair with
hockey that begins with him hunched over the set for
weeks at a time and usually ends around April with a

set of woodcuts or lithographs. "Wasn't he in some sort of trouble? He broke someone's jaw, didn't he? Or was it someone's leg?"

"The jaw incident was last year—third game of the playoffs. The leg was two years ago, a check into the boards up in Quebec."

"A busy man," I said. "So what's he up to this year?"

"Murder one," Skipper said. "Unindicted as of yet, but a serious suspect."

"That Orlando player," I said, as my memory shifted into gear.

"Correct. The Showmen's winger, Alf Rene. He was found dead right at the end of last season."

"There was no arrest, was there?"

"No, and that's the trouble. Not enough evidence and no real proof, but the business is still hanging over Parkes. He and Rene were well-known enemies."

"Also teammates, right?"

"From what I've heard that didn't keep them from having fistfights in the locker room. Anyway, Anna, I'm out schmoozing the other day at USAir Arena for that Russian exhibition game, when Sammy Allert corners me. Sammy's a sports agent, a class act in a slimeball profession, and one of the reasons I retired a rich man. We're over checking out the buffet, when he says, 'Skipper, you gotta help me.' This guy's looked out for me for a dozen years. What could I say?"

"He's Jurgen Parkes's agent," I guessed.

"Correct. And he remembers I'm in the security business now, cause Executive Security's doing the gig, and I'm walking around with a walkie-talkie."

I've seen Skipper operate. No one's ever in doubt about who's in charge.

"Sammy's desperate. He's getting endorsements canceled right and left. Worse yet, contracts are coming up soon. The owners are set to play hardball, but Sammy can't move Parkes to save his goddamn ass."

I shrugged. "What does he want?"

"Effort! Cooperation! A private investigation to clear the matter up, that's what he wants. Sammy's fed up."

"So what's Parkes doing?"

"Nothing. Stonewalling everything. The guy's got the hide of an armadillo. He doesn't seem to care."

"Maybe he's guilty. Maybe he figures living with canceled endorsements is better than a long stretch in the penitentiary."

"Maybe, but he denies it, and Sammy believes him. Sammy thinks that Parkes has just got his back up at law enforcement. So what Sammy wants is to get his own investigation going."

"Without Parkes's consent?" I wasn't sure I wanted a boxcar on skates going berserk in my office.

"No, there's the thing. After the game, we do a meeting with T-Rex himself. We hit it off; I'm absolutely in the zone. Fellow athlete—turns out he's a big football fan, turns out we've played some of the same celebrity golf tournaments. He plays at plus six. I'm a plus five," Skipper added with purely unconscious vanity. "We're talking golf games, everybody mellow, and Sammy says, 'Skipper's your man. He understands your situation, let him take the case and get things squared away for you.' You don't know how persuasive Sammy can be."

I thought I saw what was coming next.

"We've had a few beers, see, and Sammy's at the top of his game. He's practically in tears, and T-Rex says, 'Okay' and we set up an appointment."

"Ah-ha," I said. Revenge is sweet. I've been putting

up with Skipper's jokes about the benefits of exercise and the joys of physical fitness ever since I wrecked my back.

"It's not funny," Skipper said, drawing himself up. At six feet five, this is really unnecessary, but I saw his point. Skipper's great gifts come with their limitations: he hasn't the patience for detection, and he's strictly a center stage personality. That's all very fine for football and administration, but it's a real handicap in investigation, where cunning anonymity wins hands down every time.

"I don't see the problem," I said and I really didn't, because Skipper is a salesman par excellence. "Executive Security is a full-service operation. You assure him you'll coordinate every phase of the investigation. Show him our file system, our top-of-the-line computers, our well-trained surveillance teams, do the major sales act, then turn the legwork over to the specialists." Do, in short, what you normally do around here and quit worrying.

Skipper shook his handsome, dark head and looked as mournful as if the Eagles had just dropped a playoff game. "You wait," he said.

I didn't have to wait long. Sammy Allert and Jurgen Parkes arrived just after two p.m. that same day. Or rather, I should say, Sammy Allert arrived looking anxious, and a few minutes later the reasons for his anxiety were made abundantly clear when we heard Parkes hit the outer office. Allert was standing talking to Skipper and me; he heard his client and rolled his eyes expressively. Allert was maybe five feet six, a neat, compact, good-looking man with a trim beard and quick dark eyes. Soft-spoken, almost courtly, and perfectly dressed, he was the least likely companion imaginable for the force of nature that blew in the door a few seconds later.

I could see right away where he'd gotten his nickname: Jurgen Parkes was a big, blocky guy with a bold, square jaw and little light eyes. The lower part of his face was badly pitted and scarred and he had a day or so's growth of rough black beard, a match for his hair, which was ruthlessly barbered into a stiff black helmet. The rest of his attire was disheveled. He had stains on his expensive jacket, the collar of his shirt was torn and dirty, and what had been a handsome silk tie hung in a lumpy knot halfway down his chest. His slacks were dirty at the knees, underlining what his flushed face, bloodshot eyes, and pervasive odor of alcohol had already told us: Jurgen Parkes was pretty well drunk.

"T,T," Sammy Allert said soothingly, the way you'd speak to a large and aggressive dog.

"Cut that T-Rex shit, Sammy. You think Gretzky'd get named after some fucking dinosaur? Who's the league leading scorer? Two, count 'em, two lousy teams in a row and I'm near the top of the stats. Even playing in Micky Mouse Land, I'm still leading the league. I don't need this shit!"

Allert kept with the soothing noises anyway, and Skipper made himself tall and tried to bring Parkes to reason. It was not a successful effort, but I kept my mouth shut until Parkes loudly demanded who the old broad was. I told him the "old broad" owned the company and that I'd hit him for trespassing if he didn't leave our offices. Although this didn't improve the atmosphere, it did mobilize Allert to ease his client homeward. Skipper led the way, opening each door in sequence and keeping his own vast and muscular bulk between Parkes and any movables and breakables. I heard the outer door slam, followed by Allert's hasty apologies and Skipper's regrets.

"He's a piece of work," I said when Skipper returned.

"I should have known better," he said, "but Sammy's an old friend."

He shook his head and looked so unhappy that I patted him on the shoulder; quarterbacks feel responsible for the whole team. "Don't worry about it. You didn't know Parkes is a drunk."

"That's just it—he isn't. Not as a regular thing. Sammy says it's his kid again. Richie, the oldest."

I was puzzled, and Skipper said, "Cancer of some sort. Leukemia, bone cancer, I can't remember right now. Anyway, Sammy says Richie's had to go back into the hospital. T-Rex always takes that badly."

That seemed so reasonable to me that in the rush of late summer business I soon forgot about Mr. Jurgen "T-Rex" Parkes, his diminutive guardian, and our inauspicious meeting. But a few days afterward, when I was working late putting a report to bed, the phone rang. It was Jurgen Parkes, brisk, serious, and at least formally apologetic. "I gotta talk to you right away," he said.

Oh, yeah? I thought. Then I remembered what Skipper had told me about Parkes's son, and said, "My secretary's gone for the day. Call tomorrow morning and she'll make an appointment for you."

"We got an exhibition game in New York tomorrow. I'm only in D.C. till nine tonight."

I didn't reply right away. I was thinking I needed this client like I needed a gastric ulcer. "Well, Mr. Parkes," I began, thoroughly intending to put him off. Then I ran my eyes over the stacks of files and memos, the still winking lights of my computer: Baby could handle all that. And Skipper could organize those security checks and neither one would have an aching back from sitting at the console to do it.

On the other hand, I wasn't sure either one of them could manage T-Rex Parkes and his possibly indictable problem. "Where are you now?" I asked.

When he said that he was at a small steakhouse and lounge just a block away, I agreed to meet him and hung up.

TWO

IT STARTED to rain as I locked the main door, and the humid drizzle had turned to a real downpour by the time I reached the restaurant, a little faux English pub with dark paneling, menu slates, and uncomfortable Windsor chairs. Parkes was sitting near the window with a cup of coffee and the remains of a meal. He stood up when I approached and nodded without speaking. He looked as sober as a man can be, and semidrowned as I was, I regretted not telling him to come over to the office.

"Cup of coffee?" he asked.

"Fine." I hung my sodden jacket over the back of the chair to drip. A young waitress with big hair and a pretty drawl brought the coffeepot, poured me a cup, and refilled Parkes's. When she was gone, he tolerated the silence for a while before he said, "Sorry about the other day. I wasn't myself."

I refrained from asking who the hell he was then.

"Tell Skipper, would you? He's a good guy. A helluva quarterback, too."

"Sure," I said. "We all have bad days."

"Yeah," he said. "And some are worse than others. Bone marrow test days are about the worst. Richie—he's my oldest—he's got leukemia and he had to go in again for the tests this week."

"Oh, I'm sorry," I said. "How old is Richie?"

"Five. Christ, I don't know how he stands it," Parkes said, bringing one of his massive hands down on the table so sharply that the cups jumped and the saucers rattled. "I'm supposed to be tough. You know hockey?"

"Just a little."

"Tough's how I made my reputation, taking no crap, digging the puck outa the corners, checking all over the ice. Let me tell you, tough on the ice is nothing. Tough is when you're five years old, and they come after you with a hypodermic big as a knitting needle, and you're still trying not to cry." He ran one hand over his eyes in anguish and bit his lip. "I got the bravest kid in the world," he said after a minute, "and it just about kills me."

I'd been prepared for a business discussion with a pain in the ass. Instead, I was deep in the uncertain terrain of family sorrows. "How is your son doing?"

"We have hope," he said, getting hold of himself. "Don't get me wrong. Childhood leukemia can be cured. It's just that the first few years are hardest. We never know when Richie's going to relapse, when he's going into remission. Road trips—I'm getting paranoid about road trips, cause it seems he always gets sick when I'm on the road. Trish is wonderful, handles anything, but when Richie's going into the hospital, I just gotta be there. No matter what."

"I can understand that." And I did. Since Harry's heart attack a few years ago, I understand a lot more about illness and surviving.

"He expects me," Parkes added with a touch of fatherly pride. "He expects me to be with him. If it's going to be something real bad, I gotta bring my stick or my helmet or one of my gloves. He's the only kid on the ward who carries a hockey glove instead of a stuffed toy on bad days." He reached into his pocket for his wallet and pulled out a snap. A slight blond child with big eyes and thinning hair clutched a huge blue-and-green padded glove. His fingers were delicate and even in the photo, his skin looked translucent, and there was a troubling darkness underneath his eyes.

"A fine looking little boy," I said. Actually, the child looked adorable but sickly.

Parkes gave a weak smile and nodded his head. He looked at the snap for a few seconds, then returned it to his wallet. "So, that's Wednesday," he said brusquely. "Aftermath of a real bad day that I had trouble handling." I noticed that the eyes that had been bloodshot were now a clear, bright green.

"I'll explain to Skipper," I said. "He has children himself. But your legal problem? Are we discussing that or is this a purely friendly visit?"

Parkes moved his massive shoulders. Talking about his son had made him seem reflective, almost gentle. Now that he was moving on to other business, a shift in gears revealed the latent energy he carried like a psychic force field. "What I got now is a public relations problem that might get to be a legal problem," he said. "Just might." Another pause.

"You want to fill me in?" I asked.

He hesitated again before making up his mind. "Here's the story," he said. "I get traded to the Showmen two years ago when the league put a team in Orlando. Megadeal. Hartford gets some promising young players; the Showmen get their marquee attraction. The Weasel's in the package, which I don't particularly like but—"

"The Weasel?"

"The late Alf Rene, a prime son of a bitch, known to one and all as the Weasel, the dirtiest stickman ever."

"You'd been teammates for a while, then?" I found it interesting that they had moved together.

"Sure. You don't choose your teammates, you know."

"Yes, I realize that."

"My lucky day: they not only ship me to the Sunbelt, they send the Weasel with me. So, okay. I'm getting a million five a year, I can live with the Weasel. Then he gets himself killed and bingo, I'm suspect number one."

"Why is that exactly?"

"I'd punched him out in the locker room last year. That was one thing."

"What was the other thing?"

"That's what makes no sense. Alf and me we're not speaking, right? We haven't spoken since the fistfight. He's my right winger, and I haven't said anything more to him for a year than 'heads up' or 'gimme the puck.' You can ask anyone. So this afternoon when we're on our home ice he calls me up. Gotta talk to me. Wants to meet me—get this—outa town."

"Did he give any reason?"

"No, just that it was real important. And he didn't want to talk on the phone."

"And you believed him?"

Parkes paused a minute. "Yes, I did."

"Did you mention this meeting to anyone?"

"Sure. Trish was home when he called. I told her I wouldn't be back for dinner. Trish knew. And some of the guys on the team knew, cause they were getting up a poker game and they called right after Alf, and I says, 'I got a date with the Weasel.' It was no secret." Parkes's expression was blandly innocent.

"Where did you meet him?"

"There's this barbecue joint in Altamonte Springs. He

says to meet him there. Ribs are the only thing Alf and me agree on.''

''What sort of place is it?''

''Suburban. A little upscale mall with a couple restaurants, some shops.''

''Parking? Well lit?''

''Sure. Landscaped, neat, well kept. Nothing out of the ordinary.''

''I just like to get the picture,'' I said. ''Then what?''

''I get there—maybe 7:45 or so. I'm supposed to meet him around 7:30 but I don't bust my ass for Alf. Besides it's slow going. It came up a real storm. What they call a 'frog-strangler' down there. I'm driving through this shit—you'd think the whole interstate'd been turned into a car wash—anyway, I don't hang around in the monsoon, I go right in. Alf's not there, though he's reserved a table. He's already late, so I think, screw him, and I order. He never shows up. That's all there was to it.''

On the surface, it wasn't much of a story, and it hardly seemed enough to implicate a man in murder—or to cost him so much hesitation about revealing it. ''And where was he? Where did they find him?''

''I told you it was a little mall, right? There's this big plastic and steel plaything like a jungle gym, but closed in. They find him there the next morning when the rain lets up. Somebody'd walloped him in the back of the head and stuck him inside.''

''A bit of bad luck,'' I said, though I wondered just how much Parkes was keeping to himself. ''What about time of death? What did they estimate?''

''Between seven and eight, nearest they could tell. The rain kept down the heat that night.''

''And that's all? There's no physical evidence against

you? Nothing but the fact that he called you and set up the appointment?''

''Naw.''

''And there's proof he called you? I mean, you didn't call him instead?''

''Trish was right in the kitchen when he called. There's some phone company records, too. My lawyer checked.''

''And you were in the restaurant from quarter of eight or so?''

He nodded.

''What time did you leave home?''

''Seven-fifteen. It should have been a fifteen, twenty-minute drive but for the rain.''

''Which could also be confirmed. Weather records and so on.''

''Sure.''

''I can't imagine this will amount to anything more than awkwardness unless you haven't told me everything.''

''The only thing is, I hated the son of a bitch and everyone knew it. Tell you the truth, soon as I heard about it, my heart lifted. That's how I felt about Alf.''

There was a peculiar expression on his square, rather brutal face, a mix of relief and anger—and maybe regret. It was the latter that puzzled me. ''Why?'' I asked.

''Why what?''

I wondered if he was being deliberately obtuse. ''Why did you hate Alf Rene?''

''We just didn't get along,'' he said. His eyes narrowed into green slivers of glass: Alf was obviously still a touchy subject.

''Not 'getting along' is one thing. Outright hatred is something else. There must have been some reason.''

"Look," said Parkes, "you're not trying to prove I did it. You're trying to show how come I couldn't have. What was between Alf and me is irrelevant."

"You'd be surprised what can be relevant to a murder case. Maybe you had good reason to dislike Alf. Maybe someone else had the same sort of reason. There are lots of possibilities."

"I'm not interested in possibilities," he said. He leaned across the table, his eyes angry under the massive brow ridge. He was used to getting his own way, to VIP treatment, to being a star. "All I want is for you to get the media off my tail and clear my name. I'm sick of this suspect crap."

"Sure you are," I said. "But you don't want to talk about the case, and you don't want to give me any background. Since you're not indicted—what's the big deal?"

He surprised me by laughing and leaning back in his chair. "Skipper said you gave good advice."

"Which clients rarely take. For what it's worth, I'd say, sit tight. Things will blow over."

"You don't sound very eager for business." There was an edge to his voice: You don't have to look like a ballerina to be a prima donna. Parkes clearly didn't want anyone poking in his business; at the same time, the thought that I might not be interested, that I wasn't flattered to be a better sort of gofer, was somehow offensive.

"I'm never eager for difficult clients. Difficult cases can be a challenge; difficult clients are just acid indigestion."

"That's me," he said cheerfully. "A difficult client. But if it was up to me, I'd take your advice. I'd say screw the whole thing."

"What's the trouble? Is it your agent? Your endorsements?"

"Shit—endorsements just make work for Sammy and the tax collector. I can live without endorsements. It's not the money."

"So what's your problem?"

"You got any kids?" Parkes asked.

I shook my head.

"In some ways that's terrible. In some other ways that's lucky. My kid, Richie. I call him last night. First thing he says to me is, 'Did you see Mr. Norris?' Trish brings them up right, they're all polite kids. 'Did you see Mr. Norris?' He's seen old clips of Skipper on TV— thinks he walks on water, thinks he can clear his dad. You get the picture?"

I did. This tough, vain, difficult man would do anything for his son.

"Kids got expectations for you. You find yourself trying to live up to them. Richie—Richie can't imagine how anyone could suspect me." Parkes's strong jaw twitched into a wry little smile. "At the same time, it worries him. Jesus Christ, now he's worried something might happen to him before I'm cleared. He says he's gotta see me cleared. I can't have him worried. He needs all his strength, every bit. He's gotta focus," Parkes said, slipping unconsciously into the jargon of his profession and tapping his fingers forcefully on the table for emphasis. "He's gotta focus all his intensity on the disease. He's just got to." Parkes looked desperately unhappy.

"There are risks," I said. "You have to understand that."

"Listen," he said. "I need your help. Skipper told me you were the best. I gotta do this for Richie."

"And I'm willing to help you, but as I'm trying to

tell you, there are problems. There's nothing much against you, but your alibi is weak—I'm sure you see that. We can run down the people who were in the restaurant, maybe confirm the time you were there, but it's still not enough if Alf Rene was killed right outside.''

"Yeah," Parkes said. "But they got to prove I did it."

"That's right; that's why you can do nothing and hope they don't come up with any real evidence. If you want to go forward with this, there's only one way to proceed. That's to find out who killed Alf Rene. If it was you, please don't hire me.''

Parkes shook his head. "You don't know me," he said. "I'd have killed that little bastard with pleasure. But not that way.''

I was glad I wasn't his lawyer. "No?" I said.

"Naw, the Weasel was hit from behind. Blindsiding a guy's not my style. Especially with Alf. I'd have made damn sure he saw what was coming to him. You can bet on it.''

"It looks like I'm going to have to," I said.

"You'll take the case? Good." He leaned back in his chair and crossed his thick, muscular legs. "You know," he said, "I thought I could maybe go through the motions. Have someone ask a few questions, explain I'd made the effort. That's why I talked to Skipper that day. Skipper's a smart guy but not a detective—am I right?''

"Skipper's a genius administrator and salesman," I said.

"Yeah. Maybe he could've sold my kid on the idea. That would have been okay if Richie was well. But now... Do you see how it is?''

I did. This was magic. A tough guy taking a risk; an offering to the gods, a bribe to have them spare his son.

I saw that right away, and I'd have been a damn sight better off if I'd kept it in mind right from the start. Instead, standard operating procedures: I went over the ground rules, explained my fees, my general approach.

Parkes fiddled with his coffee cup indifferently. Now that things were settled, he was restless, bored with the topic, impatient to be off—or uncomfortable with the whole matter.

"Sure," he said when I finished. "Take care of it. Sammy handles my business." He produced a card. "Just send all the bills to him." When he gave a sly smile, I saw that he was not totally without a sense of humor. "Sammy's the one who's all worried about the endorsements."

THREE

"I DON'T UNDERSTAND this," I said. I was sitting in Skipper's plushy office with a sheaf of faxes and media guides, all obtained on short notice via his sports, journalism, and PR contacts. Another heap of hockey stats and press releases lay piled in my own office, and Martha, my secretary, was still sorting out the newspaper clips. Much to Skipper's distress, even his own usually immaculate desk was piled with papers and books.

He put on the pair of little gold-rimmed glasses he uses to rest his contacts and peered over my shoulder.

"Plus-minus figures," he said. "That's scoring while you're on the ice. Good plus figures means your team scores a lot when you're at work. High minus figures means you're getting scored on."

"It must depend a bit on who you play with, though? Which line?"

"Sure thing. Now Rene, here, his figures were crap until he was put on Parkes's line. As long as Parkes was setting him up, he'd get a goal occasionally, and whenever Parkes is on the ice, there's a chance the team'll score."

Player assessment was more complicated than I'd imagined. The only thing I was clear on about Rene was that he was supposedly a dirty player. "So what does that make Rene?" I asked.

"A journeyman player," Skipper said.

"Which means exactly?"

"Mediocre. Employable but not valuable. If he's

lucky he plays the big league for a few years. If he's not, back to Binghamton, St. Catharines, or Kalamazoo."

I went to the desk and flipped through a handful of records. "Alf Rene was lucky, then. He'd been up in the NHL since 1988, minus a stint in Binghamton while he was still owned by the Hartford club."

"He had some good years before he hurt his knee," said Skipper, who'd been studying the Showmen's latest media guide. "Durability's an asset." He automatically smoothed his immaculate gray flannels over his own much mended knee.

"He didn't seem to score very often," I said. "Isn't that what wingers are supposed to do?"

Skipper nodded.

"And what about his penalty minutes? Are these out of sight or not?"

"He was well acquainted with the sin bin."

"Is that really what they call it?"

"It's a somewhat evangelical league," Skipper said dryly.

"Good old Canadian Calvinists. So was he worth keeping? That's what I want to know. What do clubs pay a player like our Alf, anyway?"

Skipper consulted his notebook. "As of this year, the minimum under the union contract is $180,000. When Rene started, it was maybe $75,000 or so. Hockey's the lowest paid of the professional sports," he added with a touch of complacency. "They don't get the big TV money."

"Still, a nice piece of change for sitting in the penalty box." I was beginning to feel that my youth had been seriously misspent away from rinks and ice.

"It's harder than you might think to staff professional

teams. Lots of guys look good, are good players, skate well and all that, but they aren't able to compete with the top pros.''

''So Alf was the best of a poor lot.''

Skipper shrugged his shoulders. His glasses gave him a slightly professorial air. ''What puzzles me,'' he said after a minute, ''is why he was on Parkes's line all that time.''

''Stick him with a strong player to minimize the damage?''

''No, no, it doesn't work that way,'' Skipper said, shaking his head. My ignorance of sports is a matter of constant surprise and distress to Skipper. ''Your first line in hockey is always your best line, and your strongest players should be on it.''

''No exceptions?''

''Well, there are specialists. Like Dave Semenko. Big as a house and a punch like Muhammed Ali. The Oilers played him for years on Gretzky's line just to protect the great man.''

I rooted around on the desk for a photo of the late Alf Rene. He looked like an angel with an attitude: beautiful, even features; large, expressive eyes; a straight brow; dark hair curling to his shoulders—and a wise guy smirk. He wasn't at all what I'd expected from someone known as ''the Weasel.'' Alf Rene could have made his living as a male model, and in spite of a reputation as a troublemaker, helmets, mouth guards, and face shields had kept him unmarked by his profession.

''Five ten, one hundred and seventy-five pounds,'' I read. ''No pygmy but not nearly as big as Parkes.''

''And that's in skates and pads,'' Skipper added.

''Not a candidate for the protection racket, then. But there must have been something; he was on Parkes's line in Hartford; he was part of the deal with the Showmen, and he wound up as one of Parkes's regular wingers in Orlando.''

"Maybe that's the reason Parkes couldn't stand him," Skipper suggested. "All those great passes gone for nothing."

"Somehow I think it's more than that—with all due apologies for professional pride. What else do we know about the two of them?"

"Both from remotest Quebec. Both married."

"I want to find out where Alf's wife is now. She might be a good source. Let's get an address and a phone number. His agent, too. He must have had an agent. Get Parkes's home phone as well if you can. He insists Alf called him that night, not the other way around, but I'd still like to hear what his wife has to say. She might know the reason for the big feud, too."

"Anything else?" Skipper asked when he finished making his notes. He gave the debris on his desk a significant look. Skipper's a place for everything and everything in its place man, a demon for time clocks and perfect execution; creative clutter's a totally foreign concept.

"Not for now, unless you can think of anything else. Those police reports should be faxed up today from Orlando. Parkes's lawyer is sending us everything he has."

"I'll give him a couple hours, then call," Skipper said, glancing at his watch.

"Right. I'll tell Martha to box up the rest of this stuff. You've been a great help, Skipper. I almost feel ready to talk hockey with Sammy Allert."

Skipper looked thoughtful. "Sports is the same as any other business," he said. "Personalities and politics."

SAMUEL HARLEIGH ALLERT, sports agent extraordinaire, had his office in an anonymous building with a sleek marble foyer downstairs to impress the casual trade and plain painted wallboard upstairs where the real work was done. The agent's rooms were distinguished from the neighboring businessmen's, lawyers', and dentists' suites only by the large autographed photos of current and previous clients that decorated the entrance. The centerpiece was a particularly dramatic one of Skipper, poised for a pass against a blur of rushing linemen.

I'd never seen him play, and I was thinking how rather grand Skipper looked suited up for action, when Allert came out of his office.

"How nice to see you again," he said, shaking my hand warmly. I realized that I hadn't seen him at his best the other day. In happier circumstances, his charm of personality was immediately evident.

"I was admiring your collection. I imagine hopeful athletes are pretty impressed."

"Oh, yes, indeed. My professional trophies. Course there are not many like Skipper," he said, nodding toward the photo with real affection. "He's a once in a lifetime client."

"Really? I know he was a fine quarterback, but..."

"I represent lots of fine players," Allert said, "even star players, but not so many fine people or real gentlemen like Skipper."

"I'd agree with that," I said. "We're lucky to have him at Executive Security."

"He came a little too early," Allert said with a touch of regret. "If he was active now, the sky's the limit: endorsements, product lines—he could have been as big as Jordan."

"The NFL has been popular for years, though."

"But not black quarterbacks. Today, they're nothing surprising, but Skipper was one of the first to really make it at the position. Before that, there was the feeling only a white man could run a team. There was real reluctance, believe me. Even Skipper met some resistance, and you know the authority he projects."

"I thought football and playing on a major league team probably developed that."

"Oh, increased it definitely, but first time he walked in—he was only twenty-one. His college career was over and since his school didn't play a top schedule, most of the big agents hadn't even called him. I took one look and I saw right away he had 'it'—whatever you want to call 'it'—charisma, confidence, the ability to command. I figured if this kid has any arm at all, he'll make a fortune."

"He says you're part of the reason he did."

"I helped him keep it, that's all. It was a pleasure and a privilege." He nodded again at the photo, as if reluctant to move on to the real subject of our meeting, then gestured toward the inner office, a comfortable room with king-size leather chairs for king-size athletic bottoms and shelves lined with books and folders. "But you're here because of T-Rex. Am I right?"

"He says you handle his business affairs. He'd prefer I deal with you on all aspects of the investigation—including the financial ones."

Allert gave a short laugh. "I'll bet he'd prefer. He didn't want this at all—as you probably figured out the other day."

"Why not? He claims to be innocent, and Skipper says you believe him. Do you really, by the way?"

"Yes, I do," Allert said without hesitation. "I'll tell

you why. Jurgen Parkes's a kind of in-your-face personality, wouldn't you agree?''

"That's certainly how he struck me—though with lots
going on underneath.''

"You saw that, did you?'' Allert gave me a sharp,
interested glance. "He's by no means stupid and not as
ignorant as he sometimes likes to pretend, either. He's
a complicated man. But the surface is all macho arro-
gance and aggression—pure trouble.''

I wondered if some of that aggression was essential
to Parkes's profession. Allert agreed with a qualification.

"T-Rex likes to fight,'' he said. "I mean genuinely
enjoys a brawl.'' Allert raised his eyebrows as if his
imagination were severely taxed. "The redeeming thing
is, he fights fair and he's no bully. He'll throw his weight
around on the ice—that's part of his job, but he rarely
starts a fight and he's not the kind who goes after smaller
players. What he really likes is a knockdown-dragout
fight with someone his own size. That always seems to
perk him up and put him in a good mood.''

"There's no accounting for tastes,'' I observed.

"Indeed, no. When he was younger, he had a temper,
but now he's a real pro on the ice. He does his job and
gets on with it and confines fights to after hours.''

That was interesting. "A violent personality.''

"No, not really violent,'' Allert said carefully,
"though he's a bit of a handful when he's drinking. I
can tell you, there have been some notable bar fights,
most of which I've managed to keep out of the press.''
Allert, too, was a complete pro. The very best, according
to Skipper.

"You're saying Parkes has a problem with alcohol?''
I could see a number of scenarios, including one where

Parkes forgot a whole lot of unpleasant details, but Allert shook his head vigorously.

"He may in the future, though maybe not. He comes from a drinking culture: end of the week, it's boys' night out and time to indulge. Up where he's from, there's not a whole lot of winter entertainment except hockey and booze, so it's natural for him to have a few too many drinks after a big game. Actually," Allert said, correcting himself, "I should put most of that in past tense. Richie's illness—you know about that?" Allert's mobile face turned somber.

"We talked a lot about Richie the other day."

"Richie's illness has about put a stop to late night carousing at the moment. When the team's in Orlando, T's home all the time, Trish tells me, and when they're on the road, he calls in before and after every game. I pray to God that nothing happens to Richie."

"He certainly loves that kid."

"All his kids. The children have been the best influence in the world on him, but he just hates when Richie is sick. I would, too." Allert looked away as though thinking of his own children or grandchildren. "The treatment for childhood leukemia isn't for faint hearts, believe me, and it about drives T crazy that this is something he can't control, can't fight, can't power his way through."

I remembered Parkes's anguished eyes and nodded.

"I'll tell you this, though," Allert said. "T-Rex can be a first-class s.o.b. and a pain in the butt besides, but in justice, I must say he'd do anything for the kids. If there was a way he could take on Richie's disease tomorrow and have his son well, he'd do it in an instant."

"I can believe that." There was a pause. "But you

were about to tell me why you think he didn't kill Alf Rene.''

''I am telling you—in a roundabout way,'' Allert said, leaning back in his chair and making a tent out of his fingers. ''Given his personality, T-Rex would have gone for Alf outright. He'd never have hit him from behind. I truly believe that.''

Allert seemed a decent guy, but agents are, after all, hired to put on the positive spin. As angles went, this one was the best of a bad situation. Although Allert might be right, I couldn't see him convincing an unbiased party.

''What about the weapon?'' I asked. ''We don't have the complete reports yet. The old news clips said blunt weapon trauma. Have the police any better idea?''

''They think something heavy and metallic. A sizable piece of pipe, maybe.''

''And is there anything to connect this bit of plumbing or whatever to Parkes?''

''Not that I know about,'' Allert said.

It was conceivable that Parkes had simply been in the wrong place at the wrong time. ''Then there's nothing else but the fight last year?'' I said. ''That locker room set-to with Alf?''

''Confirmation of my theory,'' Allert said. ''Alf said something, T grabbed him by his shirt front, and Alf was foolish enough to take a swing.''

''What happened then?''

''Four of the other Showmen got hold of T-Rex before he broke Alf's neck, which is what he apparently aimed to do. That's between you and me. For public consumption, it was a locker room shoving match.''

''Do you know what they were arguing about?''

''Closed topic,'' Allert said with a sour expression.

"So he told me. I couldn't get a word out of him about it or about Rene, but, in retrospect, it's absolutely crucial, don't you agree?"

"Sure. But T's attitude is that it's nobody's business."

"The natural assumption is that the quarrel was serious enough to provide a motive. Whether or not he did it."

"Maybe so, but T's intensely private. At the time, he said it was nothing, and I spent a week making conciliatory noises about late season pressures. Richie wasn't well then, either. I mentioned that in the right quarters, and everything simmered down. T's popular with the writers, you know, as well as with the fans."

"Now that surprises me, because he seems so aggressive."

"Sure, but he's not stupid. He knows the press is important and he's clever with words. He gives good quotes, short, snappy stuff that just jumps off the page. A lazy reporter can get a story just out of listening to T-Rex."

All this was interesting but not particularly relevant. While perfectly charming, Allert was as dexterous as anyone I've ever interviewed, and in his efforts to stress the positive sides of his client's complex and thorny personality, he kept redefining the topic. "It's too bad Parkes didn't have some good quotes on that locker room brawl," I said finally. "That seems to be the chief thing against him. It's going to be important to find out some more about it."

Allert shrugged. "All I can tell you is that it made an impression on all and sundry, because as they were leaving the locker room, T-Rex told Alf the next time that he got him alone, he'd kill him."

FOUR

I LEFT Allert's office with a lot of vague ideas and nothing tangible except the name of Alf Rene's agent and the fact that Alf and his wife owned a house in Florida. By the time I got back to the office, Skipper and Martha between them had run down a somewhat longer list of names and numbers, beginning with the Showmen's coach, Jacques Laroche.

"All in Florida at the moment, I suppose."

Skipper shook his head. "They're on their exhibition road trip at the moment." He flipped open the *Post* and consulted the sports section. "New Jersey tonight. They're playing the Caps here this weekend."

"I think we ought to go," I said. "I'd like to see T-Rex with the rest of the team. And I think I'll see more if you come along for a social call."

"Lousy work but someone has to do it," joked Skipper, who came up with seats right behind the glass near center ice. We sat among the rich and fashionable, where authentic Caps and Showmen jerseys topped designer slacks and good perfume mingled with the arena smell of popcorn, hot dogs, Zamboni exhaust, and human exertion.

Close up, I had to admit the game was mighty impressive. Well-armored bodies hurtled toward us in a swirl of blue, white, and black, then slammed into the boards, shivering the Plexiglas panels in their stanchions. In quiet moments, we could hear the thin sounds of the blades slicing through the ice or a snowy screech as a skater hit the brakes before reversing into a swift and effortless backward glide. When shots went awry the puck caromed off the glass with enough force to make a whole row flinch. But if there was a breakaway or a shot on goal, every other sound was lost in the howls and stamping of the arena, and the players swept over the glittering white surface with soundless violence.

Skipper was in his element, straining to see when the puck was down at the far goal, jumping to his feet when the Showmen nearly scored in front of us, and moving his powerful shoulders in sympathy when a player eluded a heavy check. For the first time, I had some inkling of what he had given up in leaving professional sports: not just money and fame, but perfected motion, effortless grace—and the immense rush of controlled violence aided and abetted by the crowd.

Watching him, I wondered how long providing arena security and vetting new employees for celebrities would satisfy him. Perhaps having his own firm would do or expanding Executive Security. He'd already broached that subject with me: Skipper envisioned us going public, franchising, becoming a sort of upscale Wackenhut Security. Skipper'd run the figures—he and Baby agreed it was feasible, probably megaprofitable—but the idea had depressed me, and I kept putting him off. I'd really rather sell out and retire than saddle myself with big-time corporate responsibilities.

"Did you see that?" Skipper demanded. "Did you see that move!"

"Terrific," I said. I hadn't a clue, but I didn't need to worry, because Skipper proceeded to dissect the play for me as he had all game. Very helpful, of course, but even without his running commentary our client was easy to spot, unmistakable despite helmet, face shield, and pads.

T-Rex was big for a hockey player, that was the first thing—by a few inches the biggest on the ice—and fast, efficient, and aggressive. And even though his evening's work included slamming hapless Caps into the boards and banging them off the puck, Parkes had to be called graceful. He moved up and down the ice with long, clean strokes, as steady on two thin blades as most of the rest of us are on two feet.

"Beautiful balance," Skipper said, before leaping up as a sure scoring opportunity was thwarted by a fast, deft move from the Caps' goalie. "Should of been in. Carried the puck a little too far." He shook his head at this lapse from perfection and settled back in his seat, totally concentrated on the game. When it ended 3-2, Caps, but with a terrific game from T-Rex, Skipper looked as pleased as if he'd scored a touchdown.

"Great game," he said to Parkes in the locker room afterward. Skipper's own immense celebrity and a couple of VIP passes had allowed us to depart the bright glare of the arena floor for the dark underbelly of raw cement and bare girders. After the Zamboni moved out to resurface the ice with a slow groan and a cloud of exhaust, we followed the crowd of journalists and TV techies around the lower concourse to the locker area. The bulk of the press opted for the winners, but the Showmen's locker room was still busy with reporters, cameramen, mike-toting radio announcers.

While showers ran like Niagara in the background, sweating, exhausted players sat around with their shirts and skates off, showing bruised flesh and complicated pads. Others, like T-Rex, conducted interviews draped in their towels like so many Roman senators, or added to the din by working on their hair with powerful blow-dryers.

"What a nice touch on that second goal," Skipper added and T-Rex smiled. He had not been particularly pleased to see us, but he could not resist Skipper's compliments. I could see that the appreciation of a fellow superstar meant far more than all the calls of "Good game" and pleas for autographs from mere mortals.

"I got a nice pass from Luba," T-Rex admitted. "Kid can skate, can't he?"

He and Skipper were soon deep in East European imports in general and the Showmen's choice find in particular, a discussion interrupted by the arrival of a radio crew from one of the Orlando area stations. Skipper and I backed off to one side, and while the reporter asked about the game and prospects for the season, Skipper pointed out various members of the team and the coaching staff. Then he began to circulate, shaking hands, introducing me, glad-handing in such a charming and knowledgeable way that a few days later when the team returned home and I reached Orlando, various Showmen had vague but pleasant associations with my name.

One of them was Jacques Laroche, the transplanted Canadian who coached the team. I called him my second day in Florida, after I'd met the detectives in charge of the case and begun tracking down patrons of the Altamonte Springs barbecue restaurant. Laroche asked me to meet him at his golf club, an apparently essential amenity for upscale developments in Leisure Land.

Even to a Washingtonian, used to an economy built on graft, pork, and self-aggrandizement, Orlando County seemed bizarre, but I couldn't deny that it was booming. I drove past miles of golf, tennis, and retirement communities to reach Buchanan Hills, where I passed through a massive entrance, terraced and planted with a nursery's worth of tropicals like a swank cemetery, and circled a winding drive lined with large town houses and clusters of freestanding homes to a gleaming white clubhouse of vaguely Spanish inspiration. Laroche was waiting in the cool, dark bar, surrounded by overheated golfers wearing bright pastels and spiked golf shoes that rattled gently on the tile floors. He came over and shook my hand.

"Sorry I couldn't ask you to my office," he said by way of greeting. "A team gossips worse than a bunch of old ladies." He had a soft Quebecois accent that brought memories of late night French films.

"I guess they've had their reasons this year."

Laroche sat back down and rubbed his face. He was clearly of the pre-helmet, pre-face-shield era. He'd had a badly broken nose at one time, and both his forehead and his cheeks were seamed with the fine scars of old cuts. His eyebrows had suffered a permanent dissection, leaving little tufts of hair to grow in unexpected directions and giving him a candid, surprised expression. If it had not been for his luxurious golf clothes, I would have mistaken him for an old boxer down on his luck.

"Oh, you're right about that," he said. "I'm glad Sammy Allert's finally gotten onto this. He called me about your coming down. Course T-Rex didn't say anything." His sad, battered face looked even sadder.

"He would rather not think about it at all," I said.

"Not at all. Right. So the rest of us have to sweat it for him. The big guy's the franchise. I'll tell you honestly, if anything happens to him, we can pack our bags."

"He's an impressive player."

"One of the best. Our MVP certainly. But it's not just

that. We're the new guys in town. T-Rex is our marquee player, our name recognition, and they've promoted the shit out of him, excuse the language. Even this T-Rex bit. You seen the billboards?''

I nodded. Right up there with the huge three-dimensional billboards for the studios and the Magic Kingdom were colossal images of a skating Tyrannosaurus rex in a Showmen's jersey: 'See why they call him T-Rex, terror on ice!' ''Hokey but effective,'' I suggested.

''Damn right. Draws a lot of kids. And he's terrific with them. Home ice, he's a half hour later than all the other guys signing autographs. We just gotta have him,'' Laroche said, and he looked genuinely worried.

''There's no real danger of losing him, though, is there? Unless there's something more I don't know, there doesn't seem to be very much evidence, and that's strictly circumstantial.''

''That could be enough. We've marketed toward the family audience, and remember we're new here and we're up against the Magic, who've been squeaky clean. We can't afford to have this hanging over Parkesie. Hell, I'm not a lawyer. I'm not the marketing director, but I know it's not good for the team.''

''What I told Parkes was that we needed to find out who killed Alf Rene. That's what I intend to do.''

Laroche looked disconcerted and fiddled with his soft drink glass.

''Is that a problem?''

''Don't get me wrong, we'd like to know who killed Alfie, sure we would, it's just the only name on the table is the one guy we can't afford to lose.''

''You don't seem very confident about Parkes's innocence.''

"I just think it could maybe get worse before it gets better," Laroche said cryptically.

"That's often the way with murder. But I need to know some more about Rene and about Parkes, too."

"Now you're asking the big money questions. They come together, you know. I been around the league a long time, but I never coached either one before."

"That's the first thing I want to know: why they were both in the deal?"

Laroche shrugged. "We wanted Parkesie bad," he said. I was struck by his fondness for diminutives, an affectation among hockey men. "Hartford knew it and really held us up. We had to give two young players and a second round draft pick, so we knew we were going to be short on forwards. It went back and forth and they finally agreed to throw in Alfie." He scowled then as if remembering something. "Actually, we expected Wyss—he's a big, awkward kid but he'd have given us some muscle."

"But you didn't get him."

"No, and I just remembered something. I think Sammy Allert was in on the deal. Well, I know he was because of Parkesie, of course. But I think the business with Alfie was his doing. Parkesie was used to Alfie on his line, that was it."

"Let me get this straight: Alf Rene was included in the deal because Parkes wanted him. Is that right?"

Laroche's expression of surprise intensified. "Seems hard to believe now, but that's right. We went back and forth on it, cause we'd really have preferred Wyss, but they wouldn't budge. You could ask Allert about it. He'd know the whole story."

I would indeed ask him. He might have told me that story in Washington instead of going on about the charms of my head of security and the illness of Parkes's son. "So when did they stop being great buddies?"

Laroche pursed his lips and thought this over. "Damned if I know," he said finally. "Far as I could see, they never had much to say to each other. They didn't room together on the road. I don't think they socialized, either."

"Did they work exceptionally well together on the ice? Is that why Parkes insisted on Rene?"

Laroche gave a little bark of a laugh. "Parkesie can play with anybody. He's one of those players who makes everyone look good. Naw, it would have been the other way around. Alfie would've wanted to keep playing on Parkesie's line, keep his numbers up, look good at contract time."

Ah, money. I was cheered to find a concrete motivation at last; the bad thing was that it didn't take me anywhere. "So the big fight? What do you think that was about?"

"I don't know. I noticed they weren't talking." He shook his head. "I ought to have called them in and gotten to the bottom of it. Worst mistake of my career that I didn't. Had it been two of my young players, I'd've sat them down and told them both off. But Parkesie takes delicate handling at the best of times and he and Alfie were playing just fine. They were pros and grown men, after all, know what I mean?"

I did. And Parkes wasn't called T-Rex just as a cute nickname.

"Anyway, it just came up like a tornado. One minute the locker room's as usual and then—I'm in my office just off the locker area—I hear shouts and bodies thumping against the lockers. These are big strong guys, it sounds like they're tearing the place apart. I come running. Alfie's on the floor, blood running all over his face. Pierre, Tooksie, Mortie, and Emil, they've grabbed Parkesie, but all together they can't hardly hold him, and he's still got one hand on Alfie's throat. It's serious, I can see that. I start yelling. I don't even remember what I said. I think I threatened to suspend them all, call the commissioner, tell their wives. It was some crazy day.''

"Did Parkes say anything? Did he give any explanation?''

"Naw. He shut up like a clam. Alfie did all the talking.''

That rather surprised me. ''What did he say?''

"That it was nothing. That he'd been out of line, that Parkesie just took something the wrong way. He blamed himself and Parkesie didn't say anything to contradict him.''

"You said there was yelling. Did Parkes say anything then?''

"You could ask the guys who were there. All I remember is him saying, ''Enough.'' Something like ''I've had enough.''

I wrote down the names of the four players who'd broken up the fight and Laroche gave me a half dozen more who he was sure had been in the locker room. ''That's about it,'' he said.

"I heard that he threatened to kill Alf.''

Laroche looked distinctly uncomfortable. ''We didn't take it that way,'' he said.

"No? But it seems to be the one real mark against my client. Would he really be a suspect otherwise?''

"At the time everyone was upset, the guys were yelling, I was yelling. We'd just come off a bad road trip; there was a lot of tension. We all figured it had cleared the air. Alfie got a bloody nose and a cut lip—tell you the truth, he wasn't such a popular guy. Really there was no harm done.''

"Till later," I said. "Till it was mentioned in the local paper."

"A line," Laroche said. "It wasn't blown up or nothing. Just the same, I tell you I chewed the team out. There was no need to mention it to Sandy. He's the *Sentinel* beat man. But I told you. A worse bunch of gossips you'll never see."

Gossip, unfortunately, was not Laroche's personal vice. I got him to talk a bit about Alfie, who seemed to have had a taste for the high life and a knack for irritating his teammates, but the coach was not long on specifics. I did get the Renes' address, though, and after I left the golf club, I took out my map, drove two towns over, and paid the widow a visit.

LIKE THE other players I interviewed, the Renes favored a large new house in a spiffy new neighborhood. The homes were all variants of Florida Spanish: tile roofs, white or pastel exteriors, large, arched windows, and enormous front garages. Gone are the days when garages huddled modestly in backyards or rested off breezeways. These dominated the facade, so that the first thing one saw was a massive two-or three-car garage that allowed nervous owners to drive straight into their castles without ever setting foot in their professionally landscaped yards.

The Rene establishment was no exception, but its garage stood wide open. A U-Haul van was parked in the drive along with a big, flashy pickup and an assortment of cartons, suitcases, and packing crates. A thin blond woman was directing the loading operation, and two fellows I recognized as Alf's teammates were lugging cartons into the van, assisted by a tall chap with long, ropy muscles and a blond ponytail. Mrs. Rene was obviously moving out.

"I've already got an agent," she called as I started up the walk. "Their sign comes tomorrow." She took a quick nervous drag on her cigarette and turned back to the work at hand. "China goes in the van. Those two big boxes and that little one."

"Sounds like you've been bothered by Realtors," I suggested.

"You wouldn't believe. A good sign they'll be able to sell the place. This is the hot neighborhood of the moment." She was very pale, despite the Florida sun, and quite pretty with small, sharp features and a delicate frame. "So you are?"

"Anna Peters. I've been hired by Jurgen Parkes and his agent to investigate your husband's death."

"Nice of them to mention it to me," she said tartly.

"Hence my visit," I said. "Of course, I wanted to keep you informed."

"Sure you did. You need information. Well, the hell with you. They wouldn't have been so concerned if Parkesie hadn't been involved. It would just have been too bad, wouldn't it? Nobody cares about Alfie." Despite these remarks, she seemed not so much hostile as nervous.

"Look at it the other way," I said. "You're getting a first-rate investigation and someone else is paying for it."

"I know what you're here for," she said, exhaling a cloud of cigarette smoke. "To clear the big guy. The indispensable." As she was speaking the tall blond fellow walked over to us. He was pale like Mrs. Rene and he had her sharp features but a worse disposition. I guessed he was her brother.

"Get on with it, Suzi," he said without looking at me. "I want to get the truck on the road."

"In a minute, Billy." There was irritation in her voice; I guessed that he was bossy and that she was sick of him.

"Who the hell's this?" he demanded. I got a glimpse of mean little eyes and uneven teeth. "We don't have time for visitors."

"It's just another real estate agent. We're sorry," she said in a smoother voice than I'd heard so far, "we've made arrangements with Sibley and Martin."

"It might be cross-listed," I said.

"We don't need anything," he said. "You heard her. We got an agent." There was a kind of hopeful belligerence about him as if he was longing for a fight or at least an argument.

Mrs. Rene didn't comment, so I went ahead and wrote down the phone number at my motel. "Why not have your agent give me a call? Particularly if you want a quick sale, the more agents showing it the better."

Suzi Rene stuck the card quickly into the pocket of her cutoffs and turned toward Billy without answering. "Have you got that crib taken down yet?"

"I'm working on it, I'm working on it," he said. "You ought to be doing that while I help the guys with the boxes."

"You haven't started it, you mean," she said in a nasty tone. I could hear them bickering back and forth as I walked to my car. A really pleasant family.

I spent the rest of the afternoon talking to various Showmen without learning much more, and the evening reading over my notes and rechecking Alf Rene's biography. I'd almost decided to try Mrs. Rene again, when the phone rang. It was 9:30; Suzi Rene's kids were in bed and she thought we ought to talk.

FIVE

THE MOTEL LOT was still eighty degrees at a quarter to ten and damp as a wet sponge. Once I left the lights of the commercial strip, the black and starless night filled up with suicidal bugs that crashed into my windshield like insect rain. Compared to Washington's light-washed night sky, the Orlando suburbs with their sprawling live oaks, umbrella pines, and ornamental thickets seemed exceedingly dark. As I drove around the meandering circular drives of the Renes' development, I began to understand the omnipresent security spots and automatic garage openers.

I parked on the street outside chez Rene and switched off my engine. Except for tropical insects buzzing and calling in the bushes, the neighborhood was silent. There was a light on over the Renes' big Spanish style doorway and a powerful spot at the front of the garage. The U-Haul van was still parked on one side of the asphalt, but the smart pickup was gone and the mountain of boxes with it. I stepped from the cool interior of the rental car to the saunalike night air and went to ring the bell.

The door opened instantly on a dark foyer, and I knew that something was wrong even before I caught the metallic gleam of the long-barreled handgun pointed toward my rib cage. Suzi Rene was on the other end, looking pale and determined and not the slightest bit nervous. The remains of dinner touched the back of my throat before she said, "Come in," and gestured with the weapon.

I suddenly didn't care at all for Suzi Rene. "I didn't know Canadians were so big on large calibers," I said.

She glanced down at the weapon casually. "Jersey City originally," she said by way of explanation. "The Canuck accent's from living around Alfie."

"That Jersey accessory makes me nervous anyway," I said. She gave a little smirk, but she lowered the pistol and stepped aside to let me in. After she'd locked and bolted the door behind us, she flicked the light switch. A double row of tiny halogen bulbs high in the cathedral ceiling lit the large hallway and glittered off the pink marble floor. All the furniture and pictures had been taken out, leaving dark rectangles against a charming birds-and-flowers wallpaper. The imposing living room was virtually empty as well, with only a couple of over-sized couches and a large coffee table left.

"Moving van comes tomorrow," Suzi Rene said. "We got the small stuff packed and sent off today." She set the pistol down on the coffee table and settled herself brightly on one of the couches as if this were a purely social call. Small talk seemed to be required.

"You've got a nice house," I said. That was an understatement. If Skipper was right about journeymen hockey players' wages, this joint must be mortgaged to the hilt. "Will you miss it?"

"You better believe! I loved it while Alfie was alive. It had everything I'd ever wanted. Real quality, you know. Like the cornice." She pointed to the impressive molding around the ceiling. "All custom work. I had the kitchen specially designed and the whole layout's just what we wanted. A terrific neighborhood, too."

"Terrific neighborhood, but you've got major fire-power. Why's that?"

"My husband was murdered," she said, "in case you're forgetting."

"Supposedly by Jurgen Parkes."

"It could have been Parkesie," she said but she didn't sound entirely convinced. That was interesting.

"And you were thinking he might come by some dark night and do you in?"

"You never know with men," she said. "They all want their own way." She gave a little dissatisfied sniff and considered her long, well-kept nails. "Alfie always wanted to make the decisions even when I could see he was getting in over his head. And now Billy, he's my brother, he thinks he should run everything. We have awful arguments. His idea's that I should move up home, and he'll stay here and look after the house until it's sold. That's his idea."

"The house is in your name, though?"

"Oh yes. Paid up, too, fortunately. Billy doesn't know that and I'm not about to tell him." She gave a little half smile. "Billy thinks I'm broke. That's why he came down to help me move. That and he wants to know when the house sells and for how much. He thinks—" she began and stopped. "He's just interested, that's all."

I'd had a look at Billy and I thought I could guess some of his interests. I was wondering myself what the place was worth. "Is that the only reason you're moving, because Billy wants you to?"

"I've been nervous alone with the children. Ever since Alfie died. I'd never move otherwise, you know, but I've got to think of them. It's not going to do the children any good if I'm a nervous wreck. Deena and Marcel. Alfie wanted Marcel to have a real French name for when he became a hockey player. I don't know if he'll get to be a hockey player in New Jersey,'' she said and began to cry.

I made soothing noises for a while and then asked if she was frightened of anyone in particular. When she was silent, I said, ''This is a serious fears weapon you've acquired.''

She picked up the pistol and examined it thoughtfully. ''Well, there's Parkesie.''

''Do you really think Jurgen Parkes would hurt you?''

She shrugged. ''They had a terrible fight. Alfie had to get stitches. Thank goodness he didn't break his nose. Alfie was really very handsome.'' I had the feeling that damage to Alfie's appearance would truly have been a fate worse than death.

''I've seen his pictures,'' I said.

''Press photos, you mean?''

''Yes.''

She jumped up and went into the next room, returning with a leather photo album. ''Press photos don't do him justice,'' she said. ''That was our wedding.''

I'd been on the go since early, interviewing restaurant patrons and assorted Showmen, all to very little profit. Throw in Alf Rene's scuzzy brother-in-law and I'd had a full day. About the last thing I wanted to do was to look at wedding candids.

''Very nice,'' I said. The Renes had made an attractive couple, and Alf Rene undeniably had what used to be called matinee idol looks.

''He had the most beautiful hair,'' she said. She stroked the page as if she might break into tears again. ''He always looked so nice in pictures.''

I had to agree, but after we'd flipped through a couple dozen images of the happy couple—dancing, eating, toasting the assembled, kissing under an elaborate flower-bedecked arch, I thought it was time to return to business. "Did Alf have any enemies?" I asked.

"Of course not," she said. "He could be very sweet."

"Undoubtedly, but I'm told his nickname around the league was 'the Weasel,' which suggests—"

"Parkesie told you that, the prick. Don't listen to anything that bastard says. You can't trust him for a minute. They were good friends, you know. They used to be good friends."

"Really?"

"Sure. They're from the same area up in Quebec. Did you know that? Not the same town, but nearby. They played together in the Juniors. Drummondville Voltigeurs of the QMJHL. When they were seventeen."

Suzi Rene turned the pages of the photo album reflectively. "I met Alfie when he was drafted by the Devils. He was much better than Parkesie then. He was picked second round."

It was interesting how rarely anyone connected with Parkes or the Showmen answered a direct question directly. It was as if they all had some other story they just had to tell whether or not it was relevant.

"How did you meet him?" I asked.

"I got a job in the Devils' souvenir shop, and later I got to be hostess at some of the big team functions. He noticed me right away," she said complacently. "Whenever he came into the shop to autograph sticks, he always asked for me." She began to fuss with her hair, smoothing it back behind her ears: the femme fatale of the souvenir shop. "I can tell you, Alfie was a star while Parkesie was still playing in the minors."

"So they'd known each other a long time and were old friends. Parkes told me they hadn't spoken in a year."

"He's a liar. Alfie used to call him regularly."

"From home, you mean?"

"Sure from home. How do you think I know about it?"

"So they were on good terms?" Under the circumstances, I couldn't figure out why Parkes would pretend his relations with Alf Rene were worse than they were.

Suzi Rene's expression turned sour. "They weren't really on *good* terms. Parkesie forgot his old friends when he became a superstar. Like we used to go out sometimes with them when we were all in Hartford. Then Parkesie started getting big contracts, and Alfie hurt his knee, and we suddenly weren't in the same league anymore."

"Yet your husband was included in the deal with the Showmen."

"Alfie wouldn't let Parkesie forget him entirely," she said with a sly, shrewd expression.

"How was that?"

She shrugged. "That's all I know," she said. I was sure she knew a whole lot more, but having raised the topic, Suzi Rene now did her best to obscure it. I couldn't really blame her, because the thought that was lurking indelicately in the background was that Alfie had some hold over Parkes, which had materialized in the deal with the Showmen and perhaps in this overly large and ostentatious house, as well. In a word, *blackmail* was in the air, and I wondered why Mrs. Rene was hinting in this dangerous direction at all.

"Probably you're wondering why I asked you to stop by," she said at last.

"I figured you'd get around to it," I said, stifling a yawn.

"Your job's to get Parkesie off."

"My job's to find out who killed your husband, Mrs. Rene."

She made a dismissive gesture as if this was irrelevant. "I could help Parkesie out," she said. "Or I could make a lot of trouble."

"How's that?" I asked, though I could see the outlines already. As negotiators go, she was a beginner, an amateur. Back in my misspent youth, I'd cut my eye teeth on stuff like this.

"I know about those calls," she said. "I know they kept in touch. I know Alfie"—she had the grace to hesitate—"sometimes borrowed money from Parkesie."

"Really? And did he pay it back?"

I found her sly expression distasteful. Suzi Rene was an odd mixture of real grief and fear, interwoven with resentment, shrewdness, and opportunism. At the time, I had no clear idea what she was really about. "Not always," she said. "I think that's a motive, don't you?"

"Maybe," I said. "Maybe if we knew why Parkes loaned him the money. Maybe if there were any physical evidence to implicate Parkes. Without physical evidence, the 'loans' to Alfie explain that locker room fight quite nicely but not much else."

"Still, the information wouldn't do Parkesie any good," she said stubbornly, "and you know it."

"You didn't mention any of this to the police," I observed. "Who's to say you're telling the truth now?"

"I was upset," she said. "At the time I was dreadfully upset. When your husband gets killed you don't think of reasons first off." She squinched up her face as if she might cry again. With her quick and easy tears, Suzi Rene must have been a terror in marital arguments.

"And now you've remembered," I said.

"That's right. It's all clear now." She looked around

her living room with a speculative expression as if calculating future profits and losses.

"But your memory could get hazy again, am I right?"

"You just pass what I've said on to Parkesie," she said sharply. "Or better yet, to Sammy Allert. He's a gentleman who knows what's what."

"I'm not in the courier business," I said. "Why don't you call them yourself?"

"Cause I'm a lot smarter than Alfie." Suzi Rene picked up her shiny new pistol and waved it in my general direction. "And now you can get out of my house," she said.

I LEFT the Renes' in no very good frame of mind. The late Alf Rene had been a dubious operator both on and off the ice, and his Jersey City consort was set to dabble in blackmail. Sammy Allert might be a prince among agents, but he had been discreet to the point of deception. My esteemed client, who was a great talent and a pain in the butt, was probably innocent of murder but quite probably guilty of something else as yet unknown. I was sorting all this out, planning to put Baby onto the Renes' finances and Skipper onto Rene's and Parkes's past history, when suddenly the car mirrors were flooded with high-intensity white light. Someone with powerful halogen headlights had pulled out of one of the development's access roads and zoomed right up to my back bumper.

Idiot, I thought. At the stop sign for the state road, I expected the cowboy behind me to pull out around my car, but the lights remained planted blindingly in my mirrors. I wheeled onto the state road and hit the limit. The lights never wavered, and when the oncoming lane was clear and I slowed down to let Mr. Impatient pass, it turned out that he was content to wait.

There was no reason for anyone to be following me, but the roads were quiet, the night was dark, and I decided to be certain. When I spotted another ambitious development, I made a quick right without signaling. The squeal of his brakes rushed in with the night air, and I was again dazzled by reflected headlights.

At nearly midnight, there were still a few house lights, and I considered pulling into a driveway and knocking on someone's door. Florida crime fears, tales of drive-by shootings and murdered tourists first alarmed and then annoyed me. What's Orlando's crime rate compared to D.C.'s anyway? I'm a big city person and suburban crime always seems provincial. Admittedly, this did not keep me from being nervous. I had no doubt now that I was being followed, probably with felonious intent.

I'd gotten myself into a new residential development, full of cul de sacs and big circular semiprivate drives, some of which did not yet have their allotment of town houses, ranches, or villas. Doubtless intending to make it picturesque, the development's designers had laid out their streets in a long meandering course, and the big clumps of vegetation that improved the ambiance and upped the price prevented any clear view of the pattern. I didn't fancy getting trapped on a narrow dead end street, and I was uncomfortably aware that my only possible weapon, the car's jack, was out of reach in the trunk. Times like these make me question my bias against handguns, which, in better circumstances, I regard as a standing invitation to trouble.

I headed for the exit, but before I found my way out, I'd circled the whole place twice, the second time at 50 mph, giving my rented Honda's springs and shocks a workout. At last, I spotted highway lights flickering through the pines; I took the little traffic island on two wheels, rolled through the stop sign, and floored the gas, cutting out ahead of a big tanker truck. Like most Florida highways, the road was dead straight and in good repair. The Honda accelerated to seventy, and all I could see in my mirror was the rapidly diminishing tanker.

I was still congratulating myself when I realized that my heavy foot had carried me past the entrance ramp to the Greene Way. I didn't dare turn around immediately, and I'd soon cruised out of Leisure Land into a less glamorous side of the Sunbelt, where bony, unpainted shacks perched on brick columns, tiny shopfronts came equipped with heavy-duty metal grilles, and worn out junkyards and garages were lit by powerful orange-tinged spotlights.

Forget knocking on doors in this neighborhood. The streets were literally rougher, too, and the sagging sedans and battered pickups parked along the way forced me to slow down. Within minutes, hot white headlights reappeared in my mirrors. I was on the lookout for a gas station or a passing police cruiser, but before I found either, the road bent abruptly away from town into a dark stretch of agricultural land.

A warm, damp wind full of night insects rushed through the open windows. I could see deep drainage ditches on either side and dark hedges of trees and brush that parted occasionally to reveal the more open darkness of pastures or crop land. The road ran straight for what seemed miles ahead with not a spot of light anywhere. I couldn't have chosen a worse route if I'd tried.

My only hope was to outrun him, but though the rented Honda was pretty speedy, whatever he was driving was faster. He waited longer than I thought he would, a couple miles down the long dark stretch, then the lights in my mirrors wavered as he pulled out around me. I glanced away from the road for an instant, saw a man's face, indistinct and somehow nonplussed, then I automatically ducked my head and hit the brake.

He was surprised and slow to react. His car shot forward while mine slewed toward the shoulder. I straightened up with my heart knocking my tonsils, wrenched the wheel, missed the drainage ditch, and regained the road. I crossed the white line before I could control the car, then swerved right again. Ahead of me, his brakes squealed in protest; he was afraid I'd stop and turn. He wasn't expecting me to hit the gas and ram the back end of his car.

It wouldn't have been my first choice, either, but at the moment, the idea had some merit. Hondas are supposed to be well built; this one sat back on its heels like a well-trained cow pony and sprung its hood and various parts of my back simultaneously. We drifted left, then right, before I shot past the other car, which, struck again on its left bumper, caromed across the shoulder, and bounced into the ditch.

I put my foot on the accelerator and didn't lift it for a mile or so until the strained latch on the hood gave way and the whole thing popped up like a jack-in-the-box, blocking my vision and nearly stopping my heart. I slammed on the brakes, found the verge, and got out. My front fender was hanging half off; the grille was smashed, and various liquids were oozing from around the engine block. The car looked shot, and I didn't feel too good myself.

I shoved the hood down, but instead of the solid clunk of the latch engaging, I heard the sad, tinny ping of bent metal hitting chrome. Although all the muscles in my back protested, I tried again. This time, the hood not only did not engage, but sprang back upright, catching one of my knuckles. In my imagination, I saw my pursuer leaving his ditch and pulling up to offer whatever he had in mind. I decided to abandon finesse and whacked the recalcitrant hood into submission with the jack handle. Then I got back in the car and drove as fast as I dared until I spotted a bunch of well-lit advertising signs thrust high in the air like so many totem poles. I pulled into an all-night gas station to call the police and the rental company.

Neither was particularly happy that I'd left the scene of an accident. The silky voice belonging to the rental company was chiefly concerned with the damage to the vehicle. On no condition was I to drive it further. Had carelessness damaged the machine beyond the accident, I would be responsible. I pointed out that they'd have had just as much damage plus lousy publicity if I'd been run off the road and injured, but the logic of this did not impress the careful voice at the other end. No, they weren't sure about a replacement. It was still high season, cars were scarce and under the circumstances...I spotted a cruiser arriving and hung up the phone.

The solemn young highway patrolman was only slightly more interested. I suggested as politely as I could that very few people tail cars for miles with purely benign intent. He gravely reminded me that leaving the scene of an accident is a serious matter.

I said it hadn't exactly been an accident, but this did not help my case, either, especially since I couldn't tell him exactly where the incident—he insisted on calling it an "incident"—occurred. I estimated maybe five miles back, and after taking this under advisement, he got on his radio and assured me it would be "checked out." Then he collected my license number, my home and local addresses, assured me that crimes against tourists were relatively rare occurrences, and delivered himself of the opinion that while women motorists were wise to be extra careful, it was easy to overreact at night. On this example of mixed signals, we said good night.

It was two in the morning before I got back to my motel, but I called Suzi Rene just the same and let the phone ring until she answered.

"What kind of car do you have?" I asked.

"Who is this?" Her voice wavered between sleep and alarm.

"It's Anna Peters and the question's important. What kind of car and what color?"

"It's a white Honda Accord. What's this all about?"

I knew it. "Don't drive alone at night," I told her. "I almost got forced off the road by a car that followed me out of your development."

There was a silence at the other end. Finally she asked, "What kind of car?"

The Florida Highway Patrol had already asked me that. "A big dark sedan. I only caught a glimpse of it."

"A BMW maybe?"

I tried to remember the rear end of the car. I could see the shine on the dark surface, the glint of chrome, then the memory of impact erased everything else. "Could have been. Someone you know?" I asked, but Suzi Rene had quietly set down the receiver.

SIX

I WOKE UP LATE with a stiff back, miscellaneous bruises, and a bad temper. It's surprising how often one realizes one's too old for something only after the fact. I mentioned that to Martha when I called my office, but she was not sympathetic. She seemed to feel that I could amuse myself just as well at the computer and save wear and tear, not to mention rental cars.

"All anybody seems to be worrying about is the damn rental," I said, while Martha made noises about our expense account until I told her that she could handle the whole thing and gave her the rental company's local number. "Put the stress on 'accident,'" I said. "Tell them the police are investigating."

"Are they?" Martha asked. Working for a detective agency has made her skeptical at unfortunate moments.

"I called the highway patrol," I said. "Of course they were interested."

"Of course," Martha said dryly. "And what about you? Shall I set up an appointment with your physical therapist?"

"Very funny," I said. "Make it for tomorrow if you can get me back on a flight tonight." Then I had her put Baby on the line and after that, Skipper. When they were set to track the Renes' credit and some NHL past history, I hung up the phone and crawled out of bed.

I took my aching back into the bathroom, where I had to submerge it in as hot a tub as I could stand before it consented to get me down to the dining room. After breakfast, I tried Suzi Rene again, and when the phone rang unanswered, I tried car rental companies until I obtained what was apparently the last available car in the Orlando area, a subcompact Hyundai in a violent shade of purple.

An hour later, I was back at chez Rene. A van big enough to hold a shopping mall was parked in the drive, and a squad of short, muscular, bandy-legged chaps were hefting chairs and couches and lugging appliances on their backs like suburban Sherpas. A blond woman was overseeing the operation and I thought I was in luck until I realized that she was older, plumper, and considerably more cheerful than Suzi Rene.

Her name was Harriet, and she belonged to the fine local realty company whose tasteful pink-and-teal For Sale sign now adorned the front lawn.

"We want to do everything to facilitate the sale and to serve the seller," she said in answer to my question.

"Suzi must have gotten an early start," I said.

Harriet made a little face. She was maybe forty, with Dutch Boy bangs and a good deal of brio. "She called at four this morning," she said. "Well, once you're awake, you might as well get up and get going."

Now that was interesting. I suspected Suzi's early start had something to do with my late night phone call.

"I'd been hoping to see her this morning," I said. "I figured loading up would take quite a while."

"An all-day job," Harriet said cheerfully, "but there was some emergency up north, that's all I know."

"Would you have a phone number or an address for her?" I asked, even though I guessed what the answer would be.

"No can do," she said, shaking her head. "Company

policy. We can communicate with her, of course, but we don't give out client information.''

I nodded. I couldn't quite see the realty company passing on the message I had in mind anyway.

''You'd be surprised,'' she said, ''how many people try to cut out the Realtor, try to make some sort of deal on their own.''

I sympathized entirely and spent several minutes discussing property values, exclusive listings, and the beauties of the house without learning anything more than that Harriet expected a quick sale in the half-million-dollar range.

That was about par for the day. The state police had nothing new about the ''incident'' except forms for me to fill out. Their local counterparts had nothing new, either, and the barbecue restaurant patrons on my list for the day either remembered nothing or corroborated the earlier witnesses. By the time I finished these unsatisfactory consultations, my back was in open rebellion. I returned to my hotel and filled another tub. Then I made a list of BMW dealers and foreign car repair shops, stretched the phone cord as far as it would go, and lay in the hot water making calls.

Despite my miseries, I tried for bright and efficient: I was an insurance agent checking up on a client's car. I was apologetic and distressed when I called the dealers who hadn't seen a black BMW with rear-end damage, encouraging with helpful souls who were willing to consult the current work orders. What I discovered was that the Orlando area has a surprising number of dealers and repairers of luxury autos. My bathwater had been renewed several times before I finished the list and admitted defeat. The car last night had not been a dark

BMW or else its prudent owner had either delayed repairs or known a truly out-of-the way garage.

I hauled my waterlogged carcass out of the water and prepared to fly back to D.C. After three days in Leisure Land, I had only one little piece of information: Suzi Rene was sufficiently afraid of someone who drove a dark BMW to gather up her children and decamp in the middle of the night.

I SAW Sammy Allert early Monday afternoon, following a strenuous session with the physio, who gave me a discourse on whiplash injuries and put me through a variety of vaguely humiliating exercises. I was feeling more limber but less amenable by the time I got to the agent's office. This time we did not waste time on Skipper's virtues or athletic chitchat. Allert closed the door to his inner office, and I said, "Why the hell didn't you tell me Parkes and Rene were old buddies?"

"There'd been a falling out," he said. "I didn't think past history was relevant."

"The man was murdered. There was likely past history involved in that."

Allert looked embarrassed.

"I can understand you trying to protect your client; that's your job. But you say you're sure he's innocent, you want me to investigate, and then you waste my time. I can't operate this way. Now please tell me straight: Is this just PR and an attempt to look busy and console Parkes's kid, or are we trying to find out what happened to Alf Rene? If it's the first, I'm off the case and I'll send you a bill tomorrow morning."

Allert sighed and sat down heavily in his chair. "The big guy wants it done," he said. "Typical. He wants it done and thinks if he pays enough it will get done just the way he wants.''

"Meaning he avoids any personal involvement.''

"Pretty much. You might not believe it, but he's a really private guy. I've known him since he was—sixteen or seventeen. He was just signed with the juniors when the old fellow who'd been representing him retired. Patrick Motram. One of the old school, a former hockey player, former coach, former scout—done a bit of everything. He called me up and said he had a good one and wanted to turn the kid over to someone he could trust. That was T-Rex. He was maybe five-ten and skin and bones. Gawkiest kid you've ever seen. I thought Motram was pulling my leg till I saw the boy on the ice. All elbows and knees but he moved like he'd been born on skates. Two years later, T's six-two and starting to fill out and a hell of a prospect.''

Allert opened his drawer and took out a pipe and chewed on it without filling it. "That's how long I've known T-Rex and I still can't say I know him. Maybe Trish knows what makes him tick, maybe his boy—''

"Maybe Alf Rene?'' I suggested.

Allert looked uncomfortable again. "God knows. They were on the same junior team, but Alf was a different sort.''

"I think you better tell me what sort—if you want me to continue.''

"What did you learn in Florida?'' Allert asked in turn.

"That information is ours no matter what we decide.''

"Well for starters, I talked to the local police, reviewed the statements of all the people who were in the barbecue restaurant the night Rene was killed, and spoke with five of them. There's general agreement that Parkes arrived sometime after seven-thirty but not much later than quarter to eight. He was in the restaurant until nine."

"Too bad the estimated time of death wasn't just a little later," Allert remarked.

"Right, Parkes would be in the clear, because people remembered him. A few recognized him; some of the rest noticed his size and presence and wondered if he was a professional athlete. I have photocopies of the statements, and Martha is transcribing my interviews now. Frankly, nothing new there."

Allert nodded as if he'd expected this.

"I also talked to Laroche and several players. No one knows what the locker room fight was about; most only thought it was important in retrospect. That might be helpful if the case amounts to anything. Then I saw Mrs. Rene, the most interesting of the lot. In a word, she wants money."

Allert gave a little grunt. "Her usual condition," he said. He made greed sound something like pregnancy.

"She thinks she can cause Parkes trouble and maybe she can. She claims her husband called Parkes regularly, that they were still in touch even after the fight. She wanted me to pass that on to you. I told her to go to hell."

Allert shrugged and began filling his pipe. If any of this surprised him, he concealed it well.

"I also learned that Alf Rene was in the habit of borrowing money from Parkes and that it was through your good offices that Alf was included in the big Showmen deal."

"That's true," said Allert. "About the Showmen deal. I don't know about the money, but Parkes wanted Alfie included in the trade. He knew Alfie's knees were bad. He told me he didn't think Alfie had more than a season or two left. With the Showmen contract, Alfie would get a couple more years at high salary.''

''Parkes did this out of the goodness of his heart?''

''He's capable of generosity,'' Allert said noncommittally.

''I have another thought, courtesy of Suzi Rene: how's blackmail sound?''

''Anything's possible.''

I could see why Allert was a great agent; he'd be a dynamite poker player, too. ''What about probabilities?'' I asked. ''Any skeletons in the family closet?''

''Beyond the occasional bar fight and indiscreet party? No. That stuff's all pretty public anyway. Besides, this line of investigation is hardly going to help T's case, is it? I frankly think that—''

''I made it perfectly clear to Parkes that if I was hired, I was hired to investigate Rene's death. That's what I've been doing.''

There was a silence in which Allert seemed to be weighing how much he wanted to know about the murder.

''Here's another angle,'' I said after a moment. ''I think someone is after Suzi Rene.''

''Why is that?'' Allert asked. He showed mild signs of interest as I recounted the excitements of night driving in Orlando County.

''I'm sure I wasn't the target. Suzi Rene has the same kind of car as my rental. And then there's her brother— a piece of work from what I could see. A fellow who might attract trouble.''

''But you have no idea who tried to run you off the road?''

''No. And given the degree of interest shown by the police, I don't think we're going to find out—not unless he shows up again. But I called to warn Suzi Rene, and her first question was if the car was a BMW. I thought that was interesting and it narrows the field.''

Allert agreed, especially when I mentioned Mrs. Rene's predawn departure. ''I think I should talk to her,'' he said. ''So far I've been able to present this whole business as bad luck: a case of T being in the wrong place at the wrong time. I think that's going to fly, but we're still in contract negotiations....''

''She'll have her hand out,'' I said.

''I can handle Suzi Rene,'' he said brusquely. I had the feeling he'd had dealings with her before. Maybe it was Suzi and not Alf who didn't let Parkes forget his old friends. ''As for your investigation, I think we might put that on hold for a while. As you say, there's nothing really new....''

In the outer office, the phone began ringing and almost immediately, the light on Allert's receiver flashed. He listened a minute then said, ''Put her right through. Trish! How're you doing?'' His voice, which had conveyed polite skepticism with me, now became cheerful and encouraging. ''No. Not one of the kids? How's Richie? Oh, good, great.'' There was another pause, while he listened, then, ''You're kidding, Trish.'' Small talk came to an abrupt halt, and Sammy Allert's face grew increasingly serious as he listened. Finally, he said, ''You've gotten ahold of Shiffer? Do that soonest. Tell T to say nothing. Nothing. No, no, not unless he's got an explanation. Yeah, will do. She's here now, matter of fact. Right, right, chin up, Trish. We'll get through this. Right. Good-bye.''

Allert set down the phone, wiped his face and said, ''Jesus Christ, what a mess.'' He glanced at the calendar and shook his head. "Two weeks before the start of the season, and what do you think has happened?"

"Parkes has gotten himself in trouble," I said.

"The police think they've found the murder weapon. A bar from a weight set."

"Ah," I said. I could see this was bad. Not irreparable but bad. Anything suggesting athlete or athletics was unfortunate. "Where?" I asked.

"In T's garage," Allert said.

SEVEN

THE HONCHOS GATHERED in Orlando for a council of war. Old-time mobsters went "gone to the mattresses"; corporate types in trouble call for their lawyers. We all met in a fancy suite in one of the city's fancy new buildings: acres of blue tinted glass soaring up into a pyramid fit for a New Age pharaoh. We were right at the apex where the walls sloped at interesting angles and the blue cast of the glass turned the shimmering, heat-bleached whites and olives of the landscape below to a liquid blue-green. It was like living inside a sapphire, and probably almost as expensive.

Within this jewel, the cream of the sport's lawyers were huddled. We had Parkes's personal lawyer, of course, a robust man with red jowls and thick, dark hair like his client. We had Parkes's business manager, too, a thin, nervous, expensively dressed chap who fiddled constantly with his calculator. Allert, of course, was both agent and lawyer, so that brought T-Rex up to a respectable complement of legal expertise. Then there was the team's mouthpiece, a pillar of the local bar, tall, courtly, white-bearded and southern, rather like Robert E. Lee in modern dress. The owners—three of them—were present and each brought *his* own lawyer, accompanied by a junior partner to carry the briefcase and take the notes the senior partner was too important to handle. The members of this legal squadron were all cut from the same cloth: well dressed, well groomed, well spoken. Their humanizing feature was a touch of anxiety, or perhaps paranoia, visible in their preoccupation with their pagers and cell phones.

Coach Laroche was present, too, along with his assistant. The three of us were the only people who hadn't felt the need for a legal backup, but then we were very junior members of the gathering, there simply to show the flag and to reassure the owners and T-Rex that nothing was being left to chance. We were clearly to be seen and not heard, which suited me fine because I had plenty to think about.

I'd flown down early that morning with Sammy Allert, and on the way he told me what he'd learned from the lawyer and the police. Like everything else about Parkes's case, events that initially seemed clear rapidly became ambiguous.

Two nights before, Trish Parkes and the children had been alone in their house. T-Rex had been away for a preseason exhibition game and was not scheduled to return until the next morning. Around one a.m., Trish was awakened by a sound coming from the garage. Her first thought was that T had returned by himself instead of waiting for the team's flight the next morning. He sometimes did that, Allert told me, especially when Richie was unwell.

Then she heard a rattle as if something had been knocked over and got up to investigate. When she didn't see T's car in the drive, she dialed 911 and reported a possible break-in. The police arrived within five minutes, but found no one. Not wishing to alarm the children, Trish Parkes told the officer that there was no damage done.

The next morning, however, she discovered that the catch on one of the garage windows had been broken. Like many celebrities, the Parkes family was nervous about intruders and particularly concerned about dangers to their children. Since T-Rex was still not home, Trish again called the local station, and an officer came out to have a look. In the daylight, it was clear that there had been an intruder. Someone had attempted to pry open the door between the garage and the house, leaving dents and scrapes around the door frame in the process. Apparently the intruder had begun to force the door when Mrs. Parkes raised the alarm and summoned the police.

There was other evidence of their visitor around the storage rack at the back of their garage. The shelves held tennis rackets, fishing gear, a couple motorcycle helmets, both snow and water skis, plus an assortment of oversize gym bags crammed with old shirts, worn out skates, and favorite gloves that T had saved as souvenirs. Trish said it looked as if someone had been rummaging in this store, because several gym bags were lying on the floor and some skis and fishing poles had been knocked from their places in the rack. When the police officer had asked Trish if she could tell whether anything was missing, she began checking the bags. She noticed that one was partly open, lifted it, remarked on the weight, and unzipped it all the way.

"Doesn't pay to be too helpful," Allert said ruefully. Lying in plain sight on top of some team jerseys was a stout, shiny length of pipe about two feet long. It looked, Trish immediately said, as if it had been cut off the end of a weightlifting bar. That was interesting, but what really attracted the police officer were the dark brownish stains visible on one end. Knowing that Parkes was a possible suspect in Alf Rene's death, the cop put the pipe in an evidence bag and called Homicide. By the time T-Rex rolled in off a morning flight from Quebec, he found his yard full of police and his garage full of crime scene technicians.

"How did he react?" I asked Allert.

"He was frantic, of course. In case something had happened to Trish or the children. He ran right into the house."

"And the garage? What did he say about that?"

"He was furious," Allert said, "furious that someone had frightened Trish and the children, especially when Richie was sick."

"And the bar? They must have shown him the bar."

Allert's fine, mobile features managed to indicate sorrow, skepticism, and puzzlement all at once. "Trish says he took one look and shook his head and swore. 'Poor Alfie,' he says, just like that. No hesitation. 'Poor Alfie, someone really had it in for us both.'"

Against the hum of corporate anxiety and the projections for damage control, I thought that was alternative one: Alfie and Parkes had had the same enemy. Alternative two was that Parkes was as terrific an actor as he was a hockey player.

"...without a warrant," one of the lawyers was saying. "The pipe may not be admissible. We could certainly fight it...."

"The point," one of the owners broke in, "is not just Jurgen Parkes's defense. It's the good name of the team. If we fight every little legal battle—"

"Little!" exploded Parkes's lawyer. "We're talking about the only piece of concrete evidence. Everything else is just circumstantial."

"Look at the timing," Allert said now. "There's a break-in. The gym bags have obviously been tampered with. Presto, we have the probable murder weapon. If that's not a plant and a setup...."

"All we have on that is Mrs. Parkes's word," one of the owners' lawyers said. "She finds the pipe. What better way to handle it than to call the police and claim there's been an intruder?"

"You've got the damage to the door. That broken window catch, I don't think—" Parkes's lawyer began.

"How many of us have perfect garage windows?" the skeptic replied. "Besides, a few minutes with a screwdriver and you've got the 'damage' to the door. I'm just theorizing here now, but..."

We didn't get to hear the rest of his theory. T-Rex had arrived at the meeting looking like a tornado cloud. Although he was sober, his eyes were red, and throughout the discussions, I could see him tapping his fingers and shifting his big shoulders as if restless for action. Now in one swift, fluid motion he reached across the big conference table, caught the skeptical lawyer by the front of his shirt, and jerked him onto the polished mahogany, overturning water glasses and sending papers flying. "You asshole, don't say anything more about my wife."

Allert jumped up to calm his client, but Parkes struck me as being in complete control. "Trish's never lied about anything important in her life and never, never anything where the children's safety is concerned. Do you hear me?"

T-Rex had such a grip on the lawyer's tie that the poor man's eyes were half out of his head. There was no doubt he was paying full attention.

"Any more of this and you'll be off the team, Parkes." This was from the principal owner, a stocky developer with a red-blond toupee and a portfolio that reputedly included much of downtown Orlando.

"Any more shit like this and I retire," Parkes said, which made both Allert and Coach Laroche blench. "All

I'm hearing is 'damage control' and 'news management.' For your information, I'm maybe facing a murder charge. My kid is sick and I could be sitting in jail, while you dickheads worry about pulling in the family audience. You don't give a shit about me or about Alfie. I'd have liked to have pounded his face into the ice, but I didn't kill him and you oughta find out who did.''

He released the lawyer, who slid back across the table into his chair, looking pale and shaken. T-Rex straightened his jacket and tie, gave a belligerent look around the room, and stalked out.

The next hour and a half was taken up with internal damage control—a minor case of assault weighed against possible libel—followed by a more focused discussion of the issues than we'd had before Parkes's outburst: to do the man justice, he had a way of getting to the heart of a problem. The upshot was that I returned to favor, the owners even agreeing to defray some of the costs that Allert and Parkes were piling up with Executive Security. Speaking for the team, the courtly Robert E. Lee clone advised me to act promptly, and on that note, the gathering finally broke up.

It was three in the afternoon; no one had eaten lunch, and we were all feeling out of sorts. The VIPs had immediate commitments; ditto the lawyers, who were lined up with their cellular phones outside the elevators. Coach Laroche and I found ourselves alone at a little sandwich kiosk off the lobby. He looked depressed but proved talkative. I was now officially part of the Showmen operation; I was ''on the team.''

''Would Parkes really retire?'' I asked him.

''God knows,'' he replied. ''But no, I don't think so. I don't think he can afford to. Not with Richie, for one

thing. And he's still fit, at the top of his game. Still..."
He shrugged eloquently.

"You seemed discouraged," I said.

"I was thinking about Alfie, actually. I feel kinda bad
about him. And some others. Hockey's changed such a
lot. These are big money guys now. In the old days,
hockey players were all just tough, uneducated guys who
loved to skate. Me, too," he said. "What do I know
about all this high finance? I left school at fourteen. Put
on the skates and never looked back."

He studied his coffee cup for a minute. "I understood
the old guys," he said. "Fellows like Alfie and T-Rex—
they've been to school. Some of them've been to college. They're making huge salaries. Who knows what
they want? Or their wives, either? There are some smart
gals married to hockey players."

I wanted to ask if Suzi Rene fell into that category,
but Laroche nodded toward the offices and said, "I saw
Horizon Investments' nameplate in the elevator. Alfie
was working for them kinda freelance. Off and on in
sales. He came to me last October when his knee acted
up and said he was thinking of quitting. He had an opportunity with Horizon. I said I'd put him on the disabled list and that way he'd draw his pay for a couple
more months till he made up his mind. Funny, what you
think of. If I hadn't done that, Alfie might have left the
team and been alive today."

"Maybe," I agreed although I wondered. "So what
exactly was Alfie selling?"

"Damned if I understand it, some sort of shares in
this investment company. Not for me: I only understand
two things, hockey teams and farmland. I get my money
out of the one and I put it into the other."

"Did Alfie try to sell you on Horizon Investments?"

"He mentioned it once or twice. I told him I don't put money in anything I don't understand. He might have sold some of the other guys on the idea, but I don't know. Alfie wasn't really well liked. Funny, how you feel bad about that afterward. Yet if he was here today, I probably wouldn't like him any better."

"Why not?" I asked.

Laroche's ruddy face clouded, as if he was not used to dealing with subtle shades of feeling. "He was sly. I guess that was it. You felt he always had an angle, an agenda. You know the kind I'm talking about?"

I nodded. Did I ever.

"He kept his ear to the ground, too. You wanted to know anything about anybody on the team, Alfie was the one to ask."

"You'd mentioned he had a bad knee. Was he going to have to quit?"

"Pretty soon, I think. He had some disk trouble, too. Lotta hockey players get disk trouble. All that pounding against the boards." Laroche shook his head. "I thought I was doing him a favor keeping him on. It just goes to show you, doesn't it?"

On this melancholy note, Laroche stood up. I left the sandwich shop with him. He departed for the rink and business, and I crossed to the bank of elevators, located Horizon Investments, and went up to see if I could learn anything more about Alf Rene's off-ice life.

Horizon Investments' secretary-receptionist was a hefty forty-something woman with a beautiful voice, a square face, and a no-nonsense air who said Mr. Dowling was in conference. Mr. Dowling was apparently the one and only: there was no vice president, no personnel director, no executive assistant. As we were talking, I noticed a single light glowing on the switchboard, and I said I'd wait for a while. She told me to suit myself and went back to work. Her big desk had a switchboard on one end and a computer console on the other, and she was a virtuoso at both. The keyboard clicked away at warp speed and the phone never rang more than once before she flicked the switches and handled the call. In the twenty minutes I sat there, she took a bale of messages, but I couldn't help noticing that no one else seemed to be on duty. In fact, the office didn't seem very large, despite the luxury of its leather, chrome, and glass appointments and the efficiency of its major domo, who finally checked her board, switched a line, and told Dowling I was waiting.

A minute later, a tall, handsome man emerged from the back of the office. "Bennett Dowling," he said, extending his hand. He looked tanned and relaxed, well maintained, in a word. With his fair hair going gray and every appearance of health club fidelity, Bennett Dowling could have stepped from some expensive ad, perhaps one for the good men's cologne that subtly perfumed his office.

"Sorry to keep you waiting," he said. "I imagine you're working for the Showmen on this thing. It's terrible. A black eye for the area."

I agreed that murder wasn't a civic enhancement and followed him into his office. More blue-tinted glass, more mahogany, more teal leather. Teal: the official color of Leisure Land. There was a big map on the inner wall with property blocks shaded a tasteful blue-green and an equally large drawing of a development clustered around a free-form lagoon.

This seemed to be the desired plan. I'd seen half a dozen such "communities" in progress along the highways. You found a swampy area, cut the trees, leveled the brush, then dug out the swamp to make a lagoon and used the fill to support new houses.

"My first big investment," Dowling said. "Of course, we're diversified now. Property alone's too risky."

"The eighties aren't going to return?"

"Another generation, maybe, but every boom is different. You catch one, you're lucky," he said modestly. "Sit down and be comfortable. What can I do for you?"

He settled himself in one of the silky leather chairs. "Can I offer you coffee? Tea? Something stronger?"

"No, thanks. I just had lunch."

"Meeting ran late, I suppose?"

He seemed well informed already about the Showmen, and I just smiled. "I'm investigating Alf Rene's death," I said, "and I thought you could maybe help me out."

"A terrible thing," he said, adjusting his shirt cuffs and leaning back in the chair. "I'd love to help but I'm not connected with the Showmen. Naturally, I was offered the opportunity to get in on the ground floor, but hockey this far south seemed doubtful to me. I thought my money was safer with the Magic. Well, Laroche and the boys are proving me wrong, aren't they?"

"Alf Rene did some work for you, though. Isn't that right?"

Dowling frowned slightly. "He wasn't employed by Horizon Investments. Who gave you that idea?"

"You didn't offer him a job a year ago or so?"

"I did, indeed. He was having some physical problems. You'd never have known it to look at him, but something was wrong with his knees and his back. Of course, I'd kept up with the team. I make it my business to be in touch with everything of importance in town, and I'd met Alf socially. He was very presentable, well spoken, moderately famous. I thought he'd do in sales.''

"He didn't take the job?"

"No, he worked something out with the club; I believe he went on the disabled list."

"I see. And he never sold anything for you?"

"Oh, he may have mentioned Horizon as an investment to some of his teammates. Satisfied customers will do that. There's a lot of word of mouth in this business."

"Alf was one of your investors, then?"

"In a small way, yes."

"But he was never on the payroll?"

"No. Too bad." He managed to make regret look complacent.

"Why too bad?"

"Well, you know he leaves a widow, family. Horizon has a very good benefits package. Hockey now, I get the impression most of their money is up front. Young guys like that; they don't think about insurance and annuities and death benefits, do they? You have to get to our age before you think about dying, or, I should say''—here he made a charming show of fluster and embarrassment-''my age.''

There was something flirtatious about him, and I thought that he was going to an awful lot of bother for one middle-aged and ill-maintained detective. I decided to stick to business.

"You knew the family?"

"Oh, in passing. Cocktail parties, team receptions— civic events. Usually boring, but I'm always expected. And good for the firm. To be there, I mean, to be on the scene."

I agreed. I suspected civic bustle and high society were the very air he breathed.

"And Mrs. Rene," he added. "What is her name?"

"Suzi. Suzi Rene."

"That's right! I met her once. A charming little blonde. Is that right? Not too tall. Quite slim. Blue eyes."

I nodded.

"Sweet thing. Devoted to Alf. I remember now. They came to a reception. The reopening of one of our hotels, I think it was. I really feel sorry for her. You wouldn't happen to know where she's gone, would you?" Amidst all this chatter, he gave me a sharp, quick look, and I felt this was something he really wanted to know.

"Has she left the area?" I asked, all innocence.

"There's a For Sale sign up—I live quite near them. Pays to keep your eye on property in your area, you know. What's up, what's down—where the hot neighborhoods are at the moment. Even though we're moving beyond property now, it's always wise to watch the total economic picture."

He went on in this vein. He was a man who enjoyed the sound of his own voice, and his was, I must admit, a beautiful and persuasive instrument. I sat and listened. He told me about his company, which was, he said, almost scandalously profitable. Had I unused capital? I ought to think about an investment in a growth area; I could see for myself what was happening in Orlando. But every time I thought I should shut off the sales pitch, he would veer off to the Renes, to the team, to the as yet unknown whereabouts of Suzi Rene. I remembered how quickly she had asked if the car was a dark BMW and I wondered what he drove. Finally, I told him I had to get to another meeting and stood up.

"I'm late myself," he exclaimed. "Tennis date." He reached down beside his desk for a pair of large covered rackets. "Are you in the garage? I'll take you down. We've had people lost in the elevator system."

"This certainly is a spectacular building," I remarked as we walked through the lobby.

"The jewel of our skyline. And more to come. In a few years we're going to challenge Miami as the leading Florida city. They may be the gateway to the Caribbean and Latin America; we're going to be the Anglo capital of the Sunbelt. Forget Dallas, forget New Orleans; it's going to be happening right here."

"An interesting city," I said politely.

"A great place to live," he said. "I can't see why anyone would leave, can you?"

"Are we still talking about Suzi Rene?" I asked.

He was annoyed that I had made the connection, but he couldn't keep off the topic. "They had a super piece of property. Good neighborhood, decent schools," he remarked when we reached the garage level.

"And also a bludgeoning death," I said.

"Of course, bad memories," he said without sounding really convinced. "A tragic business." Then he abruptly changed gears to a more congenial topic. "Keep us in mind for investment purposes," he said, shaking my hand vigorously. "And Suzi Rene. I could advise her, help her. Let me know when you make contact with her, all right?"

I smiled. "I'm afraid I already have a client, Mr. Dowling."

"That's what I like to see," he exclaimed enthusiastically as if I'd just passed some little test. "Client confidentiality. The bedrock of any investment system. Still, you could give her my regards. Do that. I'd really like to help her out."

"I will, indeed," I said. We parted with mutual expressions of delight and esteem. I collected my rental and was waiting to turn onto the ramp, when Dowling zipped by. He tooted and waved as his gleaming black BMW rolled out of sight.

EIGHT

SINCE I HADN'T TALKED to Parkes before the meeting, I'd planned to stop by his house and see if either the great man or his wife was in a communicative mood. Dowling's gleaming sedan gave me another idea. I made a detour through downtown Orlando to the *Sentinel* offices, produced my credentials plus a reasonably accurate story, and asked to check the morgue.

In that handy repository of dead news, I collected and photocopied an assortment of clips about the Showmen, T-Rex, and Alf Rene, before I asked about Bennett Dowling.

"Dowling?" The librarian raised her eyebrows, which were very thick and blond, and pushed her oversize pink frames—the better to see me with, apparently—back up her long, thin nose. She seemed surprised and disapproving.

"Horizon Investments," I said.

"I know who Bennett Dowling is," she said with a touch of asperity. "I thought you were interested in the Showmen and the Rene case."

Nothing against them, but librarians tend to think in compartments, preferably watertight. "Alf Rene did a little freelance selling for Horizon. That's what I've heard, anyway." I did my best to look innocent and slightly confused.

"Oh, could be," she said, mollified. "It's a hot company at the moment. Bennett Dowling takes an interest in absolutely everything.'' He was apparently no slouch at PR, either.

The librarian steered me over to another drawer and began sorting the files quickly, the little metal tabs clicking against her shiny pink nails. ''Here we go. There are two, as you can see. One for his connection with Horizon and one for civic and society notes.'' She opened the top folder as she spoke, and a younger Dowling looked out at us, charming and energetic in the classic preppie mode, with tousled hair and open-necked shirt: a yuppie financial whiz posed at the helm of a snappy-looking sailboat.

''Does a lot of good,'' the librarian said, glancing at me.

''Really?''

''He's given a bundle to the community over the years. Publicity never hurts, but there's a lot with more who never give a dime.''

''Where'd his money come from?'' I asked.

''Some was his own, I gather. He started off buying up condos when the market was soft years ago and then went into investments. His advice is considered worth money.''

Be that as it may, between doing good and doing well, Dowling had taken up a lot of ink. The folders held profiles, news stories, features, and photos. Mr. Dowling appeared to be a bon vivant, a civic wheel, a financial power. The *Sentinel*'s photogs had caught him judging a local chili contest, opening a community center, appearing at a fund-raising masquerade party, and pontificating from the edge of a glossy power desk: first team all the way, All Civic, All Finance.

I thanked the librarian, packed up the clips, and departed via rush hour I–4 for a visit with my client. I had no trouble finding the development, not with the flotilla of news and TV cars with their long aerials, the studio trucks, panting exhaust like giant lizards, and the cars, bikes, and skateboards of the bored and curious public, who were anxious to see scandal and disaster "up close and personal."

They'd been circling at a distance for quite some time, but today was special. As the noisy guy on one of the All News—All Sports radio outlets had been screaming for the better part of an hour, the police had promised an announcement about the test results of the mysterious blood-stained bar. The folks on the gate were struggling to keep up with the flood and succeeding only in backing up the main road. With the entrance blocked, the more enterprising journalists and sightseers were making their way over a metal fence more ornamental than protective.

I eventually tired of breathing exhaust in the line and abandoned my car for a trek along the grassy verge of the highway. Heat shimmered off the pavement, and, in the bright, Florida sun, even the shortest blades of grass cast sharp, dark shadows. I walked along the row of idling cars and vans, pushed my way through the gawkers and sensation seekers, slipped around a semihysteric in a media blazer, and flashed my credentials.

"Sammy Allert, Mr. Parkes's agent, was going to call you," I said.

The sweating guard leaned into his hut, consulted one of an assortment of stick-on notes that covered a small bulletin board and nodded.

The Parkeses lived on the far side of the development, and as Allert had given me explicit directions, I was way ahead of other inquiring minds, who were ranging up and down the curving drives trying to figure out the numbering. T's house stood between a big artificial pond and a wide, treeless fairway. I walked up the drive, past the mandatory bed of tropical shrubs and flowers and the nonregulation swing set, and rang the intercom until a woman answered. I gave my name and waited in the late afternoon heat while the beleaguered inhabitants made their decision. Finally, the door opened. A slight blond gal stuck her head out nervously, glanced around quickly, and then asked for some identification. Instantly, T-Rex growled over the intercom: ''It's her, it's her. Let her in for Christ's sake.''

Her Master's Voice. The girl jumped aside to let me enter a big hallway, where a couple of small bikes and a bag of golf clubs shared the tile floor with a smart mirror and console set. The girl winked at me.

''A bit nervous,'' she said. Her accent was British; north of England, I guessed. ''Everything's in an uproar. Me mum will have me home, she will.''

''Wise to be careful,'' I said. ''It's a feeding frenzy at the main gate.''

''Mum's called twice,'' the girl said with barely concealed excitement. ''I told her there's been TV trucks all day. I don't dare take the kids out.''

Heavy footsteps sounded down the hall, and the Parkeses' au pair promptly disappeared. ''Keep that TV on *Sesame Street*,'' he roared after her. ''You hear me?''

We heard a door close quietly on the other side of the house and there was a long silent moment. Despite the air-conditioning, the house felt stuffy, as if the residents had been shut up with their own thoughts and their own problems far too long. Parkes was in his T-Rex mode: heavy weather on two feet and hints of storm warnings in his small sullen eyes. I decided to keep my mouth shut; it was time Parkes did the talking.

''So,'' he said, finally, ''you're here. How'd you get

in? I told them absolutely nobody, absolutely no visitors."

"I abandoned my car, walked half a mile in the heat, and used Sammy Allert's name," I said. "That's how. He wants you to have all necessary assistance."

Parkes gave a sour smile; he had an impressive range in ferocious expressions; it was amazing that children loved him, that they sensed affection underneath the tough shell. As the bell started ringing again, he steered me into a dark, wood-paneled room with shuttered windows, leather chairs, a huge TV, and lots of framed action photographs. "In here," he said. "Mindy can tend the door and the kids will be at the other TV."

"Has Sammy called you yet?"

"With the forensic report, you mean? Naw. I had to take the phones off the hook. I'll get him on my cell phone."

He switched on the TV. A green felt puppet with a large orange-lined mouth was emoting with the frenzied energy of the guys on All News-All Sports. Parkes turned down the sound and watched for a moment. "Richie loves this stuff. He gets the hockey gloves talking some days."

"How is he doing?"

"Better. He's doing better," Parkes said, his sullen expression momentarily lightening into an intense, hopeful anxiety. "Trish has him at the hospital now, but it's routine testing. Things are looking good and we're hoping no bad stuff today. Except all this shit, of course."

"And Mindy, is that her name? Mindy looks after the others?"

"Yeah. A pain in the ass sometimes but great with the kids," Parkes said. "With five brothers and sisters at home, she knows the score." He picked up the remote and flicked to one of the sports channels where two serious-looking anchors were chatting at an industrial-size desk. Behind them was a colossal blowup of my client looking like the original Immovable Object. I wondered what it felt like to be genuinely famous, a household word, a merchandising commodity. I guessed that merchandising commodities require a lot of maintenance.

Parkes brought the sound up on the announcement that we were going live to the police news conference and sat down. He looked irritated, rather than worried, and tense without seeming the least bit frightened.

The conference room was a brightly lit institutional chamber in pale green and cream with acoustic tile and folding chairs. Dave Harmen, the chief investigating officer, stood at a podium. Tall and balding, Harmen was wearing a light summer suit festooned with wrinkles; his complexion had a complementary all-night pallor. In front of him, a plain folding table held the famous pipe wrapped up in plastic like a big kielbasa. Guarding this item was a dark, round-faced woman in a white medical jacket—our forensic specialist, according to the breathless whispers of the news team. We were getting the full treatment and being teamed to death.

The detective began his media moment by recounting the indisputable facts of the case so far: Alf Rene was dead, and Jurgen ''T-Rex'' Parkes, who had had a locker room fistfight with the deceased a few months ago, had had an appointment to see Rene the night he died. Recently there had been an apparent—T-Rex stamped his feet and growled at this implication—break-in at the Parkes residence, leading to Patricia Parkes's discovery of a bloodstained pipe in one of her husband's equipment bags.

Detective Harmen then relinquished the microphone

to the pathologist, a Dr. Patel, who described the bevy of tests she had run on the pipe, progressed to blood types, degradation of samples, and other forensic topics of interest before declaring that the stains on the pipe were type-A human blood. Alf Rene's was type A, and the preliminary DNA tests indicated a match.

"Kee-rist!" said T-Rex with what seemed—and might have been—genuine surprise. The intercom bell began ringing in the background.

"This might be the murder weapon," the pathologist was saying, "but I would emphasize that that question is still open. The blood is Rene's, but the only prints belong to Mrs. Parkes. Those, I should say, are completely consistent with her having lifted the pipe out of the case."

There was a question off-camera.

"The question is, Could the pipe have been wiped off? Yes. The pipe could have been wiped off. However, it seems surprising that the perpetrator would wipe off fingerprints and leave blood stains."

Another question, barely audible.

"The blood stains are fairly evident." Here the camera prowled up close and showed, beneath the film of plastic, a faint discoloration. "There are also some paint stains, red paint, that made the pipe noticeable, but there are visible brownish stains, yes."

Trish Parkes's name was at the bottom of the next question and I saw T-Rex tense.

"Yes, as I've said, her prints are the only ones on the pipe. What? I'll let Detective Harmen answer that question."

"The answer is, Not at this time."

A murmur of disbelief from the back set T-Rex swearing.

"We haven't ruled anyone out," Harmen elaborated, "but as of this moment, Mrs. Parkes is not considered a suspect. I would remind you that further tests have to be performed. At this time, we think it could be the murder weapon, but we need a lot more data before we can say that for sure. Mrs. Parkes's prints are consistent with her discovery of the pipe. That's the situation at the moment, and that's all the information we have for you today."

A shadow moved beyond the shutters: the camera crews had arrived. T-Rex hurled his remote toward the window, then whipped out his cell phone and relieved his feelings with a high-decibel call to security on the gate. I concentrated on the ingenious speculations of the television press corps, who had commenced interviewing each other. An excitable fellow with a clipboard and big earphones repeated everything we'd just learned. His studio anchors then managed to cast doubt on the authenticity of the break-in as well as of T-Rex's alibi while piously hoping that everything would be well with the "Showmen family." T-Rex, meanwhile, was winding up a vigorous denunciation of the development, the security service, and the local police.

"They've got Sammy on," I said.

My client sat down heavily. The screen showed the corridor outside the briefing room. A woman in a snappy white suit had her mike under Allert's nose, but his impassive expression gave nothing away.

"Were you surprised?" she asked. "This must have been a worrisome development."

"It's always worrisome when you have a break-in," he said. "I want to point out that there is still no evidence that either Jurgen Parkes or his wife had anything to do with Alf Rene's tragic death. I want to remind everyone that Trish Parkes was home with her children—one of whom is seriously ill and has been undergoing chemotherapy at the Children's Hospital—and with their au pair on the night of the murder.''

"...the fingerprints.''

"I think we need to remember the situation. How many of us would hesitate to open a suitcase in our own home? Trish Parkes was asked by the investigating officer if anything was amiss. She immediately indicated the disorder around their garage—which she had quite rightly not touched until he arrived. When the bag felt unusually heavy, she opened it up and put her hand in to see what was there. I submit that is what any ordinary, innocent person would do.''

"Her husband, the center on the Showmen hockey team, has been mentioned as a suspect.''

"Jurgen Parkes was supposed to meet the late Alf Rene the night of his death. At Rene's request. Everything we can learn indicates T-Rex was inside the restaurant where—thanks to the current ad campaign—he was recognized by any number of patrons well before Alf Rene was murdered.''

"You don't sound concerned about this development.''

"Of course we're concerned. But we're concerned with the threat to the Parkes family. You have a break-in, you have evidence planted—after the forensic report we've just heard I think it's inconceivable that anyone would doubt that's the situation—so naturally we remain concerned about the security aspects and we have been ever since the incident occurred.''

"You don't feel this is going to make it more difficult to clear your client?''

"I've never felt my client needed clearing,'' Allert

said. "From start to finish, our whole concern has been with finding out who killed Alf Rene and who broke into the Parkeses' house. We're pushing for a full investigation, and the forensic evidence today only underlines the importance of proceeding vigorously."

"Thank you. That was Sammy Allert, T-Rex Parkes's agent and a lawyer by trade, making the best possible case for his client. However, serious questions remain about the break-in and about the possible involvement of one or both of the Parkeses. Back to you, Morgan."

We got a final shot of Allert pushing his way through the mob, and T-Rex abruptly switched off the set. "How the hell do you like that?" he demanded. "Some asshole breaks into my house with a blood-smeared pipe, and what do I get? My wife's a suspect, the press scare my kids. I can't even phone the hospital without wondering if some jerk is taping my calls. You'll see." A mass of kinetic energy, he stood up and began moving restlessly around the room, checking the yard through the shutters, flicking the TV on and then off.

"Sammy wants me cleared," he said abruptly. "Sammy wants to make nice with the sponsors."

"Sammy is a real pro," I reminded him. I thought Allert had handled the media pretty well.

"I pay Sammy to be a pro," T-Rex said. "But what *I* want is to find out who the fuck's playing around with my life. That's what I want to know." He glared at me. "So you. You've been 'on the case,' 'part of the team,' 'introduced to the Showmen family.' What do you think?"

"I think I need some questions answered first."

"I didn't kill Alfie," he said immediately. "With or without that damn pipe." His eyes were steady. I tended to believe him.

"Good answers but the wrong questions. Both you and Allert omitted some interesting things over the last few days."

"Listen, Sammy sticks to the essentials. He's a man I can do business with." From his expression I understood I was on the edge of the "can't do business with" category.

"You and Alfie had been good friends, old friends, right?"

"I never denied it," T-Rex said. Sins of omission, I saw, were not in his lexicon.

"At some point, you ceased to be such good friends, grew apart?"

"It happens," T-Rex said. "It's hardly indictable."

"Fortunately, not," I said. "One marries, gets new interests, wives don't always agree?"

His green eyes flickered. I realized suddenly that he was a clever man, perhaps a very clever man, who had spent most of his life around people not nearly as bright as he was. I guessed that was one reason for his air of brute forcefulness; it was also the reason for his surprise at good guesses, agile minds. "You meet Suzi Rene?" he asked.

"The other day."

"Trish is just the opposite. Down to earth. Speaks her mind when she has something to say and keeps her mouth shut when she doesn't. Suzi now," he gave me a sharp glance. "What did you think of Suzi?"

"Suzi's got an agenda."

"Right. You said it."

"So," I said, "you and Alfie ceased to be such good pals. Then he had some problems, knee first, then back. Right?"

T-Rex nodded, hesitated a moment, then, despite his

tension and impatience, turned reflective. "You should have seen him at seventeen," he said. "Perfect, just a perfect skater, wonderful shot, marvelous speed, everything. That was at seventeen."

"Precocious?"

"Yeah. By eighteen, he's no longer the biggest guy on the rink, and, by twenty-one, he's still where he was at seventeen—mentally, you know what I mean?"

I wasn't sure what that would mean for a hockey player.

T-Rex scowled and made an effort. "Alfie was lazy; he was always one for shortcuts. He hadn't developed his game. He hadn't grown into a bigger game. Like he'd been perfect at one level, the best ever, but then he didn't develop." There was something wistful, almost sad in T-Rex's expression, which I couldn't read.

"He went up to the majors, though."

"Just before me. The scouts aren't perfect," he said, "and Alfie still looked plenty good in the juniors. Anyway, he played well enough to stay up. That's what counts. Not everyone's going to get fifty goals a year."

"It helps to be on a big goal scorer's line," I remarked, "especially a big scorer who leads the league in assists."

"Ninety-three," he said. "Assists leader in ninety-three."

"You take my point."

He shrugged. "Alfie was a plenty good skater. Good as most guys I've skated with."

"Nonetheless, you did Alfie a big favor by getting him included in the deal with the Showmen. He stays on your line, he gets a good contract."

"Alfie and me went back a long way."

"Did you ever loan him money?"

"I don't know what that has to do with anything." T-Rex got up deliberately, went over to his business phone, and plugged in the line. Almost instantly the buttons all lit up. "I got stuff to do, people to call. Sammy will expect me to make a statement."

I was interested that questions of money drove him to sweet reasonableness and to cooperation with his much tried agent. I tried another tack: "Suzi Rene," I said, and he turned around. "Suzi Rene seems to be in need—or in want—of cash." I should have stopped there; I really should. Instead I added, "She—and maybe that brother of hers."

The effect was startling. T-Rex spun around. He had been irritated but preoccupied, obviously impatient for me to get on my way and out of his life. Preferably permanently. Now he leaned over with one of his massive hands on each of the arms of my chair. "Billy?" he asked.

"Billy. Tall, skinny, blond ponytail. Lovely manners. A sweetheart of a guy."

"You've met him? He's here in Orlando?" I felt that T-Rex was consuming my oxygen.

"He was at the Renes' last week. Helping Suzi move."

Parkes straightened up with a skeptical expression. "'Helping' is not what Billy does best."

"Perhaps he's turned over a new leaf," I said. "He's supposed to live in the house until it's sold. Meanwhile, she goes up north with her children, starts a new life, and forgets painful memories. It seems quite natural."

T-Rex's features underwent a swift and complex rearrangement. "Sure," he said. "Listen, you've got stuff to do. Get onto the break-in. We'll talk later. But not now. Sammy will be bent out of shape if I don't give him a call.'' He gave a sour little laugh. ''We got to meet the press and start managing the news.''

That was fine with me. I'd learned some of what I'd come for. The person I needed to see now was Trish Parkes.

NINE

I GOT TO THE HOSPITAL late—well after the press corps had flown off to make their deadlines and the sensation seekers had retired to catch the nightly news. Good riddance to both. I'd personally been offered up to the media the minute I stepped out of T-Rex's house, and a fair contingent trailed me all the way to the gate. This was a sufficient diversion for Parkes to get into his sleek little Porsche and wheel out the main entrance as I was assuring everyone for the fifth or sixth time that I was of absolutely no importance.

The hospital's silent electronic doors opened onto a big, square lobby. Overhead, banks of fluorescents dispensed a shadowless and disagreeable parody of daylight in which friends and relatives watched the television monitors or listlessly turned the pages of shopworn news magazines.

Outside it was balmy and starlit, with swaying palms and intimations of romance: holiday weather. Inside, thousands of BTU's worth of AC couldn't disguise a familiar taint of disinfectant, sickness, and fear in the cool, stale air. Medical facilities are right up there with jails and courthouses among my least favorite venues, but Trish Parkes was indeed on the premises. She'd opted to keep Richie there overnight to shield him from the media.

While my request to see her was processed, I studied the fund-raising posters plastered along the hall. The children's cancer ward with its stuffed toys, celebrity visitors, and fanciful murals was featured prominently, and the snaps of frail, balding children painting with their oversize brushes or wistfully stroking replicas of Big Bird and Barney made me thankful admittance was for parents only. Even at this range, I could see how T-Rex wound up needing the occasional drink.

His wife eventually met me in the spartan cafeteria with its fifties Formica tables and pink-and-gray molded plastic seats. Other customers sat talking quietly or brooded over acrid hospital coffee, thousand-calorie glazed donuts, and lukewarm toasted sandwiches: universal disaster cuisine, suitable for night vigils and irregular meals, for heartburn and heartache.

Trish Parkes sat across from me, toying with a hamburger. She had a large, square face with good eyes and an assertive nose: not a pretty face, exactly, but harmonious and pleasant with an air of solid competence. Unlike most of the young Showmen wives, she was not at all a glamour type. Her fair hair was cut short and pulled back behind her ears, and except for a pretty pair of blue-and-silver earrings, she'd skipped the jewelry sweepstakes. Her wary eyes were tired and her skin had a yellow tinge under the brutal hospital lights. She looked like a woman getting through hard times on guts and determination.

"Last time I was in a hospital cafeteria," I said, "I was waiting for my husband to come out of heart surgery." Despite my defenses, the nighttime hospital brought back dimly lit intensive care cubicles, the nasty sucking sound of respirators, the warning bips of electronic monitors, and Harry's chest, smeared orange with antiseptic and sutured with shiny black thread rimmed with scabs.

"And he's..." Trish Parkes tactfully did not complete the question.

"Fine," I said. "He's fine now, thank you. I was reminded, that's all. Which is why I'm sorry to be bothering you at this time."

"Sammy says you're on our side," she said calmly.

"I'm trying to find out who killed Alf Rene. So long as there's no conflict there, I'll do everything I can for you."

"Jurgen didn't kill him," she said. Her voice was level, matter of fact.

"That's certainly my working hypothesis, but I'm keeping an open mind. I just saw your husband this afternoon, in fact."

"He said you might stop by. He didn't want me to talk to you."

Parkes's reaction was too predictable to be interesting. "I'm glad you realize that you can't just ignore the business. Not with the pipe, your prints. There will be questions. And you'd better prepare yourself for the press, too. I thought I'd never get away from your house. They were literally climbing in the windows."

"I can't worry about that," she said, setting down her hamburger for good. "Sick children make you set priorities. I have to concentrate on Richie, on getting him well. I don't care about the rest."

"To take care of your son, you don't want to get entangled in a murder case. Which you will be if that was the weapon."

"It's unreal," she said. "I just put my hand in the bag and that was that."

"Yes. Fortunately, you have an alibi in any case. I understand Mindy was home that night. And the children, too. Is that correct?"

Trish Parkes nodded without looking relieved. "I hadn't considered that," she said. "What gets me is having to have an alibi. The nastiness of it, of having to think about what I'm saying, of being afraid in my own home."

"Nonetheless, without Mindy and the children in the house, you'd have a lot of explaining to do. Even as it is there will be some questions."

For the first time, she looked puzzled, and it struck me that neither T-Rex nor Sammy Allert had told her about the honchos meeting.

"One of the lawyers today as much as suggested the break-in was a fake. A way of accounting for the pipe."

"That I'd supposedly found earlier, you mean?" She gave a snort of disbelief. "I'd have thrown it down the sewer. Or straight in the river."

"You would have disposed of it?" I didn't necessarily blame her, but her reaction suggested she was maybe not as sure of her husband as she'd sounded.

"My son," she said and stopped. "My son idolizes his father. It would kill him, it really would, if anything, anything should happen to Jurgen."

"Surely his mother—"

She gave a little smile. "Mom is fallible. Mom might be forgiven."

"Do not tell the press that," I said.

"I've probably forgotten more about media relations than you'll ever know," she said sharply. "Jurgen's been a big star for nearly ten years. Believe me, I've learned the rules: Never volunteer information, smile, greet everyone by name, and ask how they're doing. Say you're excited to be moving to wherever, express an interest in community work, pose for five minutes with the kids. I can do it in my sleep."

"Sorry," I said. So her air of calm was deceptive; I admired it just the same.

She fiddled with her coffee cup for a moment. "A long day," she said. "After long days I get tired of being underestimated." I guessed that was the common fate of celebrity wives.

"Then you'll be relieved to know I'd had another more flattering thought."

She looked up.

"I thought you might have picked up the pipe deliberately. I thought you might have handled it to make sure the forensic evidence was confused."

She took this under advisement. "I don't know," she said, shaking her head. "I don't know if I'd have done that. But the break-in was for real, I can tell you that. And when I felt the weight in the bag, I thought probably a couple pairs of skates. Jurgen's been looking all over for some of his old white Bauer skates. Souvenir items, now. I wasn't thinking about what happened to Alf at all."

Well, that was certainly possible. When people are murdered, even when close friends are murdered, life goes on: the oldest cliché of all and the easiest to forget. It doesn't do to fixate on the idea that everything is calculated; it doesn't do to forget that most of the time we're just muddling through. "The break-in is still important. It raises a couple of possibilities that may help your husband."

"Sure, it has," she said. "It's probably given the police the murder weapon."

"Maybe, but a murder weapon with nothing to link it to your husband. That's a plus. Then there's the question of motive. Who wants to make trouble for your husband? What's the point of involving him in Rene's death?''

She shrugged and looked worried without giving much away.

"Does he have enemies?"

"No," she said immediately.

"Please think carefully. Your husband's personality suggests he's ruffled a few feathers."

"There are people who dislike Jurgen. There are people he dislikes. But most of that is confined to the ice. Even Reggie Synnott—he got his leg broken a year ago."

"Courtesy of a check from your husband?"

"Yes. Jurgen felt bad about that. It was a legal check, but he felt bad. He saw Reggie in the hospital. Went up the back way so the press wouldn't get wind of it. Arranged for Reggie to have a private physio he thinks the world of. They're good friends now."

"Scratch Reggie Synnott, then. Anyone else? What about the broken jaw?"

She looked slightly uncomfortable. "Haakan's back playing in Finland."

No sweetness and light there, I guessed, but a damn long plane ride. "Okay."

"What I'm saying is that there isn't anyone else. The players know Jurgen plays hard but he's a great player. They stay out of his way and then there's no problem."

"What about off the ice?"

"No. No one."

"You've thought about this?"

"Of course I've thought about it! What do you think? My husband's connected with a murder case. I've thought about everyone we've known, anyone who could have been involved. It doesn't make sense. Listen,

Alfie was an operator. Jurgen had known that for years. That was just Alfie.''

Clearly someone else hadn't been as tolerant. ''The night that Alf Rene was killed. I believe you were in the house when the call came?''

''I took the call,'' she said. ''I was in the kitchen fixing the children's dinner.''

''How did Alf sound?''

''Scared. I already told the police that. He sounded— scared may be too strong—nervous, excitable.''

''You knew him quite well?''

''Well as I wanted to. Well enough to know what was on his mind.''

That was interesting. ''You might elaborate,'' I said. ''As far as I can tell, no one knows why he called your husband.''

''He wanted something. That was usually why he called. He wanted a favor, he wanted to get Jurgen to go in on some scheme. It was always the same.''

''And these calls made him nervous?''

She shook her head. ''Not usually. Usually he was all smiles, 'Hi ya, Trish, how's my favorite gal from the north woods'—that sort of bullshit. Though he could be fun when he wanted. Alfie was a real charmer.''

''But not this time.''

''No, not at all. 'Trish,' he said, 'let me talk to Parkesie right away.' All business. I said to myself, whatever he wants, he's not going to get, and he knows it. But that's how he was. He never let up on anything.'' She looked off into the distance as if Alf Rene and the night of the murder were immeasurably remote.

''You said Alf wanted help with some business plan. Did you mean he asked your husband for money?''

Trish took a minute to come back from wherever her

thoughts had taken her. "Alfie always had something going. Investments, business prospects. Buying gold, selling hog futures. You name it. He'd tried it." She gave a slight, reminiscent frown. "Alfie felt he was entitled to be rich. With him it wasn't 'if,' it was 'when'; he expected to hit the jackpot any day."

"And your husband? Did he put any money into Alfie's projects?"

Trish looked thoughtful. "Possibly. In a small way, maybe. I know he loaned Alfie money on a couple occasions."

"What about an outfit called Horizon Investments? They're based here in Orlando."

"I couldn't tell you. Jurgen's sharp about business and Sammy's been a big help. Between them, they handle investments. I manage the household accounts, moving expenses, the family bills; Jurgen and Sammy do the heavy finance."

"I see." Maybe Sammy Allert would be able to help me on that—if I could get him to stop being Mr. Discretion. "Your husband hasn't been too forthcoming about Alf Rene or business or anything else."

"He sees it as none of your business," Trish Parkes observed. She laid her hands flat on the table and leaned forward to make sure I got her message. I could see that she would be up to dealing with my boisterous client. "Me, too. Richie's the only reason I'm talking to you. Normally, I'd tell you to go to hell. I've got enough, more than enough, to worry about, and as far as I'm concerned, Suzi can investigate her own husband's death—if she cares to know. That's how I feel about it, but this is killing Richie. I've told Jurgen: get this wrapped up no matter what it costs. It's got to be over and done with or we'll lose our boy. I just know it."

She crumpled her napkin and stood up. Her face was white; she looked bone tired. "That's all the time I can give you," she said. "When Richie wakes up, I have to be back upstairs."

I SPENT SOME TIME the next morning on Alf Rene's finances. According to the land records office, the Renes' house had been purchased for $450,000 with a loan from an area bank. A year later, the Renes had refinanced, paying off a hunk of the original loan—how?—borrowing $100,000 from another bank and then taking out a $100,000 line on their home equity. This, I guessed, was when the ultrafancy kitchen was installed and all that nice custom molding went up in the living room.

Eight months later, they refinanced again with an outfit called Bay Horizons Equity, which sounded close enough to Horizon Investments to provoke my interest. I made a note of that, and of the fact that the mortgage had been abruptly cleared about six months ago. Suzi Rene had told the truth: the house was free and clear, and she stood to gain a nice piece of change from its sale.

Next, I studied Alf's salary figures. Whichever way I looked at them, I saw more than honest thrift, and it seemed like a good idea to get on the phone to Baby. I asked her if she'd come across Bay Horizons Equity and whether the company was connected in any way to Dowling's Horizon Investments.

"Bay Horizons hasn't showed up yet," she said once we'd dispatched office gossip and the progress of some other cases. "But I think you've got a live one. Dowling's owned a couple dozen companies at one time or another."

"A big player?"

''Not really. They're all small or medium-size concerns. He's maybe a tycoon in the making or maybe he's running a corporate shell game. He's got a complicated set of holdings.''

''Wait a minute,'' I said. ''The line here is that Bennett Dowling's a community leader, everybody's favorite corporate philanthropist; there's not a discouraging word anywhere.''

''I didn't say he wasn't smart, but I'm thinking he's buying one company with another company's assets. That I don't like. He may be a sweet guy and the next St. Francis of Assisi, but don't give him your retirement money.''

''I'll keep that in mind,'' I said, though I thought she might have chosen a happier example. Did I want to retire? If I did retire, would I keep part interest in Executive Security? Did I want to worry about retirement? I was aware of the silence and shifted gears. ''Dowling seems to have kept his nose clean in Orlando.''

''He hasn't been there all that long,'' Baby observed.

''Where was he before?'' I'd been misled by the librarian. ''I'd gotten the distinct impression Dowling was a local boy.''

''He is, but he only returned about eight years ago.''

''So where was he in the meantime?''

''You'll like this: Connecticut and New Jersey.''

Alf Rene had played hockey in Connecticut and his wife was from New Jersey. ''I like it very much. The only thing I don't like is that it doesn't get us any further. Nothing quite fits. The pipe's got Alf's blood and Trish Parkes's prints. She's got an alibi and isn't a serious contender. Suzi Rene mentions a car that looks like Dowling's, but the car that runs me off the road probably isn't his. I'm pretty sure our client didn't whack Alfie, but that's only because he's such a heavy type he'd have disjointed Rene's neck.''

Baby made a soft clicking sound. Baby would like to eliminate motivation and chance. She puts her faith in the numbers. Anything else was my worry.

"I want to know if T-Rex loaned—or gave—substantial sums to Alfie," I told her. "Maybe for the house. Look since 1990. Maybe for some investment scheme—Trish Parkes said Alf always had something going.''

"All right.''

"And look for some financial troubles right before he died. Trish said the night Alf called he sounded worried, nervous, as if, I quote, 'he wanted something and knew he wasn't going to get it.'''

"Will do. By the way, Skipper ran down Rene's agent. He's based in Tampa and he's to be in town all this week.''

"Good work," I said as I scribbled down the number. I thanked Baby and hung up. Then I called Rene's agent to set up a meeting that afternoon in Tampa.

TEN

THE I-4 FROM Orlando to Tampa ran straight, flat, and crowded. Roadside billboards shilled the assorted delights of Greater Orlando: the thrilling theme parks and studio tours, the all-you-can-eat buffets, the motels with implausible combinations of luxury and thrift. Giant electricity pylons strode the fields, bringing power for the skyscrapers, the amusement rides, the megawatt special effects. In their shadows, humped Brahmin-cross cattle grazed, brown, black, and dun, while little white egrets trolled for insects in their wake. Further west, vultures wheeled in big, lazy spirals over the swamps, and lines of storks, egrets, and ibis coasted across the island-dotted rivers. Inland Florida was a curious combination of the primeval and the commercial, the one hanging on in the face of asphalt and development, the other advancing on air-conditioning and cheap power.

Tampa proved to be another Sunbelt winner, if less glossy than Disney-blessed Orlando. The highway prudentially grew stilts to cross the older, poorer sections, where tiny frame cottages crouched in overgrown yards and narrow streets were lined with shabby bungalows. But a new stadium rose on the smog-smudged horizon and an ultramodern airport sat at the edge of the magnificent bay.

Wurfel Stanford, Alf Rene's agent, had his office in a downtown sixties building, one of that depressing vintage with neither the charm and solidity of the old Florida nor the spiffy comforts of the new. Up in his little suite, I understood the plus. The higher floors had a clear view of the water. While I waited to see him, I looked out over the condos and vacation time-shares to the flat, glittering bay bisected by the thin gray band of the causeway that ran south to St. Pete.

Northward, a storm was brewing. Massive dark clouds patterned the water, turning patches to slate and deepening the milky greens and blues of the shallows. To the south, the skies were still postcard blue and the bay merged seamlessly into the open gulf.

"Million-dollar view," said a voice behind me. There was a regretful note, as if Wurfel Stanford would cheerfully have sold up if he could. "With enough capital, you could demolish this and put up condos, maybe a hotel. Balconies on every floor to maximize the real estate."

He bounced gently on the balls of his feet as if eager to get out and start demolishing and converting. From his neat curly hair to his shiny patent loafers, Wurf was young, brisk, and athletic. He was wearing a natty double-breasted suit and a bright fashionable tie, and he seemed simultaneously anxious to talk to me and eager to let me know that he was immensely busy.

"It was kind of you to see me, Mr. Stanford," I said, shaking his hand.

"Wurf, call me Wurf. Least I could do for Suzi." He spoke at a terrific rate of speed. "Terrible, terrible thing. I've been trying to do something with their affairs, but she can't expect too much. She'll be disappointed, of course, no matter what I do, though I'm already out on a limb for her, so to speak. Not that she realizes," he said, running a hand through his beautifully kept hair. One thing about sports, you get to meet a lot of well-maintained men. "She's always expected me to work miracles. Alfie was terrific, a real talent, absolutely, but so much is subjective. The numbers. You gotta have the *numbers* I used to tell her. Charm—he had charm—and looks to die for. With thirty goals a year—even thirty—and I could of done an awful lot with Alfie. Not that I'm apologizing for the way I handled his career, understand.''

I thought of Alf's fancy house and nice cars and said I was sure Alf had been in good hands. I was also pretty sure that his wife had run close herd on his agent.

"So," he said, gesturing toward a chair, "to business. You're working for Jurgen Parkes and Sammy Allert, right? Allert's one of the main men of the business, absolutely tops. Course, who couldn't handle T-Rex, eh? Numbers, he's got *numbers* and on top of it, personality. Some people don't realize that yet. They used to complain about Agassi, about him never winning the big ones. They didn't realize for selling you need personality.''

"Plus numbers.''

"Right." But his face turned gloomy. I strongly suspected that he hadn't yet snagged a prospect with both requirements.

"Rene had personality, though?" I asked.

"Oh yeah, yeah, personality to burn. But maybe not so sharp and distinct as your client. Now, T-Rex, you've seen the billboards—genius, huh? Not a pretty face but raw power and fits the motif. The kids love it. The guy's theme park all the way." His expression was avid; T-Rex as merchandising commodity was right down his alley.

"At the moment," I ventured, "he's up to his nineteen-inch neck in innuendos and bad press.''

"Tragic," Stanford said. "But you're on the case, getting the goods. You and Sammy together—I can see you clearing the great man, no sweat, right?'' He laughed without any real jollity.

''Everything depends on finding out who killed Alf Rene,'' I said. ''That probably depends on finding out why he was killed. Motive helps when you don't have much evidence.''

The agent fell silent.

''There's only one thing against Parkes after all—the locker room fight. Can you help me out on that?''

It killed him to keep quiet—I could see that right away. His well-kept hands twitched on the arms of his chair and he shifted his shoulders restlessly. ''Nothing to tell. Long season, tensions build up. Alfie said it was nothing. He could've made a stink about the fight, but he didn't want to talk about it. I was on the phone, sure. I thought maybe he'd hurt his back again—if so the club and T-Rex would have to answer for it. I thought maybe that would be the best thing. Alfie had a bad disk, you know, besides the fragile knee. Insurance claims, damages. I was ready for the whole nine yards.'' He bounced a little in his seat, ready for action even now.

''Alf didn't want to cooperate?''

''You said it.''

''And Suzi? I have the sense she's a hard-nosed lady when it comes to money.''

''No go. I couldn't get Suzi on board, either. Not at all. Drop it, forget it, not important, that's what I got.''

I found that interesting. ''Which suggests it really was nothing—or that Alf and his wife didn't want to discuss the real reasons.''

''Listen, I got other clients, other problems, know what I mean? Kid outa Bradenton-what a talent! I got the inside track soon as the hoop season's over. I'm fo-

cused on that. And guys in the NHL, NFL, the new arena
football league. As I told you, I'd be outa here except
for the view. Things are jumping. So I let it drop. I'm
telling you, Alfie could've retired right there—disability,
insurance, suit against the team, against T-Rex personally. Listen, he walks in, I see his face, I snap a couple
Polaroids. We had a case.''

The loss of this opportunity seemed to have touched
Wurf deeply. I wondered if he got an extra percentage
on suits and settlements.

''I'm told Alf Rene and Jurgen Parkes went back a
long way.''

''That was a consideration,'' Wurf said. ''That was a
big-time consideration.''

''If it wasn't just the goodness of his heart, maybe Alf
owed Parkes something. I'm wondering if he was in
debt, if he owed Parkes money?''

Wurf raised his eyebrows and nodded sagely. ''Alf's
finances—what can I say? Spaghetti.''

I didn't quite follow, but the agent was happy to elaborate.

''He had stuff coming in from here and there. No
records, just loans and fees and crazy investments. I finally refused to do his taxes. I didn't know what the hell
he was up to, that's the truth, but don't quote me.''

''It's conceivable he borrowed money from Parkes,
then?''

''Oh, sure.''

''Money Parkes loaned him—willingly or unwill-
ingly?''

Wurf looked uncomfortable. ''I don't know what
you've got in mind,'' he said, ''but I pretty much kept
out of his personal life.''

''Loans, old friendship gone sour; that locker room

fistfight and Alf's unwillingness to make anything of it: Blackmail's what crossed my mind.''

Wurf's expression relaxed into a sly half smile; he seemed relieved. ''I shouldn't think you'd want to push that angle,'' he said. ''It gives T-Rex a motive, doesn't it?''

''Depending on Alf's habits, it might give other people a motive as well—family, friends, business associates. You said yourself: spaghetti finances. And the Renes were living way beyond their means.''

''Don't look at me,'' Wurf said. ''A dead client's not worth anything.''

''What about other business contacts? You must know some of them.''

''Listen, I handle the sports aspects—player contracts, negotiations with teams, endorsements, personal services arrangements for corporations. That's what I handle and...'' He looked very deliberately at his watch and stood up. ''That's all I have time for. Interviews, meetings, gotta keep up. Kids today.'' He leaned over confidentially. ''You can't trust them. You think you've got an understanding one day; the next, someone else's got their ear. You gotta baby-sit them, keep on their tail, fend off the competition.''

I ignored the hint and stayed where I was. ''What about business? Alf was doing some work for Horizon Investments. How about that?''

''A career op. I encouraged him. Bought a piece of the action, in fact. Not just to encourage him either; Horizon's a dynamite company.''

''He was never taken on full time, though.''

I thought Wurf looked surprised. ''He certainly seemed busy for them. Course he knew Matt, mostly worked with Matt from what I could tell. Instead of with Mr. Civic Pride of Orlando.''

"You mean Bennett Dowling?"

"Yeah. He's got a partner. Pretty much a silent partner I think.'' Wurf gave another of his sly half smiles. He was not nearly so good at concealing information as Sammy Allert. "I would think silent partner would be about right.''

"And this is Matt—?"

"Spotwood. Longtime buddy.''

"And you say Alf knew him and was working for him, rather than Dowling?''

"That would be my guess.''

I tried a guess of my own. "Suzi Rene. Would she have known Matt Spotwood?"

Wurf's expression became distinctly uncomfortable. "Suzi was a sociable gal, if you know what I mean.''

"There's a lot of leeway in 'sociable,''' I observed, "but I'd better talk to her again. You must have her Jersey number and address.''

Wurf pulled a face and shook his head. "She's asked me not to release any personal data. Not even phone. This whole thing's got her spooked but good. Can't say I blame her, but—"

"Wait a minute,'' I said. "She stayed around until this week. Winding up affairs, cleaning out her house, getting ready for the Realtors. Granted she was upset...''

"New orders, what more can I tell you? Suzi gets spells of exaggerating her own importance. But I gotta run. Keep in touch. You find who killed Alfie, we've maybe got a wrongful death suit. Like I told you, I promised to do everything I can.''

He shook my hand and had the door open and the key

in the lock before I asked, "What does he look like?
Spotwood?"

"Tall, thin," Wurf shrugged. "Played some minor
league baseball, I understand. Back in the Dark Ages.
Tall, thin, and strong but couldn't handle quality pitch-
ing. You get a lot of guys like that."

Great, I thought. Certainly easy to pick *him* out in a
crowd. On impulse I asked, "Is he like Dowling? Does
he like sharp foreign cars?"

Wurf stopped, surprised. "Funny you should ask.
That's one of the few things they have in common.
They've got these identical black BMWs."

"How interesting," I said, but I could see the long
straight midnight road, the blinding lights, the man's surprised—I'm sure he was surprised—face, and hear the
fear in Suzi Rene's voice. I handed Wurfel Stanford one
of my business cards and promised to keep in touch.

He slipped the card into his wallet. "I'll be in D.C.
next week. Let me know what you find out, right? Anything I can do for Suzi, anything at all."

"Sure thing," I said, but I was beginning to think that
Suzi knew how to take care of herself.

ON THE RETURN to Orlando, I stopped for dinner at a
chain restaurant specializing in light meals and busy decor. Basically, they'd cleared Granny's attic and nailed
up everything portable, then filled in the gaps with
greenery and a nice line of Mexican tiles: Nostalgia Lite
Southwestern style. I dispatched my grilled chicken
salad, walked around the accompanying mall to stretch
my back, and found a phone booth.

"I've been on the phone all day," Harry said when
he answered.

"I know, I've tried a couple times. How are things?"

"Pretty interesting," he said in a satisfied tone. "The college called again."

"Really?" A good eastern school had been courting Harry for months, trying to get him to spend a year as artist in residence. I knew he'd been tempted, but since his heart attack, he's less easy traveling alone.

"They've offered me a semester position—three and a half months."

College administrators were getting smarter. "I think you should take it," I said. "If you think you'd enjoy teaching."

"I don't know," he said carefully. "I don't suppose you could get off for a couple months?"

"Not a whole semester," I said. "Maybe a month, three weeks. But let me check the schedule and see if I've got any jobs coming up in New England." We chewed this over for a while, but the more I encouraged him, the less willing he seemed to be. "Maybe in a couple years," he said. "When you cut back at the firm."

"Right," I said and changed the subject, sensing retirement once again in the air. I knew quite well that if I were free to go with him, Harry would take advantage of any number of interesting possibilities. The question was whether I was ready to give up Executive Security. This was delicate ground and by mutual consent, we switched to the marital small talk of the day's events and dinner menus, moved on to his artistic work in progress, and concluded with my not very satisfactory investigation. With these delays and a detour around an accident on the I-4, a spectacular Florida sunset was fading by the time I reached my motel.

Inside my room, I opened my laptop and dutifully checked my E-mail—a concession to Baby and Skipper, who have advanced ideas about efficiency. I took a shower. I switched on the TV, but the cable lineup was dismal, and my motel room, which suffered from an extra quota of mildew and a heavy line in air freshener, did not improve on acquaintance.

I was so bored that I was in danger of opening a serious consideration of my future—something I'd really been avoiding—when I made an escape via my notes. I found nothing suggestive there except for Parkes's marked interest in the news that Suzi Rene's brother was still in the area. Although Billy Deever hadn't been exactly cordial, I figured he might be worth a call. The phone at the Renes' rang unanswered, but it was still in service, meaning Billy must be staying in the house. I decided it couldn't hurt to drive past and see if his truck was still parked out front.

When I arrived, the security lights were on, but the house itself was dark except for a single dim light at the back. The building certainly looked unoccupied; no toys in the yard, no trash cans at the curb; the window curtains were tidily closed, the garage doors were shut and probably locked. The Renes' automatic sprinklers were still at work, though, because the FOR SALE sign at the edge of the lawn glistened with moisture, and there was a little pool of water on the sidewalk. The shrubbery looked neat, too, and the ornamental flowers, well tended. The Renes either employed a good lawn service or the Realtor was keeping an eye on them.

I very nearly turned around and drove back to my motel, but when I stepped out into the warm, humid night, there was something in the air. Despite the house's deserted appearance, one of those perceptions too subtle for rational thought impelled me to walk across and try the bell.

Standing on the wide step, I listened to the buzzer ring unanswered. Behind me, the neighborhood was at home behind its tinted picture windows and sun-defying blinds. Somewhere a stereo played and I could hear laughter and the sound of splashing water from a pool a few houses away. Otherwise, except for the omnipresent CRIME WATCH signs, the area appeared singularly private and unsupervised. I decided to take the light at the back of the house as an invitation. Making sure the street was empty, I slipped behind the ruffled ears of an assertive ornamental and made my way through the shadows. Bright reflections of security spots and streetlights rippled across a big glassed-in porch and then, around another clump of rampant greenery, a few lights sparkled over a gleaming marble counter and lit a fashionable, industrial-size stove. The pretty little halogen lights were probably on a timer, but better than nothing, especially combined with the big security service sticker pasted near the kitchen door.

I flicked on my penlight to check the name of the company and felt my heart jump. The door and the casement were covered with stains—red, recent, and ominously abundant. There was a handprint at the edge of the door, as if someone had grabbed it while it was half open. The doorknob was smeared, too, and underfoot were assorted drips and splotches. Someone had been bleeding, badly or just messily. He or she had come out the door and gone—where? I guessed to the garage, but back in the front yard, I found no blood on the garage door and just a few dark spots along the paving, suggesting a car left parked outside.

Since the neighborhood still showed no signs of excessive vigilance, I returned to the back. I intended to call the police, of course, but not yet. I hammered on the kitchen door, waited a moment, and considered the possibilities of an unpleasant reception. But nobody walks in Florida, and there were no cars in sight. I took out a handkerchief and, as carefully as possible, tried the knob. My guess was right. It was unlocked. I eased it open, alert for hoots and sirens, but the house remained silent as I slipped inside. I looked around quickly for the winking electronic eyes only to find that the control panel, located beside the door, had not been set. Another bad sign, but a safer entry for me. I stepped into Suzi Rene's one-hundred-grand kitchen.

I'd like to have had time to appreciate all the designer touches, but there were distractions: more splotches, an overturned chair, and, along the corridor and into the front hall, signs of a violent and desperate struggle in the spatters of blood, the cracked wall-mounted mirror, a broken kitchen chair, and a large and lethal-looking, but unbloodied, knife, which suggested that someone had either been disarmed or been injured too badly and too suddenly to make use of it.

The stains on the lower steps of the carpeted stairs reinforced these unpleasant thoughts. I went up a couple steps, avoiding the patches, and called his name. Not a sound. While I delayed my ascent, I examined another bloody handprint on the stairwell: definitely masculine and rather large. I remembered Billy as a fair bit over six feet, strong and surly looking. If it was his, his assailant had been powerful—or assisted.

I called again, then used my penlight to pick my way upstairs. The small beam of light narrowed the corridor and distorted the angles of the ceiling. When I opened the bedroom doors, the streetlights glowed through the drapes and blinds, lending the empty rooms a soft, aqueous light. The master suite, complete with a minispa in the bathroom, was empty, all furnishings stripped. Ditto the children's rooms, identifiable by their bright, patterned wallpaper, their borders of elephants and tigers, of clowns and ducks and spotted cats.

I checked the hall closets, all large, well shelved, and empty, and then approached a half-closed door at the end of the hall. My light picked up a smear of blood above the handle, as if someone had grabbed it. I pushed the door open with my foot. "Billy?" I asked.

The gauzy, filtered light from the street revealed a dark humped shadow. I forgot prints, caution, and the neighbors and felt along the wall for the light switch. A dazzling green-and-red haloed light flashed to life and only gradually dwindled to a tasteful wall-mounted lamp that cast a yellow pool onto a sofa bed. The amorphous shape was a pile of bedclothes and a leather jacket. I resumed breathing, checked behind all the doors, and made myself stir the bedclothes just in case. Then I prudently switched off the fixture and continued with my penlight.

Billy had clearly been ensconced in the guest room. Besides the leather jacket, he'd left behind an ashtray full of butts, an open can of beer, several bloodied bath towels, and a pair of sneakers. The closet was empty. I examined the adjoining bathroom reluctantly, but the nice, high-power recessed lights revealed only some drops of blood on the sink and a smear on the mirror. The shower stall was empty, if not very clean, and the half-open linen closet held nothing more sinister than a few rumpled towels. A visitor and a serious fight, followed by a hasty cleanup and departure? Maybe. That left only the big questions: Who came? Who was hurt? And where was Billy now?

Unwilling to push my luck, I switched off the lights

and went quietly back downstairs. The police would have to be notified, but not necessarily by me. In fact, best not by me, because they might start thinking along the same disagreeable lines that I was. I fished out the Realtor's card, went to the kitchen phone, and dialed into the real estate company's electronic labyrinth. I negotiated the automatic switchboard with its syrupy female voice and synthesized numbers and the multiple-choice voice-mail menu to reach pay dirt: the agent's pager number. Fortunately, Realtors work at night; she picked up on the third ring.

"There's been some damage to the Rene house on Magnolia Drive," I said. "You'd better call the police."

The agent was alert and suspicious. "Who is this?" she demanded.

"Neighborhood Crime Watch," I told her and hung up.

I wiped the receiver with a dish towel, opened and closed the door with great care, and got myself out of the Renes' neighborhood with all possible speed.

ELEVEN

"I NEED TO SEE YOU," I told T-Rex when I'd run the gauntlet of answering machine, Mindy, and Trish. "I need to see you as soon as possible."

"Yeah?" He sounded terminally uninterested. "What's up?"

"I don't want to talk on the phone."

"Where the hell are you?" he asked.

"I'm on the I-4 just outside of Lake Mary." I figured he was smart; if he was involved I wouldn't need to tell him anything more.

There was a moment's silence. "I can't see you tonight. No way. Richie just got home. Anything serious you settle with Sammy."

"I've got to ask you some questions," I said, "and I don't think you want Sammy involved."

Another long silence from T-Rex. The lights above the car phones were pulling moths and other night flyers into death spirals around the bulbs and loopy, fluorescent-drunk dives onto my front seat. Folks were roaring in and out of the 7-Eleven lot on beer and cigarette runs with their automotive stereos on high. Only when a particularly resonant system pulled away was I able to pick up the sounds behind my client. I heard a woman's voice calling him. "Yeah, yes. Right away. Nothing important," he told her. "Listen," he said to me in a different voice, very controlled, very calm, "listen, I'll see you tomorrow morning after practice. We're having a little party here. For Richie. He got home today with lots of good news.''

"I'm glad about that," I said. "You must be very relieved, but this is—"

"I don't care what the fuck it is," T-Rex said violently. "Richie's definitely in remission. The doctors are confident; the nurses applauded when he left, for Christ's sake. We think—" He caught himself. "We're sure he's over the worst. We're having a little party right now for him and the family and the kids next door. You can't know how terrific they've been to him. Hold on, he's trying to call his friend from the ward." T-Rex turned away from the receiver and called to his wife, "You get through to Chris?" A voice came indistinctly from the background. "I gotta go," he told me. "I don't want to miss this."

"All right," I said. Despite the booming stereos and the traffic hum and the voices from the party, Parkes's tangled emotions jumped right down the phone lines. Elation, anguish, and relief, plus the kind of willpower and drive that had made a small-town boy from darkest Quebec into all-everything, a megawatt merchandising commodity, and the marquee player of the decade. Whatever else he was—or did—T-Rex had a force of will second to none. "But as early as you can."

"Round eleven at the arena. I'll put you on the gate list. Tell them you're doing an article," he said and hung up.

I stretched out my car window and replaced the receiver. There are times when you're better off just to concentrate on numbers, on tidy reports and the quantifiable forms of misery; this was one of them. By rights, I should have called Sammy Allert, taken legal advice, maybe crashed the party. Instead, I drove back to my motel with a host of unpleasant permutations and the hope that T-Rex had a very strong alibi for the last twenty-four hours.

THE NU-RENA was cold. It lacked the real bone chill of a northern rink, but after the Florida heat outside, the clammy, meat-locker feel did almost as good a job. Down on ice level, refrigerant and exhaust came on strong, along with the hot smell of intense athletic exertion. I was in the Zamboni runway at the end of the arena, leaning on the boards with a few reporters who were watching for line changes and hoping for gossip. Practice was winding down. On the ice near us, enterprising radio guys had corralled a couple starters to tape halftime features for the following night's game, while some of the others were already stumping off to the locker room in their skates and their sweat-soaked practice jerseys.

The backup goalie was still busy in the nets directly to my right, taking practice shots from the reserves, who were lined up beyond the blue line. They attacked in pairs, the player on the left carrying the puck, then passing off as late as possible to his partner, who swept in from the right to take a shot on goal.

Minus the noise of the crowd, the sounds of practice were eloquent: icy chops as the players accelerated, insinuating whispers as they wheeled on open ice, a slushy scrape when they hit the brakes. A shot rattled off the pipes of the net and there was some good-natured banter, followed by the solid thock of a puck disappearing into the big catching glove, the crack of a stick as a player wound up a big shot, and the boom of a puck sailing wide into the Plexiglas: the workday sounds of big-time athletics.

T-Rex was still on the ice, too, practicing at the far end with the empty goal. He had a couple dozen pucks lined up in front of him, and he was skating down the line, flicking first one and then another into the corners of the net with methodical precision. According to one of the savvy types lounging along the boards, the great man was working on his wrist shot. He was a perfectionist, the press corps assured me, always one of the last off the ice. That made me feel better; I'd gotten the impression he was ducking our meeting.

Finally T-Rex came gliding by the boards, his stick easy in his gloved hands. He waved to the radio crew, schmoozed his way past the reporters, and told me he'd be out of the locker room in ten minutes. No temperament today; my client was all business, and the first thing he said to me when he came out and sat down in the stands was, "You got a notebook? Reporters always carry a notebook."

I dutifully produced one and looked around the cavernous arena. We were sitting ten rows up, and there was no one within earshot. Below, the Zamboni zipped up and down, noisily restoring the opaque chewed-up surface to a gleaming, transparent sheet.

"Where have you been since I left your house Tuesday?" I asked.

"I could ask you the same thing," he said.

"You know where I was. I went to see your wife. I saw the hospital, too, and lucky for you I did."

He gave me a look and clasped the seat in front of him with his massive hands. His knuckles were chafed and scratched; the right hand looked red and swollen— the usual wear and tear or some off-ice shenanigans?

"It made me sympathetic. Maybe I was foolish."

"I don't know what you're talking about," he said,

staring down over the ice. A couple of arena workers were out with their scrapers, tidying up the crease and getting ready to replace a goal.

"I went over to the Renes' house last night," I said. "I wanted to have a talk with Billy Deever. From your reaction the other day, I assume you know Billy."

T-Rex grunted. "I think he's left town."

"Under his own power?"

"How should I know?"

"That's the question," I said. "Listen, when I got there, the place was dark and deserted and the kitchen door was smeared with blood."

T-Rex said nothing.

"Naturally, I thought I'd better check out the house."

There was a flicker of interest.

"Especially when I found out the door was unlocked. I thought that was cause for concern."

"You might have called the police," he said.

"I might have, but suppose someone was hurt; better 911 and an ambulance. That was my thinking."

His green eyes watched me intently.

"Inside: total mess. There'd been a fight, obviously; quite a bad one. Blood on the floor and upstairs on bath towels."

T-Rex cleared his throat. "Facial cuts," he said in a knowledgeable way. "Head and facial cuts bleed. And some guys got tender skin. Even some boxers."

"You're suggesting minor injuries," I said.

"I'm suggesting sufficient injuries."

"Sufficient for what?"

"Billy wasn't a popular guy," T-Rex said. "Someone gave him the message he'd better get his ass out of town."

"Billy was what—maybe six foot one or two? Strong,

I'd guess, and not the most peaceable disposition. Yet there's blood all over the place and a big knife on the floor. What you're suggesting is that someone very substantial disarmed him and helped him to see the error of his ways."

T-Rex shrugged.

"At least there was no corpse in the bathtub," I said, "so I didn't feel I had to call the police. I called the Realtor instead."

Though surprised, T-Rex seemed insufficiently appreciative.

"She'll have called the cops, but better her than me. If I'd called, they'd have wanted to know why I was there and who I was working for—and all that would have led to you. I doubt it would take much effort to discover that you disliked Billy. Or that he was trouble in a small way. Maybe trouble for you?"

"How's that?" T-Rex asked. His voice was calm, but I could sense thunderclouds rolling in.

"I've been looking into Alf Rene's associates, his finances, his habits. Here's what I found: This was a guy who lived beyond his means. His finances were impenetrable even to his own agent. Besides playing hockey, Alf worked for some financial wizard's silent partner, and he probably borrowed money from old friends, money he didn't bother to repay. All this forms a pattern I could live without."

"This is Alf you're talking about, not Billy."

"Billy's a scavenger. He comes along, sees a deal, and tries to get a corner of it. Maybe seeing you're having legal troubles, he thinks he can cash in on them. How's that sound?"

"I'm not paying you for speculation."

"Don't be smart," I said. "I think you've been up to idiot games at the Renes'."

He started to deny it, but I went right on.

"You were mighty interested to learn Billy was back in town and staying at the Renes'. You were pissed off that someone had broken into your garage. It seems to me that you're plenty big enough to have taken Billy apart if you thought it would help, and I notice that your hands are all beat up. Now back to the original question—have you got an alibi for between Tuesday night when I told you about Billy and, say, ten o'clock last night?"

"I was home with the kids," he said.

"Don't waste my time. You drove out of the development while I was surrounded by the press. Be real. This could be serious."

"I went to the hospital. I saw Richie. Then I was home. Practice the next day. Time in between? Sure, I could have done it. Would I? Ditto—Billy's a slimeball. But they'd sure have to prove it."

"Your prints would be all over the place."

"The Renes and me were old friends; of course there would be fingerprints. It's your job to come up with some alternatives; after all, you're working for me."

"A circumstance I'm coming to regret. Let's, for a moment, assume you did do it. Was it because he planted the pipe?"

Silence.

"You owe me," I said. "I protected you against my better judgment. Alf's blood was on that pipe and it's a super bad thing to have show up in your garage carrying your wife's prints."

T-Rex began radiating his forceful displeasure. "He tried to involve Trish. And my kids. I was willing to put up with a certain amount from Alfie; Alfie and me went a long way back, but no way was he going to involve Trish and the family. No way. Soon as you mentioned Billy, I knew it was him.''

''So you went over and confronted him and beat him silly?'' I was staggered by the blind, impulsive stupidity of it.

T-Rex moved his massive shoulders as if surprised himself, as if his enormous strength and courage caused these occasional miscalculations.

''Why, for god's sake, didn't you tell me or tell the police?'' I asked. ''You and your lawyers are going to have to account for that pipe. If you have any reason to think Billy Deever planted it, we'd all appreciate the information.''

''I didn't know he was in town until you told me. Then it just rang a bell.''

Great: a client who's both violent and intuitive. ''So, why do you think it was Billy?''

Another big silence: T-Rex sat on information like a hen on eggs.

''Do you have any idea how bad your situation is? You're the only suspect at the moment. There have already been suggestions that your wife was protecting you when she 'found' the pipe. If this comes out, you'll be in custody for sure. Do you understand that?'' I began to wish I'd organized this meeting in Sammy Allert's office. ''No parties, no hospital visits, no kids, period.''

T-Rex stood up. ''I gotta get out of here,'' he said. ''Let's go outside.''

He hustled up the arena steps and out through the concourse doors. A brilliant sun turned the lobby glass to blue and gold. By the time I reached the exit, T-Rex was already pacing the sidewalk, sullen, even homely, but magnetic, undeniably magnetic, and I had mixed feelings about being old and wise and sensible. I watched him for a few seconds, anyway, then stepped out into the sun. He pivoted in mid-stride and said, "I couldn't have him worrying my kids. And Trish. Trish has been terrific. When I'm away—everything falls to Trish. You see what I'm saying? It was just the wrong day, the wrong time. Waiting for Richie's tests, you snooping around, that half-assed meeting with the directors, reporters pounding on the doors and sneaking in the windows—I was sick of waiting around being stared at. It was time to do something, to get some action going."

Spare us from men of action; they cause trouble every time. "You called him up? You went to the house?"

"Soon as you left, I got in the car and went to see Trish and Richie at the hospital. Coming home it was getting dark; I was chewing things over, wondering if I'd guessed right, and then I decided, why not? So I drove to Alfie's house and rang the bell. There's Billy."

"Was he surprised?"

"Naw. Scared, not surprised. I might of had some doubts if he'd been surprised. He asks me if I want a drink, a cup of coffee. He's just having a cup of coffee, he says. I says okay. He goes into the kitchen, and I'm looking at the woodwork when I see him reflected in that big fancy mirror in the hall. He's got something shiny in his hand."

"A large kitchen knife."

"You got it. I didn't have any doubts then."

"What kind of shape was he in when it was over?" I asked.

"He'd felt better," T-Rex said. His tone was judicious; his work had made him a connoisseur. "I broke his nose, I guess, and he'll lose a couple teeth. Like I say, facial cuts bleed. Ribs, too, maybe, but nothing serious. Nothing he didn't deserve, either.''

"Had you called the cops then—self-defense, provocation—"

"It was none of their business."

"Anything to do with Alf Rene's death is their business now."

T-Rex started toward the parking lot without saying anything more.

"You never answered my question," I said. "About how you knew it was Billy."

"You were right about Billy. He leeched onto his sister the minute Alfie and she were married. He was always looking for an angle."

"It's his precise angle I'm interested in."

"That's a weight bar that turned up in our garage. Alf had a set of weights. We've all got weights."

"Fine, but what about the blood? Are you saying that Billy killed him and kept the murder weapon?"

"I'm not saying anything about that; as I told the cops, I don't know zip about Alfie's death. What I do know is that Alfie took nosebleeds. He was always bleeding on stuff. He used to take nosebleeds when he was working out with weights. It used to drive the trainer berserk with all this stuff about AIDS and hepatitis, so finally Alfie worked on the weights at home. He was okay on the treadmill and the bikes and the leg lifts. Get him on the weights and bingo. Billy must have found the bar, seen the possibilities."

I thought about that. "He was helping his sister pack when I arrived the other day."

"There you go. He finds the bar, figures he'll make a little trouble."

"I'm not sure I buy that. Does he have a reason to dislike you? Does he have something else that implicates you? There's got to be something more."

"I never got a chance to ask him any of that stuff," T-Rex growled, "and by the time I left, he didn't have much to say."

TWELVE

I SPENT A FAIR BIT of time trying to convince my client to involve his agent and his lawyer. No way. "Billy didn't file any complaint, did he?" T-Rex kept saying.

"God only knows. We don't know where he is, do we?"

"Chill out," said T-Rex. "He's gone north to his sister's. He'll be in Jersey City by tomorrow morning."

"You hope."

"No one would ever have known about it if you hadn't gone blundering in there," he said, glaring at me. "We wouldn't have had to worry at all. Who'd have known if you hadn't called?"

"Don't expect me to ignore a crime scene for you. How was I to know you'd be dumb enough to attack Alf's brother-in-law?"

He had some intemperate thoughts on that, but I cut him off. "If you'd been candid at the start, I wouldn't have needed to visit Billy. It's pretty hard to investigate a case if you don't know who your client is going to beat up on next."

T-Rex tapped on the roof of his sleek silver Porsche. He looked just as big and twice as heavy as the little frog-eyed machine. "Why don't you look for another client," he said.

Lucky me, I thought, but then I was annoyed. Never do anything extra for a customer. "Are you firing me?"

"You can take it that way."

"Fine. I'll go see Sammy Allert and have him settle our account."

T-Rex pulled out his wallet.

"No, no," I said. "Everything through Sammy, that was your arrangement. Plus now the team's involved; they're picking up part of the tab—management wanted to show support for you and all that. I can explain the whole thing to them, but—"

T-Rex swore and kicked one of his tires. When I asked if he was threatening me, he said I'd know for sure when he did. We parted on disagreeable terms. If it hadn't been for his wife and his brave, sickly son, I'd have packed my bags and had Martha send a bill. Instead, I collected my rental and drove back to the Renes' house.

The driveway was full and the lawn was getting crowded. Harriet, Suzi's dynamic Sibley and Martin Realtor, was out front, mediating between a stocky bearded gent in a khaki Wel-Klean uniform and a tall, sallow, skeptical local cop, who kept trying to raise his sergeant on the cruiser radio.

Wel-Klean wanted to go in and start cleaning or, alternately, to be on his way. He had a route and a schedule; management was all over his ass about timing. "The Lapalmes have to get done before one when the maid leaves; the Hibbards, they gotta be finished by two when the Mrs. gets home. She wants everything clean when she walks in the door and no van out front, either—likes to think it just happens by magic. So I gotta move. Plus I got customers over Altamonte Springs. Either I get in now or I gotta come back tomorrow."

Harriet had another set of troubles. She had a prospect coming at three and bloodstains reduce eye appeal. At a minimum, the kitchen door had to be washed and the upstairs bathroom. The stairway carpet had to be lifted as well. The cop could have the bloody section. "Put it in an evidence bag or whatever and take it away. You can have the mirror pieces, too," she said in this pathetic voice. She could see a blue chip property going at a fire-sale price.

The cop was suspicious of the whole business and pretty sure he was going to get criticized no matter what he did. He kept moving his mouth about damage, paperwork, and possible crime scene contamination.

"Crime scene!" Harriet was almost in tears. "Crime scene—someone gets a bloody nose or cuts his hand on the mirror and it's a crime scene. I'm sorry I called the police in the first place. I should just have called Wel-Klean and complained to Mrs. Rene. It's never a good idea to have a tenant in a property you want to sell for top dollar." She turned to me for confirmation of this wisdom. "I explained all that to Mrs. Rene at the time."

"Wait a minute. You got blood damage on the property?" the Wel-Klean man demanded. "We don't handle any of that stuff. Today's market, you gotta get a specialist firm for that. See, we just don't have the technology." While he ran down his equipment, I reintroduced myself to Harriet. I had the feeling my voice rang a bell for her, but she had too many worries at the moment to look for more. I said that I still needed Suzi Rene's address for some last-minute details about the team and the insurance, and I asked if her brother, Billy, had returned.

"He damn well better not return," the Realtor said, her mouth set in a grim line. "Not with the mess he's left in the house."

"Really?"

"Stair carpet stained, hall mirror smashed, one of the

set of kitchen chairs broken—you know what it's like to try to match a set of chairs.''

''And he just left? What about his truck? He had a truck, didn't he? Is the garage—?''

''Oh, I checked all that. He left some oil stains on the garage floor, and a pile of greasy rags; I don't know what he was up to.''

Behind us the cruiser phone squawked. While the three principals reconvened, I drifted over to the neighbor's house and rang the bell. Pursued by a woman's voice, small feet pounded down the hall and small hands wrestled with an interior door.

''What's your name?'' a sturdy little boy demanded repeatedly through the screen. He was maybe three and unencumbered by the social graces. When his older sister pushed him out of the way to say ''hello,'' he tore back down the hall, broadcasting the news that I was at the door.

''Come in, Maureen,'' a voice called.

''It's not Maureen,'' I said.

''Oh. I was expecting my neighbor over. It's play group planning day.'' Mothers, like policemen, athletes, and politicians, seem to be getting younger all the time. This one was dark haired and slim in cutoffs and sandals. Her friendly, open expression turned cautious when she registered that I was not from the neighborhood.

''Anna Peters. I'm a private investigator down from D.C. I'm collecting information about Alfred Rene's death, and I was hoping to get in touch with Suzi Rene through her brother.''

She hesitated, glanced across the lawns to register the police car, my rental, the Realtor's car, and the Wel-Klean van, then unhooked the screen and said, ''Come in for a minute.''

The children were jumping around her, clamoring for a favorite TV show, for a snack, for their mom's undivided attention. Since children have an acute instinct for parental vulnerability, I guessed that the Renes were a sensitive topic. Mom broke down on the snack, ruled out the TV, and put her offspring outside in their sandbox.

"I'm Lorna Wall," she said when the little ones had departed. "The Renes weren't here long but they seemed nice neighbors. Sarah, that's my daughter, and their Deena were such good friends. We'd planned to have them over before Suzi went north. The day they left, we were all set for a cookout. Sarah was just devastated when she woke up and found they were gone."

"I can imagine."

Sarah's aggrieved mother began to explain the psychological ramifications of this disappointment, the importance of childhood friends, the evolution of the children's play group. I made appropriate comments and agreed with everything until I could ask about Billy Deever.

"I didn't feel good about Billy," Lorna said. "Of course, it was important for Suzi to have someone in the house with her, but Billy was a different sort of person altogether. I wouldn't let the children play there unless Suzi was home."

I heard a lot more along this line. Mrs. Wall was not only a dedicated mom but keen on explaining the rationale behind each of what she referred to as her "parenting decisions." I expected the kids were hellions who would give her grief.

"Have you seen Billy in the last few days? I did want to talk to him."

"Oh, I don't think he's come back. He's quite unreliable, comes and goes without thinking about the house at all.'' She leaned over her sink to check what was going on in the Renes' yard. ''I heard the truck go out Tuesday night. That was it; he left without even turning off the sprinklers. My husband, Joe, had to go over and turn them off manually yesterday morning. It's a private well, but it's drawing down the water table.''

''Do you know what time he left?''

''We'd had dinner and I was trying to get the kids quieted down and ready for bed when Billy started revving that truck motor. Sarah thought maybe it was Deena back—she isn't convinced they've really moved permanently yet—and she jumped up and ran to the door. I went after her because he's so reckless, backs up— varoom—out of the garage, down the drive, into the street without looking. The Renes were nice people, but Billy acted like he'd never lived in a decent neighborhood before. That's the attraction of this area; people are used to living in a neighborhood, they're looking out for children.''

''And you saw Billy?''

''Oh, it was him, all right, with sunglasses on—at that time of night.'' Her young, mobile face managed to suggest a variety of entertaining depravities. ''A baseball cap on, too, and holding a handkerchief up against his face, but it was him. I could have told from the way he drove the truck. No thought, no consideration at all.''

I felt immensely relieved. Billy wasn't stuffed into the trunk of T-Rex's Porsche or lying in a ditch somewhere. My errant client had told the truth, and the worst T-Rex could be charged with was assault and battery, plus stupidity in the first degree. That was not good but it beat the alternatives.

''When I saw the policeman this morning, he asked me the same thing,'' Lorna Wall continued. ''There was some sort of trouble, wasn't there? They wouldn't tell me anything, although I felt I had a right to know. We're with the Neighborhood Crime Watch and without police cooperation, we can't function.''

I was sympathetic. Half an hour later, I knew a great deal about the Walls' child-rearing practices, the friendship between Sarah Wall and Deena Rene, the structure—and most of the politics—of the Neighborhood Crime Watch group. I also knew that Billy Deever had left the Renes' at approximately nine p.m. the night he was beaten up. And though she couldn't say for sure whether he'd come back or not, she hadn't seen him since.

I thanked her sincerely. As I was leaving, I tried for Suzi's Jersey address, but although Mrs. Wall was quite willing to retail Billy Deever's faults, she turned cautious at this request. I didn't push it. Stuck to the refrigerator with a magnet in the shape of a panda was a childishly scrawled note. The only word large enough and clear enough to read was "Oradell." I thought I could pull up my fancy laptop atlas and see if that might be somewhere in New Jersey.

First, though, I had to work my way through the near neighbors, an hour's worth of effort that proceeded to complicate what I thought I knew. Billy had had visitors. That was established by the elderly gent who owned the pink Spanish-style house diagonally across from the Renes'. In recent days he'd noticed a dark, expensive sedan, a sports car, and some sort of sport-utility vehicle parked in the Renes' driveway. "Not a Bronco, though," he added regretfully. He'd followed the O. J. Simpson trial avidly, and he had a lot of opinions he managed to share with me before I got him back on track.

The sports car was a light-colored Porsche. It had been around a couple of times. I tried to get days. He was sure Wednesday.

"Yesterday?" I was surprised.

"Yesterday was Wednesday, Missus, just like I said." He gave me an indignant look behind his thick bifocals.

"What time?"

"Afternoon. About three, three or three-thirty."

"And Mr. Deever?"

My informant made a face and shook his head. "Up to all hours that one. Now I go to bed early. Nine, nine-thirty that's enough for me. Nothing but junk on TV after that anyway. Deever's never stirring till late. I heard him go out Tuesday night. Heard him come back, too. Must have been two a.m.."

"You heard the truck? You're sure it was a truck?"

"Listen, I worked in automotive. I was a supervisor in Detroit when we were making American cars instead of running these Jap imports. Sure, I heard it."

"Was the truck in the drive Wednesday?"

"Naw. Either in the garage or it went out again. If I'm on the other side of the house, I don't hear so good. I wasn't figuring it was important to keep track of that guy."

"So you didn't see him Wednesday, but you did see the sports car."

"Like I told you. This big guy gets out and goes to ring the bell. I noticed cause I noticed the car. Some of those German cars are pretty popular nowadays. Course they're built different with their autobahns and speed laws and such."

I heard about the subtle differences in national auto design while I digested what he'd told me. Billy—or at least his truck—had returned; so apparently had T-Rex.

That left a host of questions, including why T-Rex had omitted his second visit to the Rene homestead.

The very pregnant young woman on the other side of the Renes' wasn't able to help with the answers. She hadn't paid much attention to either the Renes or Billy Deever. And although she assured me that Alf Rene's death had been too bad, a real tragedy, she was glad it hadn't happened in their neighborhood. To be honest, the Renes and their troubles hadn't captured her interest, not when the heat was killing her and she was a week late on her delivery date. The only thing she wanted to know was if the fellow with the truck was coming back. I told her that was something I'd like to find out myself.

She'd seen him leave, she mentioned. Just the other night.

"Really? Tuesday? Wednesday? About what time?"

She took her time answering. "Tuesday. It must have been right after eight thirty. We watched *Roseanne* and then I went out to water my flowers. I wait until it cools off a little."

"And Billy Deever came out?"

"Staggering. I'm sure he was drunk. I'm glad my husband wasn't out with me; Kevin would certainly have said something and I never liked the look of that fellow. Anyway, he was holding a towel up to his face and carrying a bag, you know, a gym bag, and he was walking kind of unsteady. He opened his truck door, climbed in, and went rocketing out the drive."

Billy's distinctive driving style seemed to impress everyone. As for his possible return, she couldn't help. "I hear cars all night," she complained. "In and out, driving around. The Renes were nice enough, but they had a lot of cars. I just shut the blinds and ignore everything."

We talked for a few more minutes, but Tuesday and Wednesday nights were rapidly merging into the timeless miseries of late pregnancy. After wishing her good luck and a safe delivery, I headed back to my car. Every time things began to look straightforward, someone came along to confuse the issue. When I noticed the Realtor's jaunty pink hatchback still parked in the drive, I figured I should give her a chance to muddy the waters as well. I tried the Renes' bell, and the Realtor opened the door in a fluster.

"Oh," she said when she saw me. "I thought you were my prospect. I called and left a message, moved our appointment back, but you never know. I can't talk to you now; I've got a million things to do—besides firing Wel-Klean."

"What will you do about the mirror?" I asked, nodding toward the hallway.

"Oh, that." She gave me an appraising look. "I've brought a mirror. A total bear to hang. I've been wondering who I could get to help me."

Although foreseeing disaster for my back, I smiled gamely. "Maybe I could give you a hand while we talk. I don't want to make you late."

"All right! Let's get the replacement out of my car." The solution to her difficulty restored Harriet's brisk, cheerful manner. "First impressions are so vital in this price bracket. But curb appeal on this one is very good, lots of positives, don't you think?" she asked as we stepped out into the yard.

I agreed that the property was immensely appealing.

"And custom galore inside; all the hot buttons, all the goodies. It's a dream property, but that broken mirror just jumps out at you. You can see my problem."

I could indeed. "Broken by the movers?"

"Carrying a highboy down the hall," she said. "Slippery marble floor, mirror replacement expected in a week, but you can't replace that first look."

"It's a pretty big area to cover," I said.

"Wait till you see." She threw open the hatchback. The entire cargo space, including the rear-seat area, was taken up with an immense rectangle wrapped in brown paper and padded with mover's quilts. "Voilà! A decorator I know loaned it. Not a particularly valuable one but it looks antique. Really better than the effect of that passé installed mirror."

While she instructed me in the finer points of decorating to sell, we wrestled the beast out of the car. The mirror was brittle, awkward, and heavy as lead; I could see back maintenance in my future. After a great deal of effort, we muscled the package to the door and into the hall.

"I have two hangers," Harriet announced. She had a step stool, too, and a level. While I unwrapped the rather cloudy but definitely atmospheric mirror with its tarnished gilt frame, she mounted the fasteners above the ruined glass. Those in place, we each took a side and heaved. Alas, the hanging wire did not slip easily onto the hooks. We jiggled it one way and then another, while the gilt frame squealed against the remnants of the mirror below, and the muscles in my lower back twitched experimentally and considered a seizure.

"I'll have to reach behind," Harriet said. "Can you hold it just for a minute?"

"A minute," I gasped, "not a second more."

"Lean it on the wall," she said as she hauled her stepladder into range. She scrambled up and felt around behind the mirror. "Keep it straighter, I can't catch the wire."

I pulled the mirror back from the wall and felt it sway alarmingly before Harriet caught one of the hooks. "All right! One will hold it. Just keep a hand on it till I get to the other side." She dragged the ladder behind me, got up on the other side, and after a moment's struggle, snapped the wire in place.

"Can I let go?"

"All set. But not quite straight."

We now began a painstaking series of adjustments— a little to the right, a little to the left, too low, too high, before she was satisfied. The large muscles across my lower back were in open rebellion.

"A nice look," Harriet pronounced as I leaned against the banister. "Really an improvement with that birds-and-flowers wallpaper."

I glanced at the stair carpet. One of the risers was bare. "Looks like that highboy caught a bit of your stair runner, too."

"That's what I'll tell them," she said. "Actually, we think there was a fight. I knew he was trouble. I hinted as much to Suzi Rene, but what can you do? He actually left some bloodstained towels lying around upstairs. Thank god I'd been warned. Imagine walking in with a client, pattering on about this lovely property and there's bloodstains everywhere."

I agreed that would be a shock.

She checked her large, smart wristwatch. "Time for the upstairs. I figured do the downstairs first and hope for the best." She retrieved a mop and bucket from the kitchen. I followed along with a pile of plastic trash bags. I couldn't resist the opportunity to go through the house legitimately, even if it required janitorial duty.

"You'd wanted to ask me something," she said.

"I wanted to know more about Billy Deever and I want to get in touch with Suzi Rene."

"Have a look around upstairs and you'll know as much as I do about Billy Deever. Suzi—" She hesitated. "Suzi wants all communication to go through me."

"Very wise," I said, "And have you informed her about this?" I was interested to learn her reaction.

Harriet stopped on the stair landing and looked uncomfortable. "I've not been able to get in touch with her. We do handle these situations routinely: vandalism, break-ins are surprisingly common even in the nicest communities."

"Was this a break-in?" I asked.

"Well, the assumption is," she began and stopped.

"Window broken? Door forced? Security system disabled?"

She gave me a sharp, suspicious look and then, perhaps remembering my yeoman work on emergency decorating, reconsidered. "Not a thing. The security system had been shut off. No other damage. The police looked around pretty thoroughly. They didn't like the blood but basically they're not too concerned. Billy Deever seems to have gotten into a fight and left the property. No loss! I was furious about the mess, naturally, but the police have other things to worry about and, frankly, making too much of a fuss isn't going to help me close this sale quickly."

Harriet stopped halfway down the hall to check the stain remover she'd applied to the carpet, then turned into the guest room. "Let me have one of those plastic bags. If he comes back and looks for his towels he'll just find them gone, that's all."

She loaded up the soiled towels, dumped bleach into

the sink and the shower and started mopping the floor.
I offered to tidy the sofa bed.

"Close it up and we'll hope for the best."

I shook out the sheet and the light quilt and checked
down the sides of the bed. I turned up fifty cents and a
couple of matchbooks, one from a local restaurant. I
made a note of the name and left them beside the ashtray. Billy drank Coors. I found a couple of empty cans.
He smoked Marlboros. The ashtray was full. He had
made phone calls. There was a phone on the bedside
table and a local phone book underneath it with lots of
numbers scribbled in a hasty, masculine hand on the
cover. I opened my notebook and wrote them all down.
Inside, I looked for that handy list of frequently called
numbers, but those pages had been ripped out. Suzi Rene
had had a better grasp of security than her brother. I was
about to close the book, when I thought of the maps in
the back. Billy Deever hadn't known the area. Sure
enough, one had been removed.

Harriet bustled in as I was replacing the book.

"That ashtray will have to be dumped. Matches, everything out. Beer cans, too! At least the boxes of papers
are all gone."

"Papers?"

"I don't know. The house was perfectly clean and
empty the day Suzi and the children left. The next time
I stop by, Billy's in residence and he's got papers and
file folders strewn around. He said, get this, he said he
was doing his taxes. I'm trying to sell the house and he's
set up a squatter's encampment."

I wondered where those papers were now. "What
about the bathroom?" I asked. "Shaving stuff, tooth-
brushes—did he leave anything to suggest he was coming back?"

"Shaving cream and a toothbrush," she said. "No razor, no toothpaste. He was so sloppy, who knows what he'd had in mind. We'll just dump everything."

She had just finished loading up the plastic bags when the front door chimed.

"Great timing. You're going to luck out," I said.

She stripped off her cleaning gloves and ran her hand through her hair.

"Want me to take down the bags and the mop and bucket?"

"Oh, that would be kind. If you could just take them out through the kitchen door and leave them in the garage. It's unlocked. The trash cans are in there. Better not to raise questions in the client's mind."

That sounded sensible to me. I let myself out the kitchen to the sound of Harriet greeting her client with professional enthusiasm. I opened the garage, stored the cleaning supplies, and checked the trash can, which held a couple sacks of plastic-bagged garbage. I opened these up and sorted through the contents carefully. Ten minutes later, I closed up the garage and walked back to my rental. For what it was worth, I knew where Billy went to eat, I knew the numbers he called, and I had a few dirty, torn, spaghetti-smeared snapshots, the debris of family pictures, showing various members of the Rene family, including Billy Deever himself.

THIRTEEN

I GOT BACK to my motel thoroughly fed up with T-Rex Parkes and his evasions and omissions. The case was taking more than its share of time and keeping me in Leisure Land far longer than I'd anticipated. Had things been different, I'd have flown home to have a row with Allert and to pursue Alf's finances through data banks, credit bureaus, and Baby's files. That would have been the sensible MO, but when I tried to get out of my car in the motel parking lot, pain clenched across my lower back. With one foot poised over the blacktop and one hand on the door, I dropped a gear and found my body in neutral. I swung my leg back in, edged around carefully in the seat, and, on the second try, managed to get both feet on the asphalt. Triumph, except that I was bent over at a nearly 90-degree angle. I leaned down on the door frame and levered myself upright to the accompaniment of shooting pains. Getting back down to pick up my bag and papers was agonizing, and the walk across the lot to the motel lobby convinced me that upright locomotion was an evolutionary mistake.

A consultation with the desk clerk and several phone calls produced a small spare room at Suntime Physical Therapy, where I was diagnosed with back spasms, plunked on a table, and loaded up with a saddle of hot towels to await the physio. Half an hour later, a muscular young fellow in a "Go Gators" T-shirt, a spectacular tan, and a revolting air of health and vitality breezed in, clipboard in hand. He poked my back, examined my stance, and clucked regretfully over my follies.

"Glass is darn heavy. And lifting anything over shoulder height has got to be a no-no for you."

"It was in the line of duty," I said.

He observed that we all have to be careful of our body mechanics, especially as we get older.

Lucky him. He was clearly at the age when such cautions are still theoretical. "I need to get out of here. I'm due back in D.C. by the weekend. I have people to see, appointments to keep."

"We'll loosen up the muscles with massage," he said, "but you're going to have to stick with the exercises and keep walking. Within reason, walking is good. Sit as little as possible. Chairs are death to the spine. No lifting, goes without saying. Absolutely no sudden stress on your back. Otherwise you'll regret it."

I winced as he touched a particularly tender spot.

"You've got some damage," he said, "but nothing yet that can't be rehabilitated. Stay off muscle relaxants. Your G. P. will advise, but the problem is you feel okay and then you're apt to reinjure the muscles."

I decided to call my physician as soon as I escaped from Go Gators' sadistic clutches.

"There're no shortcuts," he said, as if reading my mind.

"I've been doing my exercises pretty faithfully," I said.

Go Gators grunted noncommittally. "A healthy spine is the patient's responsibility," he said. "Here at Suntime, we really believe in having the patient take control of her back."

Thirty minutes later, having imbibed the physio's moral imperatives along with his skillful massage, I was up and ambulatory, my rebellious muscles stretched, toned, and reassured. Nonetheless, flight was out. I knew that even from the drive between the physio's and the motel. Airplane seats, luggage: my back went spastic at the thought. Maybe tomorrow. Maybe the next day. In the meantime, I decided to lie on my bed and work the phone. When attempts to corner either my client or his agent failed, I decided to try Billy Deever's numbers.

The first ones were unrewarding: a local pizza and sub shop, a transmission specialist, a video rental place eager to offer the best in "adult entertainment." The one out-of-area number eventually rang unanswered in Oradell, New Jersey. His sister's place, I guessed, but when I tried to confirm that by calling directory assistance, I was told "S. Rene's" phone number was unlisted. No listing, no answering machine—celebrity caution or, combined with her sudden early-hours departure, outright fear? I would like to have known for sure.

I called my office and told Baby to have someone find Suzi Rene's address in case we needed to get in touch with her, then I worked through the rest of the numbers. I recognized one as T-Rex's home number, also unlisted. It was no real surprise that Billy knew the Parkes's number, but vaguely disturbing that it turned up among numbers he'd been calling regularly. Another number rang the Lakeside, a restaurant and bar where Billy had collected some matches. The ad assured me of "fine cuisine in a gracious lakeside ambiance," which somehow didn't sound like Billy's scene.

I revised that thought after I'd tried the last number. This one was answered by a Southern voice at once soft and precise, "Spotwood residence."

Now that was interesting. "Could I speak to Mr. Spotwood?'' I asked. "This is Anna Peters. I'm trying to contact a friend of his.''

There was a pause, buttons clicked, and a flat, northeastern voice came on the line. "Who's calling?" he asked. His chilly tone didn't suggest "gracious ambiance.''

I introduced myself. Mr. Spotwood was not impressed.

''This is an unlisted number. How did you get it?''

''It's important that I contact Billy Deever,'' I said. "He left me this number as a place where he might be reached.''

''I've never heard of him,'' Spotwood said. "Don't call here again.''

''Surely you have heard of him,'' I protested. "He's the late Alf Rene's brother-in-law. I believe Alf Rene worked for you.'' The line had already gone dead.

I called my secretary in D.C. and had her check our extensive collection of city directories: Spotwood lived on a big rural spread northeast of Orlando and quite near Lake Monroe. Maybe near the Lakeside Restaurant? I flipped back to the phone book maps, comparing the full assortment to the ones I remembered in the Renes' phone book. The missing one covered the Lake Monroe area. I got up, stretched experimentally, and decided my back could manage a short drive to dinner.

The Lakeside was an eatery hovering between chic and seedy. Smack on a largely undeveloped stretch of lakefront, the wood frame structure with its big screened and glassed porches and private dock suggested an earlier, pre-air-conditioning prosperity. The neglected paint, crumbling parking lot, and tired interior testified to the inroads of cheaper chain restaurants and swanky theme eateries, as well as to the irresistible attractions of Disney World and its Orlando satellites.

Inside, the dining room was large—oversize, really, for its location, and half empty. I took a menu but stood at the bar. I could see right away that the bar stools were impossible—wrong height, without back support, "death to the spine," while the metal cafe chairs in the dining area were only slightly better.

Over mineral water and a beer, I checked out the clientele. I suspected most were elderly boaters attracted by the dock and the nearby marina, for there were considerably more people in the Lakeside than the nearly empty parking lot suggested. A few diners looked like tourists off the beaten track; the rest, family parties, locals on a night out.

After the bartender had refilled all the orders and started mopping his counter, I produced a tattered snap showing Billy and the Renes and asked if he'd ever seen either of the men in the restaurant.

The bartender set down his towel, took the photo in hand and studied it curiously. He was young with pale, alert eyes behind little round anarchist glasses. His long, thin face ended in a square, determined jaw.

"Looks like you need to buy a photo album," he said, eyeing the stained and torn picture.

A rogues gallery, I thought to myself.

"He looks kinda familiar." He tapped Alf's face. "But I don't think he's been in the bar."

"Minor celebrity," I said. "You might have seen a news photo. What about the other guy?"

"No. But I'm only on end of the week and weekends. You'd have to ask Steve. He's on nights the rest of the time."

"All right, thanks," I said.

"Course the woman, I know," he added offhandedly. "Least, she used to be a regular. In every other weekend and lunch once a week. I work the afternoon shift ordinarily."

"Really. Did she come in alone?"

"Naw. Comes in with a big guy who's got a boat on the lake. A really nice sailboat, that's all I know."

"Ever mention his name?"

"I don't remember. I'm good with faces, not so good with names. People come in, you know, they talk to you, they don't necessarily want to introduce themselves."

I slipped a bill out of my wallet and slid it under my glass. "You said she used to be a regular. When was that?"

"About a year ago. Couple times a week, you could count on it. Then, I don't know, from late spring, early summer—no show. Maybe she goes up north."

"What about this fall? Have you seen her at all?"

"Once or twice, but like I say, maybe she's just changed her day. You'd have to ask Steve."

I clarified Steve's schedule and retired to the dining room to check out the patrons and try the grouper, characterized by the bartender as "pretty reliable." I chose a window table where I watched the last of a photo perfect pink-and-orange sunset close down ahead of anvil-headed storm clouds boiling up in the east. Across the lake, a white toylike sailboat raced for the shore. Then the late-day clouds darkened, the sky turned to slate, and lightning shot toward the water in blinding white flares.

In contrast to the ultra-managed landscape, weather in Leisure Land had a pleasingly primal aspect. Within minutes, the rushing storm reached the Lakeside. Sheets of rain smashed against the porches and decks, setting the marina lights bobbing and obliterating the lake. Fac-

ing a gray wall of water, I opened my map and found
the road where Spotwood lived, a meandering secondary
running along the northern shore. If he kept a boat on
the water, it would be an easy sail down to the dock at
the Lakeside. To meet Suzi Rene?

I decided it wouldn't hurt to have a look at Mr. Spotwood, and when the short, violent storm dwindled to
sporadic showers, I paid my bill and got in my car. Spotwood's residence was hard to find in the dusk. A black
Florida night had set in well before I reached a long
cement driveway that wound through swamps and pastures toward a thick grove of trees along the water. The
house was another oversized pseudo-Spanish number
with big arched windows and doors. There were lights
on around a pretty courtyard terrace visible through a
wrought iron grille, but otherwise no signs of life. I rang
the bell and waited, listening to the drip of rainwater off
the eaves and to the slap and rustle of the palms in the
lakeshore breeze.

When there was no answer, I rang again. The house
was fitted with tinted, reflecting windows that gave no
clue to what was inside, and another fine iron grille
locked over the exterior door, creating an effect that was
half authentic Spanish, half neighborhood under siege.
Somewhere nearby a heron squawked and cattle moved
in the fields around the house. This was a thoroughly
deserted area, and I had time to consider the merits of
the whole idea before the door opened. I was surprised
to see Bennett Dowling. He was in his bon vivant mode,
holding a cocktail in one hand and a cigarette in the
other, but he didn't look at all happy to see a visitor. He
made no move to unlock the grille, leaving me standing
under the drips from the roof.

"Anna Peters," I said. "I spoke to you in your office the other day. About Alf and Suzi Rene."

"That's right!" he said attempting joviality. "Found any trace of our Suzi yet?"

"Not yet," I admitted.

"You'll let me know," he asked. "You'll let me know the minute she turns up?" A powerful smell of bourbon wafted in my direction.

"Sure," I said. "But actually I came to see Mr. Spotwood. Is he in?"

"Incommunicado," Dowling said with a nervous laugh. He swayed gently back and forth on the balls of his feet. Behind him, I could see the dark wood and Mexican tile of the hallway: conquistador chic. "Matt's incommunicado at the moment."

"How so?"

"Business calls. The modem's the curse of the modern office."

"I'm able to wait."

"No, no." This seemed to be the last thing Dowling wanted. "I mean he's out, summoned at the last minute. I'd come over to discuss the restaurant fest—have you seen our posters? The Great Orlando Cookout. That's this year's theme, and Matt Spotwood has an interest in a barbecue restaurant. I have to recruit the restaurateurs individually," he said in a confidential manner. He elaborated on this with a sort of desperate, almost frightened, garrulity.

With the distinct feeling I was being stalled, I said, "Since you're here, maybe you can help me. I'm actually trying to find Billy Deever, Suzi's brother."

"Our Suzi?"

"Suzi Rene, yes."

"She has a brother?" This seemed an extraordinary piece of intelligence to him.

"They're fairly common," I said. "Brothers."

"I only met her once," he said. "Once or twice." He waved his hand to indicate the vanity of social life, the impossibility of exact knowledge.

"My feeling is Matt Spotwood knows her better," I said.

Dowling's eyes narrowed. "What gave you that idea?" Perhaps he wasn't as drunk as he seemed.

"Conversations here and there," I said. I waved a hand to indicate the tenuousness of information, the futility of his asking more. "And Billy, of course, knows your friend Spotwood, too. No question."

I thought he was alarmed by that idea, though he hid it pretty well. "Matt meets all sorts running a restaurant. Casual contacts, you know how that is."

"The thing is, Billy's disappeared. Suddenly and mysteriously."

"He was maybe that sort of guy," Dowling said, forgetting that he'd supposedly never met Deever and had been ignorant of his existence. "Here today and gone tomorrow."

"I hope not," I said. "I think he's vital to the investigation. To my client's defense. I trust he isn't 'gone' in any permanent way."

"I didn't mean that," Dowling said, genuinely alarmed. He really should have stayed off cocktails. He was a lot sharper in an unaltered state.

"You sure Spotwood isn't around?"

"No," he said. This time he closed the inner door, and when I rang the bell again, he opened up just enough to advise me to leave.

I drove away in a thoughtful mood. When I spotted a

side road leading through some scrub, I pulled off the driveway and doused my lights. The night was noisy with insects and with the wind-rustled palmettos. I got out and started carefully along the wet, sandy track, trying to remember where Florida's poisonous snakes resided and hoping there was no water around deep enough for alligators. Out of the trees, the farm track ran along a fence toward a water tank and some feed troughs for the cattle. I was afraid I was destined for a tour of Spotwood's extensive agricultural property, when I came around a group of trees and saw the lights of the house glimmering through a screen of pines. A hundred yards further on, the track petered out at another fence line.

Standing in the dark, listening to the steady hum of mosquitoes and their larger brethren, I asked myself what I was doing. Even if Spotwood was in residence, I was unlikely to be admitted. So why was I standing out in the middle of an isolated property, chock-full of possibilities for a permanent disappearance? On the other hand, that very idea was suggestive. I'd thought from the start that Bennett Dowling was too good to be true, and Suzi Rene wasn't running away from Santa Claus.

I decided it wouldn't hurt to stretch my legs for a few minutes. The grounds really did look deserted, with neither security guards nor large mammals on the premise. I checked to make sure the fence was not electrified and after an immense effort, I got my recalcitrant back, and the rest of my anatomy, over the wire, and set off to take another look at Spotwood's residence.

It was slow going. The ground was damp, and balmy Florida has a surprising variety of thorny, spiny plants. I reached the pines just as lightning began flashing again and made the edge of the lawn as the rain started. I took shelter under an ornamental pergola close to the pool and waited.

Twenty minutes passed; the lights were still on all over the house. From my vantage point, I could watch the storm advancing across the lake with thin jagged flashes of lightning. The rain that had been energetic for a while dwindled into drips and sputters. I was half soaked and beginning to feel cold despite the muggy heat, when I heard voices—angry, I thought, but not loud. Footsteps, a silence, a car starting up, then another conversation, short and tense, from which I could only make out isolated words, before the car accelerated away from the house. Bennett Dowling leaving?

Time for a talk with Spotwood, I thought, but I had just stepped out from under the pergola when a second car left the garage. I moved back as the headlights swept across the lawn. In the glare, I could see no more than that a man was driving, then the red taillights winked down the drive and disappeared behind the palms and live oaks. I had to assume I'd missed the elusive Mr. Spotwood, because when I went to the door, the bell rang unanswered.

I stood on the step considering my options, until another sinister rumble of thunder decided for me. I tried the bell one last time, then slogged back down the driveway to my car. A ridiculous evening, a stupid excursion; I could probably have found out most of what I'd wanted to know right in Baby's data banks. Most of, but not all, and I suppose that was the whole point: proving the efficacy of the way I've always done things, going back to basics, committing, in short, one of the fallacies of—let's just say—middle age.

After two false starts, I located the right road, found my car, and, with a certain relief, left the dark fields for the well-lit and well-traveled state road to Orlando. Although there was nothing particularly sinister about either Dowling or Spotwood, it was peculiar that they should both claim ignorance of Billy Deever.

Still, I had other resources. Back at my motel, wet, stiff, scratched, and insect bitten, I tried the next best bet and attempted to contact Suzi Rene. Repeated calls to New Jersey were unsuccessful, however, and I switched attention to my client. Trish Parkes answered their phone with the information that T-Rex was on the road. "Panthers tomorrow night in Miami," she said. "He'll be back Saturday for a day. Is there any message?"

"Ask him to call me when he gets home, please," I said, but by then so much had happened that T-Rex didn't feel like calling anyone and I had to track him down in person.

THE FIRST BAD THING arrived via the morning papers. I'd worked my way through the national news and the labyrinth of Florida state politics to the local headlines. Certain anxieties lurking in the back of my mind drew me to a bylined story, and the dateline sent me to my map. I read the article over again and drank a second cup of coffee before deciding that my need to know outweighed caution. I phoned Detective Harmen.

When he came on the line, I reminded him of my courtesy call two weeks before and asked if he had any identification yet on the body washed up on the western shore of Lake Monroe.

"You got an idea?" he asked.

"Caucasian male, early thirties, long blond hair, thin, maybe six-one, six-two?"

"On the money."

"Try a chap named Billy Deever," I said. "He's the brother-in-law of the late Alf Rene, the Showmen hockey player. I have a photo if that would help."

"What about you come down and take a look at the evidence?"

"I only saw him once," I said. I'm not really into forensics, and I'd barely finished breakfast.

"That's once more than anyone else around here," Harmen said and started giving me directions.

Right then, I had reason to regret my momentary civic mindedness. To start with, there was Harmen's attitude, half collegial and half condescending. He wanted whatever information I could give him. At the same time, he was suspicious of me and couldn't resist making it clear that he disliked private investigators in general and women investigators in particular. If that wasn't enough to complete his résumé as a nineteenth-century cop, he seemed amazed that any female over fifty was still gainfully employed. I couldn't help feeling miffed at that, especially since he was looking pretty old, tired, and rumpled himself that morning.

"I imagine this is all new for you," he remarked as we left his office.

"White-collar criminals get killed, too."

"It's different when you see the results," he said and mumbled something about "real investigations."

I remembered the unpleasantly grisly end of one of my recent cases and suggested we get a look at the deceased. Harmen promptly switched his tack to my "line of inquiry." He was curious as to how I was "getting on." He hoped I wasn't "muddying the waters," and observed that it was easy for "civilians" to complicate an investigation. I told him that I was sure I was working on different lines altogether and referred to Executive Security's sophisticated corporate and fiscal data banks.

Seeing he'd taken the wrong approach, Harmen marched away toward the morgue elevator. We got out on the storage level and walked down the row of big coolers off the brightly lit autopsy room. "Just finished him up," the technician said as he opened one of the stainless steel cabinets and rolled out a tray with a zippered body bag on it. He slid the body onto a steel trolley, maneuvered the trolley out of the way of the doors, then undid the zipper.

Stretched out in heavy-duty plastic, Billy looked swollen, clammy, and battered. Not a good thing at all. As an occupational hazard, dead people don't frighten me, but they sure depress me, and even the unlikable Billy was no exception. His fight with T-Rex had bent his nose and deposited an assortment of bruises; the autopsy had left industrial-size surgical scars, and the warm, murky waters of Lake Monroe had turned his pale skin to dough. He looked like incipient decay, and I wondered who had hated him enough to think that this transformation would be an improvement.

I handed Detective Harmen the photo and shrugged my shoulders. "It looks like him, but I couldn't swear to it. I saw him for maybe three minutes a week ago. His sister's up in New Jersey. If you don't want to wait for her, maybe one of the neighbors or Harriet Sloan, the Sibley and Martin Realtor, could give you a positive ID."

Harmen studied the photo. "Looks like him to me," he said. "It looks pretty good that this is the guy. You say his name's Billy Deever?"

I tapped the photo. "The late Alf Rene, his wife, her brother, Billy Deever."

"How'd you get this?"

"It's a long story," I said.

Harmen indicated that his morning was mine and that he wanted information straight up; I was thinking more in the nature of a swap. The trouble was, I didn't know what was safe to trade. "I'm curious about the time of death," I said. This was the one thing I needed to know pronto.

"The usual uncertainties," Harmen replied.

I pretended a knowledgeable interest in the bruises on Billy's side and said nothing.

"At least forty-eight hours in the water," Harmen offered finally, and Tuesday, two nights ago, jumped into my mind.

Even though the neighbors saw Billy leave and claimed to have heard his truck return, the timing was bad. And if T-Rex had told the truth and it wasn't a serious fight, why did he return the next day? There were too many possibilities. "There's a lot of bruises," I said. "How was he killed?" That was suddenly crucial. Beaten to death—put money on T-Rex. Anything else...

"I need some information," Harmen said.

He held a winning hand, but I gambled that he didn't know it. "Locate Suzi Rene soonest," I said. "She's in danger."

"More work I don't need," Harmen said.

"My guess is she's next on the list and she knows it."

"I gotta have some supporting evidence," Harmen said.

"First tell me how Deever died."

"You're helping with a police investigation," Harmen reminded me. "I can give you major grief."

"I've given you an ID. That's saved you a bundle

right there. I've given you the Realtor; she's the only way to contact Suzi Rene—in itself a suggestive detail. Just out of interest, as one investigator to another, I'm asking, how did Deever die?''

Harmen's expression told me what he thought of this appeal to collegiality. ''Somebody knocked him around, that's obvious. The doc thinks a fight. Then—maybe later—he gets knocked in the back of the head with a blunt object.''

''Same as Alfred Rene,'' I said, but I was wondering if I could lose my license in Florida for helping clean up a crime scene. Even a crime scene the police had pretty much dismissed. Harmen was going to be livid when he found out that the local constabulary had let Sibley and Martin scrub the joint and resume house showings. He wasn't going to be too happy with me, either, if he ever found out I'd been through the house Tuesday night. I was suddenly very glad I'd helped Harriet tidy up. If my prints were found, I had an easy answer.

''The actual cause of death was drowning, probably while unconscious.''

That opened other possibilities. I'd have to find out if my client had a boat, went boating, knew boat people. ''Maybe you ought to look for someone who sails,'' I said.

Harmen wasn't amused.

''I'm serious. Suzi Rene had a friend with a boat and a fancy black BMW.'' I explained how I knew this and referred him to police reports of the ''incident'' when I was nearly forced off the road. ''No one took that too seriously,'' I said, ''which has made trouble for me with Mama Hertz and my insurance company. 'Tourist hysteria' was pretty much the investigating officer's opinion. But Suzi Rene has the same kind of car as I was driving, and when I called to warn her, she asked right off if it was a black BMW. The next thing she did was pack up her children and decamp in the middle of the night."

Harmen's expression turned serious. "Any candidates?"

"Two. Her husband had connections with Horizon Investments."

"No way, you're wrong on that. Not Dowling's company. We checked that angle. Rene was considered for a job, then continued with the Showmen."

"Right," I said. "That's the official line. But people around the team keep mentioning that Alf was working for Horizon and his agent let slip that Alf was working, not for Dowling, but for his more or less silent partner, Matthew Spotwood."

"He's been mentioned," Harmen said with more interest than he'd showed so far. "A man who keeps a low profile."

"Perhaps for good reason. My office has been looking into Horizon Investments. Let's just say the researcher involved has raised some questions. Since everyone assures me Dowling's pure gold, I've started wondering about his partner, Spotwood. He has a black BMW and he's maybe the fellow Mrs. Rene used to meet for lunch and dinner dates at the Lakeside Restaurant, which is just across the water from where Spotwood has a big ranch."

"Pure conjecture," said Harmen.

"Sure," I said, "but you wanted my 'line of inquiry' and that's it. As you've pointed out, my field is white-collar crime. I doubt I can be much help to you with a violent, unexplained death."

Irked to find himself boxed in, Harmen reached over and abruptly zipped up Billy Deever's high-tech shroud. "We'll be keeping the photo for the time being."

"Sure. I always believe in cooperating with local police departments," I said, knowing I had a copy and two other snaps in reserve.

Harmen wasn't pleased with my compliance. I sometimes think the more cooperative you are, the less you're appreciated.

"Where did you get it, by the way?"

That I decided to leave vague. Harriet of Sibley and Martin would doubtless recount our meeting, but by then I'd have moved on. "It was a bonus. I needed some photos of Alf Rene. Fortunate, as it turned out."

"Oh, very," Harmen said, but I sensed he was being sarcastic.

"And Suzi Rene?" I asked, but now it was his turn.

"We'll take care of it," he said, with a superior smile. "Don't worry about her at all. I think we've got this under control."

I'll bet, I thought, but I shook his hand as one suspicious investigator to another and wished him luck. At the first phone I saw after leaving the morgue, I called my office and asked Skipper to get someone to track down Suzi Rene in New Jersey. "I want to talk to her and I want to make sure she's got protection. I'm not sure the police here sense the urgency."

"I'll go myself," he said. "I met her husband once. Fellow athlete, you know, maybe she'll talk to me."

"Right, but stay alert. She talked to me over a nine-millimeter Glock."

Although Skipper is not one to court unnecessary danger, he seemed positively enthusiastic. "It'll be good practice," he said and hung up.

How about that? I thought. Practice for what? I began to think that Skipper was serious about his plan to learn every aspect of the business. And then to make me an offer? I didn't know, but if I couldn't start making a better job of the case I was on, I might just consider it.

FOURTEEN

I DON'T KNOW what made me call Alf's agent again, probably just the general uneasiness and paranoia aroused by life around T-Rex Parkes. On ice he was twenty-four carat, a genius; off ice, he took bad situations and made them impossible, so that there were days when I was afraid that I had a thug at best and a psycho at worst for a client. Working for Parkes was like trying to walk over hydrilla: nice green carpet on top but plenty of mud and water underneath.

Then there was Bennett Dowling, who hadn't employed Alf Rene, and Matt Spotwood, who apparently had. Without having anything concrete against either one of them, I didn't trust them. Anyway, as soon as I said good-bye to Skipper, I dialed Wurfel Stanford in Tampa. His answering machine came on in a blare of self-advertisement with recorded stadium sound and a snappy pep band. "This is Wurf Stanford," the message continued. "I'm out signing the top athletes in America. Leave a message at the tone and Stanford Associates will call you back as soon as possible." Another blast of cheers and applause signaled it was time to talk.

"Anna Peters, calling at eleven a.m. Alf Rene's brother-in-law, Billy Deever, was found drowned and probably murdered this morning in Lake Monroe. I'm worried about Suzi and I think we should talk." I gave him my motel number and said I'd check my messages there before noon.

I called my husband at his workshop in D.C., gave an

edited account of my activities; then, realizing I couldn't keep postponing the inevitable, I dialed Sammy Allert's number. I was in luck. He came on the line to tell me that it was raining in D.C. Maybe he was delaying bad news, too. I looked out at the glaring white pavement and sunstruck street and said rain sounded pretty good. He wanted to know how the case was going. I said it was developing and asked if T-Rex had a boat.

"A boat? No, a ski-do thing—I think he had one of those but Trish made him get rid of it. Too dangerous for the children, she thought."

"But he likes the water?"

"They take the kids swimming. He can water ski, but again, the club doesn't encourage. Back injuries, knee injuries—you can see the picture. I'm a big golf advocate, myself. Fitness without too much danger." He gave a laugh that wasn't quite easy. I wondered if T-Rex had spoken to him. I figured I couldn't entirely trust Allert, either.

"What about friends with boats?"

"I'm sure a few of the Showmen will have boats. But T's not a sailor, if that's what you're asking."

"It is what I'm asking. Alf Rene's brother-in-law was found drowned early this morning. The death is listed as suspicious, most likely murder."

"I see." Allert didn't sound inclined to share his vision with me.

"Did you know Billy Deever? Have you had any contacts with him?"

"Where are you calling from?" Sammy asked, ultra-cautious.

"Sorry about the background noise. I'm on the street down from the morgue. I had to do the ID first thing this morning."

Another pause.

"There are other complications," I said. "Maybe you know about them?"

"I don't know what you're talking about," Allert said.

"T-Rex thinks Billy planted that pipe in his house. My feeling is that's a possibility with blackmail as the motive."

Allert grunted noncommittally.

"T-Rex went over to Billy's on Tuesday night. Broken bones and blood on the floor. According to our client, Deever pulled a knife on him without warning."

"Was T hurt?" Either Allert was a pretty good actor or this was all new and unwelcome information.

"Bruised knuckles, which I suppose he can pass off as a hockey injury. Deever's injuries were more extensive, but apparently he left the house under his own power a little later that evening. I get conflicting reports as to whether or not he returned. The coroner says he was at least forty-eight hours in the water. T-Rex is going to need a pretty good alibi for Tuesday night—especially if his visit to the Renes' comes to light."

Allert wanted to know how I'd learned about the fight. "I stopped by and found the evidence," I said. "No one else knows yet that T-Rex was involved, but the fight itself is no secret." I explained about the Realtor and mentioned the local police and the cleaner. "This is a mess," I warned him.

"We're looking at damage control," Allert murmured.

"I think we're going to need more than that," I said. "Plus some more information. Starting with a whole lot more about Alfie and T-Rex."

"Does T know that Billy Deever is dead?"

"No, unless he did him in."

"You'd better let me handle this whole thing, Anna," Sammy Allert said briskly. "I'll get on the first flight I can. Don't proceed any further until I talk to T."

"I have a couple of promising leads. This is the time to follow up...."

"I don't want anything more done until I can talk to T. Who knows what more you're going to stir up."

Uh-oh. Blame the messenger time. "Look, Sammy, I took this job only on the condition that I had free rein. I warned both you and Parkes about that explicitly."

"This is different," Allert said. "This has nothing to do with Alf Rene's death—which is all that we hired you to investigate."

"You're kidding," I said. "T-Rex thinks Billy was trying to blackmail him. And Suzi left town in a panic and is now incommunicado. Of course this is related. We can't ignore—"

"Yes, we can," said Sammy Allert. "And that's just what we're going to do. No reflection on your work, but submit your last bill as of eleven-fifteen this morning." His voice was calm and polite. He really was the complete gentleman, even when he was being unreasonable.

"Fine," I said. Good-bye to 100 percent humidity and Leisure Land. Did I really need this when my back was killing me? It must have been force of habit that led me to say, "Detective Harmen will be delighted that I no longer have conflicting obligations. I've been guilty of some sins of omission, but—"

"We'll have to talk," Allert said. He changed gears like a Formula One racer, fast and smooth with no telltale rubber on the road. "Face to face would be best. You're standing right on the street and after your distressing experience this morning—"

"The only distressing experience is if you've lost confidence in our client," I said. "Unless you know something else you haven't told me, I see no reason for that."

"That's your professional opinion?"

"He needs a good alibi for later Tuesday night. Otherwise, he's not guilty of anything more than giving Deever a broken nose and some cracked ribs."

I could feel Allert wince all the way down the line in D.C.

"The trouble is some mud will stick."

"For sure. Unless we find out who killed Alf Rene—as I've said from the first."

"Right," said Allert, sounding deeply skeptical. "T's not due back until tomorrow; I'll be down by then. We'll keep Executive Security on retainer until we can all talk. Just don't be overly energetic. We'll work something out." He was clever, decent, and shrewd, and his voice carried the residue of hundreds of deals, arrangements, and compromises. I hung up with mixed feelings and returned to my motel to find a message from Wurfel Stanford. I was to contact him immediately, and he must have meant that literally, because he answered the phone on the first ring.

"Anna Peters," I said.

"I have to see you right away," he said. "Today. This afternoon."

"Regarding?"

"Your earlier message. I'm due up in Washington, but I can delay my flight."

"All right." Tampa and return? The low ache at the base of my spine flared experimentally. "We can't talk on the phone?"

"No, no. I'll meet you partway, okay? I got someone to see in Plant City anyway. Coach there has spotted a prospect. A long-term interest, so to speak. Gotta keep watching the young ones coming up. No contact, of course, everything on the up and up. But showing interest, putting my name about. You gotta hustle in this game.'' Wurf sounded rather desperate.

''Where is this Plant City?''

''You passed it on the way to Tampa.'' He gave me directions for the center of town. There was a sandwich shop he favored. ''I hate chain food,'' he said. ''You can be there in an hour. We'll have lunch.''

I was strongly tempted to refuse, to tell Wurf to stop playing mysterious and give me the information, but something in his voice changed my mind. ''All right,'' I said, resigning myself to an hour each way in Disney World traffic. ''This had better be good.''

I FOLLOWED Wurf's instructions off the Interstate onto a straight, flat secondary with burger joints and sandwich shops on every corner. There's a disorienting sameness to central Florida: the same chains, the same signs, the same clusters of gas stations, convenience stores, and fast fooderies, separated by swampy meadows sporting hopeful COMMERCIAL FOR SALE signs or black-and-green rows of plastic mulch for young strawberries, celery, and iceberg lettuce.

The town itself was largely preboom, the buildings too small to balance the wide thoroughfares and broad, mostly empty sidewalks. I found the sandwich shop tucked away on a side street. A large red Chevy truck with a trailer hooked behind was parked in front. The truck had a bucking bronco as a hood ornament, and the trailer sported a rodeo design advertising Slim Jenkins, a stunt riding act. While a border collie dozed under the axle, a thin, bowlegged black man wearing a stetson and chaps methodically washed white Florida dust from the sides of his truck. Mr. Jenkins had his gear set out on the sidewalk and a hose running from somewhere behind the Lite Bite. He gave me a friendly, proprietary nod as I opened the screen door and went into the restaurant.

No chic at the Lite Bite. The decor was shabby but functional: a counter, a half dozen booths, and as many tables. The menu board touted vintage diner food, and the ambiance featured a faint but pervasive smell of mold. I didn't see Wurf Stanford.

I ordered a BLT and drank the powerfully sugared house lemonade while I watched the street. When it got to be one-thirty, I paid my bill and went outside to stretch my back and wait some more. At two o'clock, having tried to raise him on a nearby pay phone, I decided Wurf wasn't coming. Or perhaps had come and gone.

"Could I bother you for a minute?" I asked the rodeo rider.

He straightened up. "Don't need much excuse to stop washing a truck," he said. His accent was western to go with his gear.

I described Wurfel Stanford as well as I could and asked if he'd been around.

"Talks a lot, always got some deal going?"

"That's the guy."

"Sounds like Wurfel Stanford," Jenkins said.

"Exactly." I was surprised.

"Yeah, I know him. He was my agent for a while, but he don't know shit if he steps in it. Excuse me. Maybe good enough on the basketball and football racket, but no damn good for rodeo. I do mostly my own bookings now and I got a guy who helps me with the legal end of things."

"He was supposed to meet me here this afternoon."

"This would be the place. He comes around regular. He likes Milli's corn chowder. You have some of that?"

When I guessed it was too hot for soup, I got a pitying glance. "Only thing she cooks right, but she sure cooks up a good corn chowder. You should try it."

"On my next visit," I promised, then eased back into the subject at hand. "Have you seen Wurf today by any chance?"

"Naw. Not today. He's been in town, though. He's got a prospect, he claims, right here in Plant City. Wurf's always got a prospect," Jenkins added slyly. He had a dark, skeptical face and vivid sapphire eyes.

"If he shows up, could you tell him Anna Peters was looking for him?"

"Sure thing. But one thing with Wurf, he's always on time. If he stood you up, it was deliberate."

"He seemed very anxious to see me," I said.

"Oh, that's Wurf, all right. All hot and bothered for whatever's on his plate at the moment. Something else comes up—good-bye."

I agreed that was probably the case, and, heading back toward the I-4, I had every intention of turning east for Orlando. But at the last moment, I found I didn't quite agree with the knowledgeable Mr. Jenkins and selected the westbound ramp. Half an hour later, I parked just down the street from Wurf's building and stepped into the afternoon heat.

The lobby had a beauty shop on one side, a coffee shop on the other, and a little stand that sold papers, magazines, cigarettes, and souvenirs squeezed up against the elevator. I passed on the chance to acquire a Tampa Mutiny T-shirt or a Go Gators hat and went upstairs to the seventh floor, where I found Stanford Associates locked up tight. I hammered on the door, then inquired at the adjoining offices. "Wurfel Stanford" drew only vague disinterest from the CPA next door. The lawyer in the next office "hadn't talked to Wurf in weeks," and the orthodontist's receptionist in the corner suite could only tell me that she'd seen him that morning. I took the elevator downstairs and after considering my options over a cup of coffee, I decided to trust that Stanford Associates' neighbors would remain unobservant. I returned to the seventh floor, where I slipped on a pair of latex gloves, picked Wurf's lock, and let myself into his rooms.

The blinds were down against the afternoon glare, creating a dusky twilight broken by bands of blue-and-silver glitter. I hesitated in the doorway, expecting troubling silhouettes and unpleasant discoveries, but the outer office was empty and orderly, smelling only of elderly air-conditioning and stale cigarette smoke. Ditto the inner office. Maybe ex-client Jenkins had been right after all.

I pushed the button on Wurf's answering machine. Several of his clients had called; my own voice piped up from Plant City. The first of the athletic hopefuls had phoned in at 12:40. If Wurf had already left the office, he'd have had plenty of time to get to Plant City. Had he possibly gone home first? I was looking through the phone book to see if he had another number listed when I heard a key rattle in the lock. I stepped into the outer office in time to meet a woman with short, vivid hair and a multitude of rings, earrings, and chain-link necklaces. She was wearing the ubiquitous Go Gators T-shirt and a short denim skirt, and she was carrying a mailing tube.

"I've been waiting for Wurfel Stanford," I said, hastily stuffing the rubber gloves into my pocket.

"Sure you were. How'd you get in?" Her features were sharp and not quite symmetrical, which gave her a piquant, alert expression. I'd recognized the proprietor of the souvenir stand and begun to relax when she tilted the mailing tube and a long, slim machete slid into her fist. I decided against premature optimism.

"Anna Peters," I said. "Executive Security Services. Let me give you my card."

"Put your purse down," she said. She was small but her arms and legs were muscular and the machete looked razor sharp.

"You can't be too careful today," I agreed, trying for cheerful professionalism. I slipped off my shoulder bag and set it carefully on the magazine-covered coffee table. "Wurf wanted his office security checked. I thought I'd throw in a little demonstration of the weaknesses of conventional locks."

She unsnapped the bag with one hand and looked inside with such a tough, professional air that I began to worry that she was undercover. "You got some ID?"

"You're holding my wallet. Help yourself."

"You gotta license," she said. Clearly a novelty. That removed one problem and set up others.

"Of course."

"It doesn't give you the right to break into Wurf's office. I know it doesn't." I could see that she was tempted toward citizen heroics, summoning the police, making a scene.

"Look, Wurf was supposed to meet me for lunch today. He was really insistent that we get together, but he never showed up. I was going to say the hell with him and drive back to Orlando but I was concerned."

Her face took on a pinched, anxious look as if I'd just confirmed her worst imaginings. "Why should you be worried?" she asked.

"You're a friend of Wurf's."

She nodded eagerly. "Sure. He stops by the stand every day. I run the souvenir shop in the lobby."

"Yes, I recognize you. A nice line in T-shirts and Gators souvenirs."

"Our best sellers at the moment."

"So you maybe know about Alf Rene, the Showmen hockey player Wurf represented?"

"Yeah, Wurf felt real bad about that. Wurf thought Alfie would be his breakthrough player. He'd done very well for Alfie. Better than anyone realized. I saw him play a couple times." She seemed set to recount the excitements of Showmen hockey, but at least the machete was at ease.

"I'm investigating his death," I said.

"Wurf was brokenhearted. He had nothing to do with that."

"I didn't for a minute think he had," I said. "I need his help because something serious has happened." I explained about Billy Deever, but when I mentioned that the late Mr. Deever was Suzi Rene's brother, the souvenir proprietor bristled.

"You can't trust her. Smarmy bitch. She was always making up to Wurf and then behind his back she was complaining that he wasn't doing enough for her Alfie."

This hint of rivalry reminded me of Wurf's many expressions of concern for Suzi Rene. Had that femme fatale cast her chilly eyes on Wurf? Anything was possible. "Nonetheless, her husband and now her brother have been murdered and she's left no forwarding address. Your friend Wurf wanted to tell me something.

He was very insistent that we meet today. When he didn't show, I decided I'd better check up on him.''

She wiped her expression and pushed my bag toward me with the tip of her machete. ''He probably got a call. A prospect. You know how it is, he can't neglect his business for Suzi Rene and all that old news.''

''Sure,'' I said, ''just like you can't close your stand and come running with a lethal weapon to check on his office.''

She shrugged. ''It's none of your business anyway.''

''After Wurf gets me to come all the way to Tampa to tell me something important, of course it's my business. You see everyone coming in and out. Did he have visitors today? Anyone unusual in the lobby?''

She thought this over, twisting the length of hardware store chain she wore as a necklace. ''A guy's come a couple times,'' she said finally. ''Too old to be an athlete. I asked Wurf about him, but he said it was nothing.''

I pressed her for a description, but ''tall, middle aged, well dressed'' covered a multitude of sinners. ''Not today, though. You didn't see him today?''

''No.'' She looked doubtful.

''Are you sure there's nothing else? No one who's maybe hanging around, not visiting Wurf, just keeping an eye on the place?''

She thought a minute. ''We did have something odd a couple weeks ago,'' she said. ''I don't know if Wurf knew about that.''

''What was this?''

''The satellite company was here. Apparently someone up on the ninth floor wanted one of those little data dishes installed. Something about the way the chase for

the wires ran. He had to get into Wurf's office for a
minute.''

Great; a minute or two would have been enough to
bug the whole office. ''Why don't you put away that
weed whacker and give me a hand.''

''I don't know why I should help you,'' she said.

I put my finger to my lips and went into Wurf's office.
I looked behind his Buccaneers' wall calendar and his
autographed photo of Trent Dilfer. I checked along the
baseboard and behind the file cabinet then ran my hand
under the desk and came up lucky. ''Hand me my purse,
would you?'' When she brought it, I took out my small
camera and snapped a couple pictures. Then I set the
bug on the desk and snapped a couple more.

''Oh,'' my friend with the machete said.

''Best to have photographic evidence.'' I unscrewed
the phone receiver and extracted another small trans-
mitter: Wurf really should have hired Executive Security. ''Anything said in this office plus any phone calls
would have gotten picked up. We need to find him,'' I
said.

She put the machete back in its mailing tube deci-
sively. ''Let's check the back lot. That's where he parks.
Then his apartment. He might have gone home for something. He might be all right.''

''We'll hope so,'' I said. She led the way at top speed
down to the rear exit and out a short hallway to the
parking area, where she began a methodical sweep up
and down the rows.

''What does he drive?'' I asked.

''A black Nissan with a vanity plate: SPTSMN.''

There were vans and sedans and compacts, a topless
four-wheel drive, and a repainted school bus. A very

dark blue Nissan gave us a start, but at the last row she shook her head. "No, not here."

"My car's down the street. Do you know where he lives?"

She did and followed me through the lobby and out to my rental. She got in, still carrying the machete in its mailing tube. As I fastened my belt, I noticed the name on the address label: Jennifer Galinda. "Jennifer," I said.

"That's right. But no Galinda any more. That was my ex. I'm Jennifer Thomas at the moment."

"You don't sound too certain."

"Naw, it may not work out. I don't mind marrying," she said reflectively, "but I get sick of changing my name. Turn here. We've got to get up onto the interstate."

Five minutes later we were in the afternoon rush hour traffic, a Roman circus of souped-up pickups, fast-moving commuters, and business vans running the obstacle course of clapped-out old junkers, disoriented travelers, and time-on-their-hands snowbirds in pastel Town Cars. Every time I had to hit the brakes my back double-clutched.

"Couple minutes," she said. "Wurf found a pretty nice place. Neighborhood's on the way up. He's thinking of buying the apartment to keep from getting stuck with rent increases. Next exit."

We dropped down the ramp to a wide boulevard. Jennifer directed me across four lanes onto a grid of side streets. "Look at that," she said, as we passed an abandoned van. "That damn thing's still there. Wurf's been after the city about it half a dozen times. Whoa! You're past it. The pink building."

I pulled into a driveway and turned around. The

neighborhood was a mixture of rather handsome old two-and three-story apartment buildings with larger, newer ones that hadn't taken neglect quite as well. The shabby stuccos wore their faded pinks, fawns, and creams with an almost Mediterranean charm; the fifties and sixties metal panels went to rust and dents in a way that suggested lousy maintenance and structural weaknesses.

Wurf had picked a pseudo-Spanish building with an arched portico and a tile lobby. Jennifer stuck her mailing tube machete case under one arm and checked his mailbox. When Wurf didn't answer the intercom, she produced a key and we went upstairs.

"I collect his mail when he's away. He's out of town a lot and I stop by. You have a problem with that?"

I certainly did not, though I wondered to myself if husbands Galinda and Thomas might have. "Wurf's lucky to have someone looking out for his mail," I said.

"I don't want you to get the wrong idea," she said. "My life's complicated enough already."

"Right," I said.

"This is his apartment. Wurfie?" she called.

Wurfie! There must be something in the air. First hockey players, then our own Chairman Newt, now Wurfie Stanford. But if he was in residence, Wurfie wasn't responding, and Jennifer unlocked the door and pushed it open nervously. "You in, Wurfie?"

I stepped inside, figuring if anyone had damaged Wurf, he hadn't stuck around. The hot, closed-up apartment was small enough so I could see most of it at a glance: living room with TV and big double-hung windows that would be hell on the AC. Kitchen off with ceiling fan. Bedroom to rear with double bed, built-in cupboards and bureau. Bathroom down a short corridor from the living room. Everything was fine and dandy except for the faintest lingering odors of human exertion and gunpowder.

"Do you smell that?" I asked.

"Roach spray?" she guessed. "You got to spray all the time down here. I kill it with air freshener."

"I think gunpowder. Does Wurf have a handgun?"

"He's got a license," Jennifer said defensively. "It's all legal."

"And where would his car be parked?"

"Out back—or on the street. I already looked. It's not there."

"My feeling is to call the police," I said. "For sure if he doesn't turn up by tonight."

Jennifer looked doubtful and uneasy. "He was going to fly to D.C. tonight," she said. "He'd talked about the trip. There's a Georgetown kid he's watching. Wurf's sure he's going to get him signed come March."

I pointed out that Wurf had told me he was willing to delay the trip to talk to me, but she was unconvinced. We were still arguing about it when we got back to my car. "You're sure there's nowhere else he might park?"

"I told you already." She gestured irritably toward the abandoned van. "That piece of junk is taking up a space and a half in front as it is. Wurfie's been frosted about it."

I walked over to the van, an artifact fit for some future urban archaeologist. Layers of body paint revealed that at some time in the distant past it had belonged to a dry cleaner. Then it had gotten religion as a runabout for the Full Gospel Church of the Redeemer before its final transformation as a hauler for vegetables and melons.

The passenger side was locked, the driver's side was unlocked but cranky. I went around back and tried the rear doors. They opened to a buzz of flies and a hot smell of human waste and blood. Wurfel Stanford was lying in the cargo bay with a nasty round black wound over one temple.

Jennifer said nothing for a moment; then she sucked in her breath.

"I'm so sorry," I said. "You'd better—" I couldn't finish the thought because just as I turned there was a rustling sound and a gleaming metallic streak. I jumped to avoid the blade, which bounced off the edge of the van and connected on the rebound with the back of my wrist, scoring a long stinging diagonal. "It's all your fault," Jennifer screamed. "It's all your fault for coming around!"

She was getting up a pretty good head of steam when she saw the blood and stopped. She looked at me in shock and surprise. I was halfway behind the van door when she started to cry. "Oh, Christ, I didn't mean to! Poor Wurfie!"

She'd cut something fairly big: my life's blood was running down my hand and dripping on the asphalt. I grabbed my wrist to stanch the flow and sat down dizzily on the curbing. "Call 911. And get me a towel or something. Wurf will have towels and a phone in the apartment," I said as she began to look wildly about. The machete dropped to the sidewalk and I heard the sound of Jennifer's running feet behind me.

FIFTEEN

THE EMERGENCY ROOM was a warren of well-lit cubicles and mysterious little bays hung with scrub-suit-green curtains. A strong disinfectant overlaid the aroma of nervous bodies. I sat around half chilled in the AC with my shirt off until a nice young intern with mocha-colored skin and a thick braid of black hair stitched me up. She was in her first year of training but already skillful. The neighborhood produced an abundance of slash wounds, and she'd had a lot of practice. I got a tetanus shot, too, and half my arm painted with disinfectant.

"I think it was a pretty clean machete," I told her as she slopped vivid orange from my wrist to my elbow.

"Best to be on the safe side." Her voice carried a rhythmic island lilt.

"That antiseptic's a bit conspicuous," I complained.

"Infections are no fun, so it's best to be safe," she said sternly and slapped on another coat. I don't know why doctors, even beginning doctors like this one, are so suspicious of me. I was told to rest, take fluids, keep my bandage dry, and consume a bovine-size dose of antibiotics. I promised everything, but as soon as I heard her in the next cubicle, I escaped to the pay phone.

I called the office first on the chance that someone was still around and got Skipper. Connections had been lousy to Jersey, so he'd sensibly contacted Solly Franco, an investigator we sometimes used in Newark. Solly had driven to Suzi Rene's house and found it empty.

"Damn! Any ideas?"

"Neighbors say she was all moved in, then bingo. Suitcases in the car and hasn't been seen since."

"Papers stopped? Mail?"

Skipper gave a confident grunt; he was way ahead of me. "Both piling up. It could be a holiday, Anna," he said but he didn't sound convinced and I wasn't, either. "We're trying to contact her family. That's the best I can do at the moment."

"Right. And I'll call some of the Showmen wives down here. Somebody may know. The police are also looking to notify her about her brother."

"There's another thing, Anna. Wait a minute. Baby had some material. She left a message for you to call. Something interesting, she said."

I waited on hold, resolutely avoiding eye contact with a thin, yellow-faced man bobbing up and down impatiently in elaborate high-topped sneaks and a sullen woman in a bathrobe voluminous enough to conceal a dozen machetes. Both wanted the phone.

"Here it is," Skipper said after a few minutes. "It's that data on Horizon Investments you wanted. It's just a list of companies." He sounded disappointed, but by the time he finished reading Baby's memo, I understood the possibilities. I thanked him, relinquished the phone, and returned to my cubicle, where I was supposed to await a representative of the Tampa Police Department's Homicide Squad. Instead, I took off the hospital smock and put on my blood-spattered blouse. Then I reconsidered, replaced the smock, tucked it neatly into my slacks, and headed for the exit. Let Jennifer of the machete handle the police.

Three hours later, I was outside T-Rex's home. I'd stopped at my motel for a clean blouse, a dose of painkiller, and a dozen phone calls. At the moment, I was tired and hungry. Every mile of the long drive was sitting on my lower spine and none of the analgesics had quite taken hold. I extracted myself from the car in no very good frame of mind and rang the bell. When Trish opened the door, I saw that she was in a similar mood. "What couldn't have been handled on the phone?" she asked.

I stepped inside and looked around before answering. "Suzi Rene," I said. "She's left Jersey. Where would she go?"

"How am I supposed to know that?" Trish's voice rose in exasperation. "I've hardly talked to the woman in the last couple years. Believe me, I've got more important things on my mind than Suzi's whereabouts."

"I've called the wives of two complete lines plus the goalies and the coaches. They all agree you've known her the longest. If she's got to hide, where's she likely to go?"

"Hide?" Trish asked. Then she looked down at my arm. I followed her glance: the thickly padded bandage showed a little red seepage: I had been warned to take it easy.

"Machete wound. Basically an accident, coinciding with the discovery of Wurfel Stanford's body. Did you know Wurf? He was—"

"Alfie's agent. He's dead?"

"Worse. He was murdered—one shot to the head. And with Suzi's brother found this morning—"

"Come in here," she said. She led me into the same little office where T-Rex and I had watched the news conference. It seemed a much bigger room without my oversize client. "There was nothing in the paper about Billy."

"Yes, there was. The body that washed up along Lake

Monroe turned out to be Billy Deever. I had to identify him this morning."

Her face had not so much gone pale as dead, as if she'd withdrawn from it and left flesh and bone to their own devices. "What happened to him?"

"He drowned," I said. "Probably a couple days ago."

"He drowned." She seemed unbelieving. "He just drowned. He hadn't been hurt?"

"He'd been beaten up," I admitted, "but that wasn't what killed him."

She looked as if this was sinking in a long way.

"Suzi's got to be told," I said finally. "And she's probably in danger. Husband, brother, husband's agent: it doesn't look very good for her."

Trish dropped into a chair and stared out at the streetlights shining through the palms and live oaks. She seemed to have had a terrible shock. I took a seat and waited. This was a woman who was surviving a child's major illness, murder accusations, and legal troubles, not to mention life with T-Rex Parkes on a daily basis, yet the death of this obscure and unsavory character had obviously hit her hard. I wanted to tell her that Billy had been seen up and mobile after a meeting with her husband, that at least T-Rex was in the clear for Wurfel Stanford. At the same time, I sensed this was my best chance for information.

After what seemed a long time, Trish asked, "Have you tried her house in New Jersey? They bought a small house while Alf was with the Devils."

"In Oradell? We've checked that. She moved in, then left abruptly."

"Well, I suppose she would," Trish Parkes said. "They all knew each other there."

"Who's they?"

"Her friends, Alf's friends. Business contacts, I don't know." Trish spoke in a calm, detached manner as if none of this had anything to do with her. "She wasn't used to that life; it kind of knocked her off the rails. Alfie, too. Money, success, bright lights. They got to feel it was all more important than it really is."

"She was a big city girl, though. Jersey City isn't exactly Manhattan, but it's plenty big."

"Is that what she told you?"

I nodded and Trish raised her eyebrows. "I've known Suzi Deever next to forever," she said. "She didn't get to Jersey City until she was thirteen and her family collapsed. The father was a drinker; her mom held things together as long as she could, but she died of cancer when Suzi and Billy were just getting into their teens. Suzi got sent south to New Jersey to her mom's sister's. I guess they were poor enough, too, because I know she left school and went to work. At the time, I'm sure that job in the hockey shop was the height of her ambitions."

"That's where she met Alf."

"Oh, she'd known Alf long before. Knew all about him, but what are you going to do?" Trish asked. "You count on the people who you've known; they may not be perfect but they've done things for you, they've gone through hard times with you. They owe you and you owe them; that's just the way it gets to be."

I had the feeling she was talking about herself and T-Rex. "Where would she go if she had to hide?" I asked.

"She'd go home," Trish said promptly. "To the old farm. There's still a house, barns, I think a trailer, too, on the property."

"You'll need to give me directions," I said.

She stood up as if she was thinking this over, then

went to the desk, where she not only wrote out the address but also drew me a map. A darn good thing, because I would never have found the place otherwise.

"And you," I said when she was finished and I'd thanked her. "You look as if you've had a shock. Is there anything I can do?"

"No," she said.

"It's not T-Rex," I said. "Wurf was shot this afternoon. Billy Deever was last seen up and about Tuesday night late. Your husband's thrown his weight about in a particularly stupid way, but I still don't think he killed Alf and I'm pretty sure he hasn't killed anyone else."

For just a minute, her expression softened, before she stiffened up as if putting her emotional armor back on. "Let me tell you something," she said. "You're trying to be kind, but there's nothing new you can tell me about my husband. I've known Jurgen since we were in primary school. We grew up together and he saved my life, literally. I sometimes have to remember that." She looked across the room, away from the trophies and the expensive leather furniture and the shadows of the tropical night to a different, distant place. "We were out on the ice when it was coming spring, when the river was starting to break up. The ice was spongy and the river's deep where we went through. I'm a poor swimmer even without heavy winter clothes on, but you know how strong he is. Even as a boy he was amazingly strong. He got hold of me somehow, and he had the strength to wrestle us both up onto solid ice." She gave a little wistful smile. "And then later, all this and the children. He adores the children. It would break his heart to be separated from them or even to disillusion them. And Richie. You'd have to see them together to understand." She shook her head. "You mustn't blame him too much.

Or me, either,'' she said, then she moved abruptly to the door and, without another word, showed me out.

Back at my mildew-steeped motel, I called Harry, my secretary, and Skipper.

"I should go with you," Skipper said when I told him I thought I knew where Suzi was. I was momentarily tempted. A back-destroying flight to Quebec, a long drive basically one handed, possibly trouble at the other end—Skipper would be good company.

"No. I think you'd be better here."

"Doing what?" He sounded so disappointed that I wondered if he was developing a taste for investigation.

"Soothing your old agent, for one thing. I'm supposed to meet him here tomorrow morning. So see how early you can fly down. The other thing is to talk some serious business with T-Rex. He doesn't want to tell me anything; maybe he'll tell you. There's never been any real motivation for Alf's death, has there? And now his brother-in-law and his agent—it's too much. Parkes doesn't make sense for either of those, and he was safe with the team all yesterday."

"You're sure?"

"I called the team, talked to the coach. Checking up is how it's gotten to be ten p.m. and I've still not had dinner."

"Okay, okay," Skipper said. He didn't know the rest of it; I didn't trust him not to worry my husband.

"I've been thinking about Baby's note. She clearly thinks Horizon Investments is a kind of Ponzi scheme."

"Ponzi scheme?" Skipper asked.

"I'm dating myself. You know the type of thing: Initial investors are paid high returns from the money invested by later investors, who are lured by what looks like the promise of exceptional dividends."

"A pyramid," Skipper said.

"Right. The lucky organizers and a few early investors sometimes make fortunes...."

"Paid for by the losses of the many folks down along the base of the pyramid."

"Correct. What I think is that Alf persuaded T-Rex to put money into such a scheme."

"That hardly makes his situation any better," Skipper observed.

"It may even make it worse, depending on what he knows. We need to find out for sure and we need to keep an eye on him, Skipper. I have a bad feeling about this."

We got our schedules straightened out and a story organized for Sammy and T-Rex. Then I hung up and called a half dozen airlines until I managed a direct morning flight into Montreal.

WE LEFT SUMMER, leisure, and the Sunbelt behind in the radiant white clouds and blue skies of 35,000 feet. By the time we descended toward Dorval, we were deep into fall and heading for winter. The trees were bare, the grass was brown; our silky-voiced stewardess announced the temperature as –3 degrees Celsius, and while we did our conversion arithmetic, added that the wind chill was running –20. The returning vacationers congratulated themselves on brief, satisfactory respites and enjoyed the groans and consternation of thin-blooded visitors like me underdressed for serious cold.

To encourage my already stiff and recalcitrant back, I stopped at an airport souvenir shop, where I paid outrageous sums for a thick wool sweater, a scarf, and a ski hat. Nodding sagely, the clerk thanked me in French and assured me I was going to need them. Quebec was having an early winter.

That was evident as soon as I hit the road. The air held flurries, and the ground, slush. After the vapor-soaked heat of central Florida, I was freezing in my rental car. I pushed the heater as far as it would go, pacified my back with ibuprofen, and set out to find Suzi Rene.

Trish Parkes's guess was a farm halfway between Montreal and Quebec City on the flat, windswept plateau running north from the St. Lawrence. On a November day with a gray sky and hit-and-run snow, it was nobody's idea of picturesque. The lonely farms glimpsed from the highway were functional at best, windburned poverty at worst. I began to understand teal, pink, and lavender as vacation colors, and Florida with its heat, color, and artificiality as a destination. Up here, life was a bare-bones affair, with farming as unadorned hard work.

My navigation landmark was the village coffee shop, but though I was tempted to stop, I thought better of it. Any rental car meant a stranger, and Suzi might still have friends willing to pick up the phone. Prudently forgetting about coffee and sugar-laden snacks, I stuck with a secondary road that ran between the brown-and-white snow-splotched fields. With the help of Trish Parkes's map, I located the right country lane. There was a school bus shelter on the corner and a farm with three weathered barns and a colossal boulder in the front yard. A mile or so further, I spotted the narrow dirt track Trish had described. A battered mailbox listed from a post; I was just able to read "Deever" in the faded paint.

The track led toward a thick shelter break of pines, and I nursed my rental over the potholes and washouts to find a rotting barn, an old metal trailer, and a silvery, paint-stripped farmhouse beyond the trees. From a distance, the house might have passed for rural charm, but I guessed the trailer was warmer, for a white plume of wood smoke was blowing off the metal vent. There was no other sign of life. If Suzi was in residence, she must have put her car in the barn.

I shut off my motor, unfastened my belt, and pushed open the door. Immediately, a shooting pain raced up my thigh and over my lower back, preparatory to a general seizing up of my whole mechanism: too much cold, too much sitting—too bad for the spine and its ancillary muscles. I stretched to one side and then the other, thinking of maintenance and flexibility. I can honestly say that therapy saved my life, because while I was getting into gear a metallic ping turned my windshield to a sunburst of cracks. I dived onto frozen barnyard mud, my back unspeakable, my cut arm throbbing.

In the reverberant silence, I raised my head, straightened my arms, and found my back refused to engage. Damn! I considered the idea that I'd been beaten to the trailer, that whoever had killed Wurf had located Suzi first, that I was in deep and total trouble, an idea that inspired me to grab the frame of the car and haul myself back into the seat. The windshield was a spiderweb with a round, sinister hole in the center, but I could see that the trailer door was partially open. Suzi Rene had aged ten years, but she still had the same pistol and a pretty good aim to go with it.

"It's Anna Peters, Suzi! I need help. I've been hit." Although not strictly true, this notion was dramatic enough to lure her out onto the step. I hung onto the frame and attempted to get my feet on the ground and my spine vertical.

"Don't move," she said. Despite looking pale and frightened, she went into a respectable shooter's stance.

"I can barely walk," I said as I lurched out of the car. "For god's sake put that away. This is the second rental I've damaged because of you."

"You don't sound shot." She seemed almost disappointed.

"Only in a manner of speaking. My back's seized up. But I've got to talk to you," I said as she made to return to the trailer. "I've got some news about your brother."

She stopped and looked at me. I was hanging onto the door frame to keep from being blown across the field. She was bundled in a down jacket with the Glock at the ready.

"Billy."

"Yes, Billy. I left Orlando at ten this morning to come find you. Which is the reason I'm barely able to stand."

"You didn't tell anyone you were coming?" There was no mistaking her anxiety.

"Only my office. In case I don't call in tonight," I added on the chance I'd figured her wrong.

She bit her lip in displeasure.

"I couldn't count on finding you first, could I?" I asked. My scarf flapped across my face and my light parka billowed and shuddered in the cold wind that was screaming down from Hudson's Bay and points north. I wondered if she was hoping I'd freeze to death and save her the trouble of an interview, but finally, she slid the gun into her pocket. Listing at a forty-five-degree angle, I set off toward the trailer. Suzi watched my progress, then came over and took my arm.

"Muscle spasm," she diagnosed. "Alfie used to get those." She described the late Alf's symptoms, which, I had to say, sounded familiar, and recounted the arduous therapies of professional athletes. While she held the dented aluminum door against the wind, I managed the steps on the second try. Inside was a dirty brown carpet, a variety of brown and green vinyl-covered chairs, and a potbellied wood stove of ancient vintage. I made for that and lay down flat on the floor.

"You haven't really been shot," Suzi repeated.

"It was only good luck I wasn't. What the hell were you thinking of?"

She set the pistol on the divider that ran between the living room and the kitchenette. She took off her coat and hung it up behind the door. I studied the ceiling, dark as tea around the stove vent and stained and blotched from rain and rust in a dozen places. Seeing the trailer, I could understand the fancy house and that six-figure kitchen makeover. "What did you come to tell me?" she asked.

"Your brother is dead. You'll have to make a positive ID, but I'm afraid there isn't much doubt. I'm sorry."

She sat down on one of the vinyl chairs. I was eye level with the ankles of her substantial winter boots. "I don't believe you," she said.

"He drowned. I've got—" I patted my coat pockets. "There's a manila envelope in the car. I brought you some newspaper clippings."

Suzi watched me for a minute, but as I hadn't the slightest intention of moving, she finally got up, retrieved the pistol, put on her coat, and ventured into the bone-chilling wind.

"He drowned," she said reproachfully when she returned, as if I hadn't just told her that, as if I'd claimed he'd run off and joined the circus.

"Drowning's a leading cause of death in Florida. All

that beachfront and all those lakes." I thought she didn't sound terribly grieved—nor terribly surprised, either.

"He couldn't swim," she said sitting down with her coat still on. "He wasn't fond of the beach."

"He wasn't at the beach," I said. "Read the story. He was found in Lake Monroe." I thought that startled her but it was hard to tell. I'd never before had to interview anyone while lying half paralyzed on her carpet. Let me tell you, it changes your perspective—in more ways than one. "Any ideas about that?" I asked when she'd finished the news story.

She shrugged. "Maybe a fight. You know what Billy was like. And then he maybe got thrown in the water."

Not a bad guess, but I had something else in mind. "You know that area pretty well," I suggested. "You used to go to the Lakeside Restaurant, didn't you? That's right on the water."

"I don't know what you're talking about. Alfie and I went to a lot of restaurants."

"This wasn't with Alfie. This was with a friend who has a boat—and maybe a black BMW, too. I've got some guesses as to who that friend was."

She didn't want to talk about that, and I wasn't really in a position to insist. "You don't know everything," I said finally, and I told her about Wurfel Stanford. She couldn't have been more shocked if I'd pulled out a gun and shot her.

"You're lying!" Her face had seized up like my back. "Nothing's happened to Wurf."

"Check the rest of the clippings," I said. "This morning's *Tampa Tribune*."

She ruffled nervously through the news cuttings then stopped. "Oh, my God!" she said. She was so white she'd turned transparent and I could see a thin blue vein jumping in her neck. She'd hardly turned a hair when I'd told her about Billy, and she'd sure hidden any concern about almost perforating me.

"He knew where you were going?" I guessed.

Her answer was to take a deep breath.

"And the children? He knew where your children are, too?"

"I thought I could hide them better," she said after a moment. She started to say a name and then changed her mind. "No one knows what they look like. You know how it is with little kids," she added as if trying to convince herself. "They all look kinda alike."

"But Wurf knew," I repeated.

"I had to have some help," she said frantically. "To make arrangements. And Wurf has—had—contacts. He knew coaches, youth league basketball guys, hockey camp people—people with no obvious connection to me. You understand, don't you—relatives, friends—they're the first people anyone would think of."

I remembered her saying that she was smarter than Alfie, and I thought that you can get caught by being too smart almost as easily as too stupid. "Have you been calling? Have you checked in with them today?"

"Not yet. I will, I will right now." She jumped up and grabbed a cell phone. Lousy security, but if she'd been followed this far it was only a matter of time, anyway. While I worked on my back muscles, she punched in the numbers—for Tampa? Orlando? New Jersey? Other points south or east? Suzi disconnected and tried again in case she'd dialed incorrectly, then paced up and down nervously. Her call was not going through.

By the time she gave up, I'd gotten my coat off and was sitting upright, thawing out by the stove.

"I'm sure they're all right," she announced. "Maybe

they left the phone off the hook. Maybe one of the kids knocked off the receiver." She looked at her watch. "I usually call a bit later." Her voice was defensive.

"For how long will they be all right?"

"You said Wurf was killed yesterday around noon. Someone would have been here by now."

I could see she was prepared to gamble on that and shrugged.

"Wurf didn't say anything," she insisted, her voice tightening. "I know he didn't. The children are perfectly safe."

"Would he have gotten himself shot for you?"

"It might have had nothing to do with me at all," she protested. "I'm not to blame. I don't know why you want to blame me for this. I liked Wurfie. He wasn't the best agent in the world, but if you kept after him, things were okay."

"Wurf had something he wanted to tell me as soon as he learned about your brother's death. He was upset and very insistent that I meet him. Have you any ideas about that?"

She looked as if she might, but she shook her head.

"He said he'd gone out on a limb for you. Does that refer to the kids or to something more?"

"You've wasted your time coming here," Suzi insisted. "I just had to get away, to be by myself for a while." She went on in this vein, experimentally, I thought, and I finally told her to save it for the press.

She got angry then and began waving the Glock around. I'd just begun to think I'd made some fundamental miscalculation when the door boomed open. Suzi fired off a round into the wind and storm, and my heart jumped to aerobic speed. I had to hope she'd run out of ammunition soon, because she was going to kill someone for sure. We were still breathing up gunpowder when the door swung closed, caught the wind again, and banged open a second time with enough force to loosen the hinges. With snow dusting the rug all the way to the stove, Suzi bounded over to slam the door shut and flick down the lock.

"How long do you think you can stay here?" I asked when she'd caught her breath. "Shooting at everyone who comes by. I understand that Canadian police don't take kindly to firearms in the first place."

"I'd be a whole lot safer if you hadn't poked your nose into my affairs."

I took that under advisement. On the whole I agreed with her—but not entirely. "Was it me, or was it Billy?" I asked.

She sat down and examined her pistol. I could see that the combination of my news, her failure to reach the children, and the otherwise trivial fright of the wind had her spooked.

"Billy interfered, didn't he? And he was stupid. He tried to involve T-Rex, am I right?"

"I don't know what the hell he was doing," she burst out. "I'd gone back to New Jersey to get away from him and all his nonsense."

"And also to get away from whoever tried to run me off the road the night I came to see you. I'd guessed Bennett Dowling at first. Now I'm leaning toward his silent partner, Matthew Spotwood. You knew him, didn't you?"

She made a little motion with her shoulders.

"He employed Alfie. Wurf told me that and it made sense. And Alf's death began to make sense when I learned more about Spotwood's business dealings—and about his relationship with you."

Suzi started to deny it, before abruptly jumping up and trying her cell phone again. "It's nearly five o'clock. Where the hell are they?"

I didn't say anything. She punched in the numbers a couple more times before slinging the phone onto one of the chairs.

"Maybe just as well," I said. "Those things are really insecure."

"Shut up!" she screamed. "Will you just shut up and get out of here!"

I made myself comfortable near the stove. The carpet gave off the cloying odor of embedded dust, mixed with the smell of wood smoke and ashes. "You're forgetting you destroyed my windshield. I doubt I could see to drive to the end of your road."

She had some opinions on this, then burst into tears: I hadn't been wrong about her MO in tight spots after all. I worked on loosening my back until I thought we'd had the best of the performance. "Why don't you cut that out and we'll get down to business," I said.

She picked up the pistol and began to toy with it ominously.

"Forget it," I said, trying to sound serene. Given my present situation it was important not to let her see how many cards she held. "The ground's already frozen and my office knows I'm here. You've got a brain. You can see that won't work."

I had a couple of bad moments before she shrugged petulantly. Suzi crossed her legs, leaned back on the chair and set her face in hard, shrewd lines. "Make it good," she said.

The wind was beating on the sides of the trailer and screaming in through the vents. When big gusts hit, the whole trailer quivered like a boat in rough seas. "We each have a problem," I explained. "I need some information. You need some protection."

"No one's going to find me," she said. I wasn't convinced about that, and I didn't think she was, either.

"I managed in two days. Whoever's after you has already invested in three murders. Do you think they're just going to give up and go home and forget you?"

"I had nothing to do with any of this. Alfie…" Then she stopped.

"Look," I said. "I run a security firm. We provide protection—for a fee, of course. Very good, very exclusive, very expensive. Exactly your kind of place."

"So?"

"I propose a swap. You give me the information I need. I'll call Skipper Norris—you'll have heard of him, former pro quarterback, all-everything. He's in charge of security services for us. He knows what you've been up against—publicity, fans, nosy press—right? We'll have him lay on the works: twenty-four-hour bodyguards for you and the kids, a safe house—the whole thing. Think it over."

Instead, she jumped up and tried the phone again.

"Before it's too late," I added.

Her mouth twitched and she glanced at the pistol, before sitting down again nervously.

"We can handle it," I said. "I'll call Skipper. We can send someone to check on the kids personally. There may be all sorts of reasons why you can't get through."

She rubbed her hands together and blew on her fingers, then went over to poke at the fire in the wood stove. I could see that her mind was going like crazy. Finally she said, "So what do you want to know? What's so all-important?"

"Alfie and T-Rex," I said. "They quarreled, they

didn't get on, but T loaned—or gave—your husband money and even saw that he was included in the Showmen deal. I want to know why and why they had that locker room fight.''

"He didn't give Alfie the money," Suzi said indignantly. "It was all commissions Alfie earned."

"Commissions?"

"Yeah. Horizon Investments. Alfie got T-Rex in on the ground floor. He made him a lot of money. It was no gift."

"Sure," I said. "How come Sammy Allert who handles Parkes's money doesn't know anything about that?"

"These guys are all the same," she said with weary cynicism. "They all want to think they're financial geniuses. Show off to their agents, surprise their wives. Selling athletes investments is a piece of cake, Alfie always said."

"There's more to it," I said. "You as much as told me that the other night. Besides, why was Alfie included in the Showmen deal? That was long before Horizon Investments."

Suzi looked tired suddenly. "Of course you wouldn't know," she said with an irritable sigh. "That's kind of funny, really." She sat without speaking for several minutes then gave an unpleasant laugh. "I guess it's time for ancient history. Ancient history only a few of us know. The big, useful secret of T-Rex Parkes's life." She paused for dramatic effect, and I had to resist the temptation to tell her to get on with it. "He and Alfie'd been lovers."

That was one idea I hadn't considered: stereotypes will get you every time.

"Surprised, huh?"

I shrugged. On reflection, it fit the facts quite nicely.

"All this was long ago when they were just kids," Suzi said. "It wasn't serious with Alfie. Just loneliness and experimentation—Alfie was kind of a wild kid. I wouldn't have married him if I'd thought…" Her voice trailed off and she looked uncomfortable.

I began to see some of the complexities and compromises in her own marriage. "And T-Rex?"

"T-Rex has a real weakness for handsome guys like Alfie," she said. "That's just the way he is."

I digested this. Painful, sure, for Trish, maybe awkward for the children, later, but I didn't see the problem. "We're in the nineties," I said. "Gay liberation, queer theory, civil rights. Who cares, really?"

"Oh, you don't know hockey," she said. "The ultimate macho establishment. Ever watch Don Cherry? The Canadian hockey commentator?"

I searched my mind and came up blank.

"Mouthy guy, fancy suits, stiff collars—you've seen him."

"Ah," I said. "One of my husband's enthusiasms."

"That's Canadian hockey," she said. "Canadian hockey players are men who are men and eat raw meat—that whole thing."

"I'd think T-Rex would fit the bill no matter who he goes to bed with."

"You don't know them," Suzi said. "And you don't know Parkes. He's one angry guy. Dishonest, too; he can't face himself the way he is. He wants to be—I don't know what he wants to be or what his problem is and I don't give a shit. Ask him, don't ask me."

"Was this ancient history generally known?"

"No. But of course Alfie knew," she said slyly. "And I found out."

"Right." She didn't have to say anything more; I could see the picture. Hints and suggestions were enough. T-Rex had kept Alf with him out of fear and, perhaps, affection. Then one day Alf went too far and there was a fight. Then what? I was still thinking about that when Suzi jumped up. "Call your office," she said. "And let's get out of here. I want to leave right now."

SIXTEEN

I CREPT DOWN the road after Suzi's white Honda. The wind whistling through the hole in the windshield defeated the heater, and the mess of cracks combined with the driving storm to reduce visibility to her red taillights and a narrow cone of snow-crossed light. When we reached town, I abandoned the damaged rental at the local gas station and got into Suzi's car. We stopped at the coffee shop long enough to call my office and put all the wheels in motion, then we headed for Montreal and some hard bargaining.

The trip should have taken an hour; in early season snow, it took nearly three—plenty of time for us to hammer out an agreement. In exchange, I got bits and pieces of information, but the real bonanza didn't come until we were installed in a downtown hotel. By that time, my office had contacted Solly, who'd located the family in Morristown, where Wurf had stashed the children. No crisis, Solly assured us, just a power outage—squirrel on the wires or minor accident. He'd dropped off a cell phone and organized for discreet guards.

"Good work, Solly."

"You'll get my bill," he said, "and here's that cell phone number. You got a pencil?"

"Hold off on that," I said. "We're still in negotiations here. We'll call you back in a little while. Tell Mrs. Rene what you've found—everything but the phone number."

I handed the receiver off to Suzi, and she started in

on Solly. While I lay in the bathtub reviving my back, I heard her squeezing out every detail about the children and trying to get around him. Whatever he told her must have been accurate, because when she hung up she was reassured if not satisfied.

"I was worried," she said from the other room when she put down the phone. "I was real worried."

"I don't blame you." I was feeling more sympathetic, having drifted into a pleasant sensory limbo thanks to aspirin and hot water. The hotel tub was large enough to stretch out in and, half asleep, I admired the handsome fittings, the marble sink, the big mirrors, the king-size expanse of tile and brass. Martha would complain about the expense account again, but I'd been in no condition to comparison shop.

"Of course, I would feel better if I could talk to Deena and Marcel."

"And you will," I said. "When you fulfill your end of the deal."

"You can't imagine the anxiety," she said from the doorway. If she was trying for sympathy she'd come to the wrong place. "Going back home—I figured who knew? And then, I began to feel paranoid. When you showed up, I knew I could be trapped there easy."

"You're safe here," I said, "And Solly's topflight. He'll make sure the kids are okay."

"And then?"

"What did I tell you from the start? We have to find your husband's killer. T-Rex is the big suspect, but I'm still betting against."

"It wasn't T-Rex," she said reluctantly. "It could have been, but it wasn't."

"You know that for sure?"

"I thought it was him at the start, I really did. I'd have said something otherwise."

Sure, I thought. "Do you want to tell me about it?" I asked. Although I hated the idea of getting out of the hot bathwater, this was what I was being paid for.

She leaned against the door jamb and considered. "Let's call room service first."

"All right."

She fetched the menu and read me our choices. I opted for pasta; she'd have the chicken. She added a bottle of white burgundy, French pastries, and coffee. Twenty minutes later, I was out of the tub, our food was on the table, and we were both feeling newly civilized. Beyond the gold-and-white-striped curtains, sleet pattered against the windows and the storm blurred the city lights. Safe inside after the trailer and a long, cold ride, we had a new appreciation of central heating, thick carpeting, and room service.

Suzi refilled our glasses and raised hers ironically. We had reached one of those odd moments in investigations that produce a sometimes dangerous rapport, and Suzi was in a reflective mood. "Alfie would have been a great player, a real star, if he hadn't hurt his knee back in 'eighty-seven." That was her premise; probably it had been Alf's, too. If Trish had a story of old debts and old loyalties, the Renes had one of high—and thwarted—expectations. Alf had been destined for greatness; his late-blooming friend, Parkes, had been cast in the supporting role. I could believe it; T-Rex had pretty much told me the same thing.

But the rawboned and awkward center had talent, too, and, as important, durability. Parkes had never been seriously hurt, and as he grew bigger and stronger, he was the one who inherited the megacontracts, while Alf dropped into the precarious ranks of journeymen players. "It wasn't fair, was it?" Suzi asked.

"So Alf began to right the balance just a little?"

"There was nothing *wrong* with that. He just made sure Parkesie didn't forget him. Nothing heavy handed. Just like when we really needed things."

I could see the easy beginnings of what had become a bad habit. "Like house deposits, maybe?"

"Stuff like that, yes. Parkesie never missed the money, let me tell you. And at contract time—what did it cost him to say to Allert, 'See that they keep Alfie. I'm used to having him as a winger'? Nothing, right?"

"But all this goodwill wasn't entirely voluntary, was it?"

Suzi gave me a sour look. "It wouldn't have done us any good to be broke, and it wouldn't have done Parkesie any good for the press to learn about his sexual habits."

That was certainly a neat arrangement, and the Renes had not felt much need to justify their conduct. "Parkes eventually got tired of it, though, didn't he? Was that what that locker room fight was all about?"

"Alfie didn't have much sense," Suzi said regretfully. "When Richie got sick, Parkesie wasn't himself. He had the feeling that maybe it was his fault."

"His child's illness, you mean?"

"When your kids are sick, you don't think logically. He was still running around the way he always had, getting into fights in bars, drinking too much—and picking young guys up once in a while, Alfie thought. Then Richie got sick. Have you see him? He's a cute little fellow. When the diagnosis came in, Parkesie went on the straight and narrow. Literally, in his case."

Yes, I could see that. Terror drives you to magic, to

random, desperate offerings to the gods such as hiring Executive Security. Given T's personality, he wouldn't have done anything halfway. "And Alfie?"

"Listen, Alfie had his troubles, too." She discussed them at length, but the interesting angle was that at some point last year, Alf had, indeed, gone to work for Horizon Investments.

"So why did Bennett Dowling lie about it?"

Suzi waved her hand, an airy, dismissive gesture. "He and I had a thing about a year ago. Nothing too serious. Not on my part, anyway. It was just that Alfie was away such a lot, and Bennett was always after me." She gave a sly smile as if those attentions had not been too burdensome. She had a strong suit in vanity as well as calculation. "But Bennett felt awkward; he didn't really want to deal with Alfie, so he had everything go through Matt."

That seemed an odd way to run a business, but I let that go for the moment. "I'd picked Matt for your friend at the Lakeside."

"Matt? Not likely." She seemed genuinely offended. "Matt Spotwood's a certifiable creep."

"But he's from New Jersey, right?" Sports teams, I knew, attract all sorts of wheeler-dealers. "You knew him before?"

She moved her shoulders eloquently. "Slightly."

"And he introduced you to Bennett Dowling?" I suspected that wasn't the only time Suzi had helped herself and Alfie, too, through friendship with a wealthy and powerful man.

"I think that's right," she said reluctantly. "At one of the big Showmen parties. All the civic wheels were there. Matt and Alfie got along okay, and they went back to when Matt used to run the concessions for the Devils.

That's how Matt started, but he's into a lot of different stuff now. He's an operator.''

I knew that and also that some of his businesses had already crossed the line. Baby had uncovered fraud charges and claims about bad debts. Nothing proven, as the Scots say, but there was a kind of lingering odor. ''He and Dowling were running some kind of operation here, am I right?''

''Bennett has such plans,'' she said with such a wistful note in her voice that I wondered if she regretted leaving, if she'd considered being serious about Dowling, if Alfie'd had a serious rival. ''He really, really wants to do good things for the community. And he'd made commitments, promises.''

She sounded like his PR agent. ''Civic betterment costs money,'' I observed.

''Matt Spotwood came in and promised capital,'' Suzi said. ''It was only temporary, a temporary cash flow problem, and Bennett believed Matt could help him.''

''Spotwood had cash to invest?''

''A little, yeah, but I think what he really wanted was to get his hands on Horizon Investments. Bennett has amassed quite a lot of land and with Disney working on that new planned town...''

''Bennett Dowling has holdings near Celebration?''

''He claims. So,'' she said, ''profit down the road but not yet; he needs money right now, right away. You know how it is.''

I did, sort of, but I wasn't about to go into that with her.

''Anyway, Matt had lots of ideas, and he and Bennett went in together and started buying and selling companies, moving assets back and forth, creating what looked like a lot of profits.''

A corporate shell game, I figured, using companies and lots as super Monopoly counters.

"On the strength of that, they sold a pile of shares in their investment company. That's when they took Alfie on. They really went after the athletes, the community celebrities, trying to create this glamour image."

"T-Rex was one of the buyers?" I asked.

"Yes. Exactly the high-profile buyer they wanted. That's when Alfie was promised full-time work whenever he was ready to leave the Showmen. One more year. He wanted to play one more year and then retire. We'd have been pretty well fixed by then." She sniffled tentatively though her eyes stayed cold.

I decided to ignore this. "So what was the problem?"

Suzi pulled herself together. "They had some losses," she said briskly. "The property market is still volatile—and they guessed wrong on a couple things."

"Big losses?"

"Not that big. They could have recovered them, I think. They could have waited for a turnaround in property values, but Bennett wouldn't do that. He couldn't stand not being on top of everything. I told you," she added with a hint of exasperation, "he had plans. The youth camps, the local restaurant fest, minority scholarships. All those things. Bennett loves helping people, organizing events, and Matt kept saying that he could fix everything, that he could keep the cash flow healthy. Alfie spotted what was happening; he saw Matt gradually taking over the operation and just giving Bennett enough to play philanthropist with."

"Alfie knew a fair bit, then, about Horizon Investments?"

"Yeah." She sighed and poured herself another glass of wine and studied it with a melancholy and regretful expression. "Alfie could be real stupid for such a bright guy." There was a long pause before she added, "We got thinking about the farm—the trailer and the old house and how they would make a nice summer place for the children. That was just after Alfie hurt his back the last time and it looked like the Showmen might cut him. Sales were flat, too, just at that time, and Alfie figured, he figured he'd ask Matt Spotwood for a loan."

She said this with a straight face. I wondered if she had been entrusted with the negotiations. She certainly could be cool enough when she wanted to be. "Did he have anything to back up his request?" I asked.

"He had some papers," Suzi said with a half smile. "He had copies of some letters, balance statements."

I was doubtful. "Salesmen don't usually handle compromising company documents," I observed.

"Well, you know, I was in and out of the office," she said. "I sometimes met Bennett at Matt's house. And the Lakeside—you were right about that. I was around."

What a team! No wonder Bennett had wanted to know where she was. My near car crash made a lot more sense, too. "And did the partners come across with the loan?"

"No, they did not." Her tone was aggrieved. She'd apparently been surprised that not all the world was as blackmailable as T-Rex Parkes. "Things got a bit nasty," she admitted.

"You realize this gives a number of people a motive for Alfie's death, don't you? If any of this had been brought up, Parkes probably wouldn't ever have become a serious suspect."

"I didn't want to get involved," she said. "I had to think of the children. And then Billy insisted that we didn't owe Parkes anything. Why should we get in trouble for him? I was in shock and didn't know what to think, but Billy said to keep quiet and everything would be fine.''

I could see that this was going to be her first line of defense: she'd been grieving widow misled by domineering brother. I wasn't sure I bought that notion, but I let it pass. "Why should Billy care?" I asked. "How was he involved?"

"He wasn't *involved*," she said so quickly that I began to wonder. "I think I should call the children now."

Ever the optimist! "We've got some more work to do yet," I said. I didn't know the half of it. It took another twenty minutes to discover that, in an ironic parallel to Alf's arrangements with T-Rex, Billy had apparently been leeching off the Renes' good fortune for years. Lately, though, Alf had "drawn the line" as Suzi put it. "We had bills for the house, two kids," she said, but, fortunately, Billy had "picked up work" from Spotwood. The exact nature of his duties escaped her, but Billy'd been right about things being fine, for despite their own financial troubles, Horizon Investments had quietly paid off the substantial mortgage on the Renes' house. Although Suzi had previously indicated Billy knew nothing about that windfall, I wondered if he hadn't had some idea—or if he'd had other reasons entirely for staying on after she left so abruptly.

"When did he start to work for Spotwood?" I asked. She was vague about dates.

"Before or after Alfie was killed?"

"Maybe a few months before."

"Maybe?"

"All right, yes," she said irritably. "Yes, a few months before. Billy refused to understand that we had our own troubles."

"Where was he living?" I asked.

"He had his own place by then."

"By then? He'd been living with you earlier?"

"Well, when he first came down.... He needed time to get up a security deposit, the extra rent money."

"Sure," I said. "And when did he move into his own apartment?"

"After he got work."

"With Matt Spotwood?" Matt Spotwood seemed to have represented a bonanza.

"The only work that was available. Billy had a record, and no one was ever willing to give him a second chance." Suzi sounded defensive and upset. She wanted to call the children right away; she didn't trust me or Solly or Executive Security. She went on in this vein for quite a while.

"Listen," I said, "you're a businesswoman. You want high-priced security for yourself and your children. Fine. We can provide. But what I want in return is your husband's murderer. Nothing less."

We got some tears then and a whole lot of drama, all of which gave me some new ideas about what might have happened to Alfie. Finally, we reached the night of his death. "So what did Alfie want to talk to T-Rex about?" I asked. "Assuming he did call him?"

"Oh, yeah, he called Parkesie. Alfie saw trouble down the road for Horizon Investments—this was just after he'd talked to Matt about the loan. He wanted to warn Parkesie."

I thought that was the first attractive thing I'd learned about Alfie; his consort didn't agree.

"I'm not sure why he bothered," she said. "I told him that's not what salesmen did and that he was asking for trouble, but I sure think that was what was in his mind."

At last, I began to see a logical pattern emerging: the Renes were worrisome, both personally and professionally, and what better way to eliminate Alf than by contriving to cast blame on a large, famous, and potentially troublesome investor like T-Rex? I remembered again that Suzi had complained of Alf's fecklessness. "Who else would have known that your husband was going to talk to T-Rex?"

"I don't know if he told anyone," she said evasively.

"You knew," I said. "What about Billy? Was he around the house?"

She jumped up. "It had nothing to do with Billy!"

I was interested in her reaction. "I didn't say it did. I just asked if he was around."

"He was in and out, you know."

"Was he 'in and out,' as you put it, the day Alfie phoned T-Rex?"

"He was over at Daytona that day. Billy liked auto racing."

"So he wouldn't have known what Alfie planned to do?"

Suzi Rene reached a higher level of exasperation. "I hardly knew what Alfie had in mind, never mind Billy. I warned him and I warned Alfie, but would either of them listen to me?"

I knew the answer to that one. She was a sly, indirect person surrounded by impatient and impulsive men. "How did Billy meet Spotwood, anyway?"

When she didn't answer, I said, "It was through you and Alfie, wasn't it?"

In the silence, I had another thought.

"Did Alfie use him to relay messages? After the 'loan' didn't go through? Did he hint through Billy that trouble might be coming?"

"I told Alfie to leave everything to me; I told him that, but he wouldn't listen."

"He maybe didn't know you had an inside track," I suggested. This was nasty but my back was aching again and she was trying to outwait me. Sooner or later the phone company would get the phones back on. Then she'd call her kids the usual way and clam up, figuring she'd already given me enough.

Suzi stamped around the room. I was insensitive; she'd adored Alfie; Bennett Dowling had been just a passing thing.

"Nonetheless, your brother probably knew what Alfie had in mind. And at the same time, Billy was working for Spotwood. This strikes me as a recipe for trouble."

She blew up into another minor tempest: I didn't understand anything.

"Who are you protecting?" I asked. "Or are you still hoping for more? The way things are going, you'll be lucky to get out with what you've got and your personal health intact."

"People owe me," she said stubbornly. "For Alfie."

"Be real! You're on the run, your kids are in hiding. Your husband, his agent, and your brother have all been murdered, and someone took a crack at you, if I'm not mistaken, that night I was nearly run off the road. All that matters anymore are your kids, but if you think I'm going to foot the bill for them without the evidence I need, you're very much mistaken."

"You wouldn't," she said. "The children had nothing to do with anything."

I was afraid she was going to pull out their pictures, but she was still an amateur. "Try me," I said. "T-Rex has a cute kid, too. A cute kid with cancer. That ups the ante."

"I always knew he was the only one you cared about," she said bitterly. "He's the star. That's all anyone cares about."

It's surprising how passionately we cling to the idea of fair shares and turnabout; even folks who are on the shady side themselves dream of universal equity. "I have clients who'd prefer Sherlock Holmes. The world's unfair. So what?"

We considered the nature of things and my undesirability as an investigator for some time. At the end of our discussion, she agreed that her brother probably had known about Alfie's plans and had probably confided them to Spotwood.

I asked the next logical question: "Would Billy have killed Alfie?"

She was pale to start with and went paler. I saw that this was what she had feared. "You'll do anything to get T-Rex off," she said.

I found it interesting that she didn't deny it outright. "You were worried about the possibility?" I guessed.

"He and Alfie had argued," she said in a small voice.

"About what?"

"The usual—money."

"But it was a serious enough argument to have worried you—after your husband was killed?"

She moved her shoulders nervously. "It crossed my mind, but I had no proof, none at all. Billy said he was at Daytona and didn't get back till late."

"They don't race at Daytona in bad weather. The night Alfie was killed there were heavy rains and thunderstorms."

"Billy said something about waiting them out on the way home. He's my brother, after all, my own brother," Suzi burst out. "I didn't cross-examine him. And then everyone was talking about the fight with T-Rex, and the little argument Billy had with Alfie didn't seem so important.''

I could see how T-Rex with his heavy temper and his candor had been a godsend. ''But Billy had that pipe—the one that showed up in T's garage.''

''Oh, that was nothing.'' She confirmed Parkes's story that Alfie suffered nosebleeds. ''Billy was out of control. He said he had to have money to make a fresh start. He could see there wasn't going to be much more from us. I wanted him to go to Jersey, to get out of the way. When he wouldn't listen, I thought that meant he hadn't done anything.''

''Maybe he didn't; we've got several possibles.'' I had another thought. ''And what happened to those interesting papers?''

''I'm not sure,'' she said evasively.

''Would Alfie have had them on him?''

''No,'' she said as if she didn't want to talk about this, either.

''You have them?''

''I had them,'' she said irritably. ''I had them and I'd made arrangements.''

''What kind of arrangements?''

''I had Wurf speak to Matt.''

''Wurf Stanford?''

''Sure. Horizon owns his building. He knew both Matt and Bennett.''

''When was this?''

''Just before you showed up.'' No wonder she lit out for Jersey after I was nearly run off the road.

''Where are those papers now?''

''Billy got his hands on them. I told him he didn't know what he was doing, but of course, he wouldn't listen. We had a real fight about those papers but he was just out of control.''

That put Billy's death in yet another light. "The papers are gone," I said. "Cleaned out of your house."

She shook her head as if regretful over lost opportunities. "He may have tried to sell them," she said. "Matt or Bennett would have wanted them back."

"Possibly," I said, but I had another candidate. I got on the phone and made reservations for a flight into Orlando.

SEVENTEEN

"YOU'RE PERSONA non grata," my usually unflappable head of security told me when I stepped out of the steamy airport gangway into the cool, artificial breath of Orlando Airport.

"Hello, Skipper. I thought you were supposed to soothe all those athletic temperaments." I handed him my carry-on and attempted to straighten my back without sending it into spasms. Considering that I ached all over, I was in a pretty cheerful mood. I had Suzi's notarized statement and, with it, enough information to undermine T-Rex's status as suspect number one.

"T-Rex is on a tear," Skipper reported. "Trish's moved out, and Sammy's apoplectic."

"Really? Let me guess: T-Rex is pulling his cash out of Horizon Investments; Trish thinks her husband killed Billy Deever; and Sammy wishes he'd never heard of either one of us."

Skipper looked momentarily surprised, then laughed. "Pretty good for an old lady," he said.

"Damn right, but you might ease up on my age."

"Not that you're moving well at the moment," he observed. "You look like a linebacker after a tough game." He nodded toward my arm.

"That's the small stuff; it's my back that's totaled. Injury in the line of duty compounded by nonstop travel."

When we got to the car, my mechanism seized up again.

"I've got the cure," Skipper said.

"A large whisky with a Valium chaser would probably do it."

Skipper shook his head in disapproval. I have somehow surrounded myself with moralists and fitness freaks. "I have a friend," he said. He picked up his cell phone and punched a variety of buttons. As I edged into the car, I heard him joking, cajoling. "I know it's game day. We're on our way there! Business." Pause. "Can't say now, but important, Pappy, super important. For the team, too. Well, you know my new line of work..." There was more persiflage, gossip, hints, but within five minutes, Skipper was behind the wheel and we were pointed toward the city. "The Showmen trainer," he said to me. "Hands of genius. He'll have you feeling better in no time."

TUCKED AWAY deep in the interior of the vast arena, the trainer's room was white, clean, and functional, with a big massage table and assorted benches. A portable radio brought in R&B, while a whirlpool in the next room provided a watery obbligato. The masseur was short and compact, with surprisingly long arms and large, strong hands. He clucked with disapproval when I described the train of events that brought me to the point where I could hardly clamber onto his table.

"I see a lot of back spasms," he said as he attacked my frozen muscles. "Mostly boarding injuries. Unavoidable. But lifting! Course players can be careless, too." He commenced a catalogue of back follies: snow shoveling, water skiing, motorcycle riding, other extravagant recreations. I felt no attraction to such spectacular diversions. None at all.

"Some injury here," he said. I winced. As he warmed

to his work, he digressed to the evil competition of mechanical massage and regaled us with an account of a friend's work with racehorses. "They like massage," he said. "More sense than some people." I agreed wholeheartedly. I was beginning to feel better already. Skipper was right; this man was a genius.

While I lay on the table getting maintained, Skipper sat reading notes off my laptop and consulting Suzi's notarized statement. Every now and again he gave an eloquent grunt. When he was finished reading, he said, "With what Baby ran down, I think we've got them."

"We've got our man off, anyway," I said. "I'm sure of that."

"Keep your head down," said the trainer. "Relax, relax. I can't loosen muscles if you won't relax."

"Sorry," I said. I took his point but I had a few other things on my mind.

"I think I ought to call our client's wife," Skipper said delicately. I'd already figured out that Pappy, the genius masseur, was a world-class gossip.

"Right, plus our client and his agent, too."

"The big guy'll be on his way already," Skipper said, checking his watch. "An hour or so. Preskate at six, Pappy?"

"That's right. You'll need to relax a bit more," he told me, "if I'm to get you off the table before the guys come in for taping."

"Right," I said. "I'm relaxing, I'm relaxing. But we'll need to keep an eye out, Skipper."

"Don't worry," he said. "I'll get everything set up."

"And that Detective Harmen. Take my laptop—his number's in there. Don't tell them I'm in town, though, would you?"

Skipper looked quizzical.

"I'm in his good graces—I think—but the Tampa police are still waiting for a statement. Otherwise, the sooner they're involved, the better."

"Absolutely," said Skipper, who is a true believer in the conventionalities, a lover of management, organization, and coordination. He left, happy, with his cell phone and my computer. He would be good with Trish and with Sammy Allert, too, and he'd soon have Executive Security back in everyone's good graces. I had no worries about that. T-Rex was another matter. He had personal problems, a hot temper, and, I guessed, at least some of the compromising documents that had cost his old buddy Alf and his least favorite person, Billy Deever, their lives. I really couldn't relax until I saw him safe on the ice, preferably with round-the-clock protection, and until Spotwood and Dowling were explaining themselves to the police.

I GOT OFF the table shortly before the players started arriving for their pregame skate and found a place to stand in the back of the arena. Skipper soon joined me. He'd missed Trish Parkes, but he'd contacted Sammy Allert. "Sammy will keep trying to get her. She's staying with a friend in Vero Beach. Not too far away and everything's fine there, Sammy says. He was relieved."

"He damn well should be," I said.

Skipper had gotten to the Orlando police, as well. Although Detective Harmen had been difficult, he'd finally shown some interest. "Your name was not magic," Skipper said reproachfully.

"I'm not running a PR business," I said. "All will be forgiven if we're right on this."

Skipper remained noncommittal.

"And T-Rex?"

"No luck. We'll see him come in."

"If he comes in."

"He never misses a practice, certainly not a game. Work ethic in spades," Skipper said.

"I'm not thinking of his playing hooky. He did have some of those papers, didn't he?"

"Yeah. Sammy said he'd come in like a tornado, ordered complaints filed with everyone from the SEC on down and personally threatened Dowling—poor Sammy!"

"I'm betting Spotwood's the lethal one."

"T-Rex probably called him as well. It was vintage tyrannosaur behavior. He's promising to sell every share he owns in Horizon Investments and he's going public with the complaints—not that I blame him."

"How big an investment?"

"A million-five, he told Sammy. Sammy thinks maybe twice as much. Enough to do damage. First thing Monday morning, Sammy's got to put out the sell orders. Of course, Sammy's ripped. He'd never have let T-Rex invest so much in a speculative company, and if T-Rex takes a loss, you know who'll get blamed."

We chewed this over, while I wondered what the odds on T-Rex were and how long we should wait for him to show up and, if he did get here safely, how best to approach the subject of his personal protection. There was his family, too. Though I disliked broaching the subject with him, Trish and the children were going to need some watching as well.

"There he is," Skipper exclaimed, just as I was about to give up. I could hear the relief in his voice. "That's T-Rex just coming around the boards." Skipper stood up and waved.

"Is there somewhere we can talk with him privately?

If we get more tyrannosaur behavior, the whole team will know about it.''

"Why don't you let me handle this? He seems to associate you with bad news.''

Skipper's face was carefully noncommittal. Our head of security is nothing if not tactful, but I was aware of being managed, and I hesitated a moment, expecting professional pride and possessiveness to get the upper hand. Instead, I realized that if Skipper was going to run Executive Security, he'd have to deal with the T-Rex's of the business on bad days as well as good. "All right,'' I said, realizing I'd just made an important decision. "Pacify the client. Meanwhile, I'll try to get hold of the head of security here. No matter what T-Rex wants, we've got to take every precaution.''

ALL THROUGH the preskate and into the first period, Skipper was busy on his cell phone. He'd somehow gotten us into a luxury box unused for that day's game, and while I watched the arriving crowd through a pair of binoculars, he kept trying to contact Trish Parkes. Trish was the key, he'd said when he came back from what he described as a "gale force" confrontation with T-Rex.

"He does understand how much we've improved his legal position?''

"Somewhere in his tiny brain pan,'' Skipper replied sourly.

I knew then that it had been a truly unpleasant meeting; Skipper does not usually run to satire or sarcasm.

Beyond the glass, the crowd noise rose in a deep, muffled roar. The Showmen had a clean breakaway, but, at the last instant, the Bruins' goalie blocked a sure goal and robbed them. As the arena exhaled a collective groan of dismay, I heard Skipper say, "Trish, it's Skipper Norris. How're you doing? Listen, we've got some pretty good news." While the surf of crowd noise ebbed and surged in the background, Skipper summarized the efforts of Executive Security.

"Yes, a signed statement. What it does, is it just really opens up the field. The assumption's got to be that all three killings are related and all by the same person. Right. And we've put T out of the loop on two of them. What's that? No, Anna's found a witness. Well, sure there'll be questions, but we can handle those." Skipper's buoyantly optimistic temperament really belongs in sales. "The main thing is, Trish, we've got to get everyone protection until we run these guys down. And the other thing is you've got to get home to handle T. You know how he is, he's pleased in *one* way..."

The rest was drowned out by the crowd, ecstatic about a shorthanded Showmen goal. I swept the binoculars over the arena and checked out the on-ice celebrations, before following the players back to the bench. T-Rex sat down and hunched forward, still intent on the action. It was good to have him where I could keep an eye on him. Just the same, I scanned the arena and checked that security personnel were still stationed at the top of each aisle.

"Success," Skipper announced when he disconnected. "I think she just wanted to shake him up, get this thing resolved. She knows he's been dragging his feet."

"Good. She'll be back?"

"Tonight." Restless with satisfaction, Skipper walked over to the window and studied the ice. "Even T-Rex will be pleased. I know he didn't think I could do it. I'm going to go downstairs when the period ends and send a message into the locker room.''

I could see that T-Rex Parkes had once again become Skipper's client. Well, he was welcome to every ounce of the skating monster. Meanwhile, I returned to my binoculars and circled the stands. When I refocused on the bench T's spot was vacant. I felt my heart jump. ''Skipper? Has there been a line change?''

''Not yet.'' He rocked easily back on his heels and glanced up at the scoreboard. ''TV time-out's coming up pretty soon. They'll switch lines then.''

I felt a cold little ripple of anxiety. ''Are you sure? He's not on the bench.''

''Extra shift?'' Skipper suggested, but he held out his hand abruptly for the binoculars. He scanned the ice then shook his head. ''A cut maybe. He'd go into the locker room if he had a cut.''

Maybe, but I was unconvinced and the whole setup made me nervous. ''I don't like this.'' Although the big scoreboard hanging over the ice still showed 1:05 left to play, I said, ''Let's get downstairs.''

''Elevator's on the left,'' Skipper said, picking up on my anxiety and moving quickly toward the door. ''We want arena level.''

Downstairs, we found security in the hall and a serious-looking fellow with linebacker's shoulders and bouncer's eyes on the locker room door. It took a call to his supervisor before he opened negotiations. That was good policy, an operating procedure Executive Security endorses and I personally approve; at the same time, we could see that T-Rex wasn't in the tunnel, he wasn't on the ice, and, when the wall monitor showed the bench, he wasn't there, either.

"He went to the locker room, didn't he?" Skipper demanded.

"Yeah."

"He's in the locker room now."

"Message about his kid," the guard said. "It's happened before. When the hospital calls, he wants to be informed right away."

"The hospital?" Maybe test results, I thought, along with certain other possibilities that sent my anxiety meter skyward.

From being laconic to a fault, our security man now seemed ready to bury us in details. "I seen the runner come down a few minutes ago," he continued. "Pressbox guy I know. Richie, that's the kid's name, he's been taken to the emergency room...."

I knew right then that someone very cruel and very savvy was after T-Rex. "Where did he go?" I demanded.

Skipper pushed past the guard as if he were heading for the line of scrimmage and banged open the locker room door. "Parkesie! T! You in there?"

"Where is he?" I repeated.

"Like I been telling you, he's changed and gone. Took off his skates and pads and pulled on a pair of shorts. I saw him leave."

"Which way did he go? Where's his car?"

The guard started gesturing, but Skipper grabbed his arm. "Show us and bring that walkie-talkie."

The guard protested. He couldn't leave the door, he had orders.

"We just talked to Mrs. Parkes," I said. "The little boy's safe at home."

The guard's face changed expression slowly, as if realization was a prodigious physical process. He switched on his walkie-talkie and started shouting into it as he ran down the corridor, "Al, it's Steve. Major problem! Get someone onto the locker room door pronto. I'm heading for player parking."

Ahead of me, Skipper crashed open the metal doors to an outer corridor where the Showmen's trademark teal carpeting ended and plain concrete announced the guts of the arena. Here was where pumps, siphons, and refrigerant created the ice, and the technicians, cleaners, and Zamboni drivers stowed their gear.

"Right and then left," the guard yelled. Another corridor with fluorescent lights and anonymous doors. I ignored distress signals from my back and tried to figure out how much time we'd lost. The Showmen had scored with 1:08 left. T-Rex had left the bench sometime before the 1:05 mark, when Skipper and I headed downstairs. A minute or two for us to reach the locker room; a couple minutes for T-Rex to change.

"How far?" I gasped to the guard.

There was an elevator ahead, and Skipper was already pounding the button, but the guard indicated the stairs.

"One level down!"

Skipper plunged ahead, unmindful of his aging knees, his feet ringing on the bare concrete steps. I scrambled after him down the hot, airless stairwell, while the guard brought up the rear, slowed by the necessity of broadcasting our every move to his supervisor. I sure hoped his boss had taken the warning and was dispatching reinforcements. Down the stairs to the landing, two steps and down again. Skipper jerked open the heavy door at the bottom and we charged into a dark, cramped parking area tucked under the stadium. Orange sodium lights lit the recessed bays formed by the pylons of the great building. At the end of a long narrow ramp, a white rectangle of Orlando sunshine shimmered over asphalt, but our whole focus was on one of the "Reserved— Player" spaces halfway up to the second level.

"Holy shit! Security breach!" the guard announced to his unseen boss.

That was one way of putting it. The other was that a whole lot of things had gone wrong simultaneously. We'd gotten things wrong, I mean Skipper and I, because our client was standing backed up against his beautiful Porsche facing a tall, thin hollow-eyed man with a formidable handgun. The gunman's face was frozen with tension, giving him a remote, artificial expression. I guessed this was Spotwood.

But Spotwood—or whoever—had gotten things wrong, too. Although he'd been smart enough to understand that Parkes would do anything for his son, he'd clearly believed that T-Rex was a rational man who'd be impressed with double-figure calibers and maneuverable to somewhere less public than the Showmen parking area. Mistake. T-Rex was of a different order than the rest of us, and, in his single-mindedness, he was simply ignoring the gun, editing it right out of his awareness. Instead, he was banging on the roof of his car and hollering that he had to get to the hospital right away and announcing to all the world that this shit better stop because Richie needed him and he was getting into his car this minute.

Meanwhile, Bennett Dowling, clambering from the driver's seat of a handsome black BMW, had miscalculated, too. I suspect that he'd seen himself doing chauffeur duty and keeping his hands clean or maybe conducting discreet business negotiations with a semidissatisfied customer. Instead, facing two crazies and a possible homicide, he was vainly appealing to reason, pleading, "Everything was a mistake! Things can be worked out! For god's sake, let's not panic," when Skipper let the door bang shut behind us.

There was a moment to think about Richie, on the verge of losing his father, and about stupidity and greed and the failure to check the obvious, before the security guard set up a squawk for reinforcements.

Hearing our arrival, Spotwood turned, but even in a rage, T-Rex had the top athlete's ability to stay focused. As soon as Spotwood moved, T-Rex was on him. I'd seen Parkes take off on skates, zooming after the puck or racing to check an attacking winger, but he could never have accelerated faster. He closed the gap before any of the rest of us had a chance to move. The gun discharged, a sonic boom in the enclosed concrete shell of the garage, but Spotwood had already been struck by 240 pounds of angry muscle. The pistol hit the floor and skidded under a nearby car. While we waited, appalled, and Dowling dithered half out of his car, T-Rex Parkes lifted Spotwood bodily like some hapless opposing defense man and slammed him into a concrete piling.

"T!" Skipper cried, "Easy, easy, man," and started toward them.

I told Dowling to get out of his car. He was so surprised, he complied. He didn't begin to sputter until I reached over and tapped his pockets quickly.

"Hey, what are you doing? What is this?"

"We've nearly had a shooting," I said.

"I had nothing to do with that!" he exclaimed, his voice rising. "You have no official role here." Dowling had friends, contacts; I was to understand that he was a genuine luminary, a public benefactor, a VIP. Somewhere a mistake had been made; I was petty cash and he was an unlimited credit line.

"Watch him," I told the security guard, who, with less patience and a stronger back, jerked Dowling away from his still running car and onto the walkway around the edge of the garage. I hurried toward the group of struggling men, almost tripping over a hockey stick lying a few yards from the Porsche. T-Rex, I remembered, took bits of his athletic paraphernalia to comfort Richie when he was in the hospital. Whatever they'd told Parkes today, he'd figured it was bad enough to require the stick. I bent and picked it up.

Over against the piling, T-Rex was still trying to dismember Spotwood, and it was taking all Skipper's considerable strength to prevent him. "Don't damage him," I heard Skipper say as he struggled to get his shoulder between them. "That message was a phony. Listen to me! I just talked to Trish. Listen! Richie's home. He's fine. Absolutely all right."

All at once, there was a pause, a sudden silence, a suspension of activity, as T-Rex absorbed that intelligence. He loosened his hold on Spotwood, who shook himself free and began defending himself with noisy accusations.

"Save it," Skipper said. "We're calling the police. We'll get this sorted out."

Spotwood burbled for a minute more about his lawyer, his rights, his injuries, but he'd only been waiting for the right moment, because as soon as Skipper and T-Rex released him, he leaped away with surprising agility and raced down the ramp toward the waiting BMW. The security guard behind me shouted; Skipper made a dive and missed, tumbling onto the concrete. T-Rex tripped over Skipper and lost a step. Spotwood was set to charge by me, when I swung the hockey stick like a baseball bat and caught him across the midsection.

He gave a gasp and stopped, clutching his ribs. I swung again, aiming for his legs, but this time my back turned to mush, the blow was trivial, and he grabbed the stick. I hung on to it just long enough to feel an assortment of muscles parting company with my lower back. Still gasping, Spotwood fumbled with the hockey stick, intending mayhem, but this time T-Rex got it right, for he caught Spotwood from behind in a no-nonsense bearhug and told him that if he moved as much as his little finger, he would break his neck.

Sirens howled at the end of the ramp and an assortment of uniformed security personnel burst from the arena, followed within minutes by the first inquiring minds of the press corps. Skipper limped heavily down the ramp, favoring his long-damaged left knee. As soon as the security people took over, T-Rex went to his car. Over the hubbub in the garage, I could hear him talking to his wife, demanding to speak to Richie, checking on the younger children. "Of course I'm all right," I heard him say to his son. "No danger at all! All straightened away. You never doubted your dad. Sure I will—if they'll let me. The police are here now, so there'll be questions. But I'll get in there for the last period. Right!" His face was shiny with sweat and tears, and he angrily waved off the first officer who approached him.

Skipper hobbled over to the policeman. "It's his son, officer. They told him his son had been taken to the emergency room. The child's a cancer patient."

"And you're?"

"Skipper Norris, from Executive Security."

Even with his tinted glasses and his big hat, I could see the cop's face light up. They like celebrities and interesting cases and something to gossip about, as much as anyone. "Eagles, right?" he exclaimed. "Big touchdown pass against the Cowboys!"

I could see this was going to work out smoothly no matter what I did, and I asked one of the security people to please hand me the hockey stick.

"They'll want it for evidence, maybe; besides it's Parkes's."

"Just give me the stick," I said, "unless you want to have to carry me out of here."

I leaned on the butt end and hobbled over to talk to T-Rex. He was standing beside his car with the phone still in his hand and an exhausted, faraway expression on his face, as if the last few minutes had depleted even his immense resources.

"You've talked to Richie," I said.

"Yes," he said with immense relief. "Yes, Richie's fine." He gave a slight, shy smile.

"They would have killed you," I said.

He focused on me for the first time and scowled. "That's what you were hired to prevent," he said.

Gracious as ever! "Actually, I was hired to find out who killed Alf Rene. Your protection was just a by-product."

T-Rex gave a quick, ferocious smile. "So I owe you."

"You do, indeed. They wanted some papers from you," I guessed.

He said nothing.

"Papers you collected from Billy Deever."

"I didn't get them all," T-Rex grumbled.

"Hence your second visit to the Renes'?"

"He was already gone when I got there."

"I need those papers," I said. "They're your best chance to keep everything on a strictly business level."

I got one of his killer frowns. Sammy was right;

Parkes was a very private man. I would have done well not even to hint at his private life, but I wasn't feeling full of sunshine, either. "Suit yourself," I said. "You started this."

"I didn't know how far it would go," he said. He meant into his life and Alf's.

"Proof, knowledge, you pay for those things, one way or another, but, believe me, incriminating material on Horizon Investments puts Alf's death in a whole other light."

T-Rex thought for a minute then reached into the back of his car and pulled out a manila envelope. "Remember my family," he said, which was as near an appeal as he was ever going to make.

I nodded and tucked the envelope under my arm just as the officer approached.

"You're wanted over in Tampa," he said.

"Tell them I've been out collecting evidence," I said.

EIGHTEEN

WE WERE IN Florida for five days. I spent most of my time talking to semihostile police officers, while Skipper worked with Sammy Allert on media relations and damage control. We got a big break when Forensics found evidence that Billy Deever had been on board Spotwood's sailboat, and more evidence, in the form of bloodstains, when they pulled apart the ship's cabin. That got law enforcement interested in Spotwood's earlier relations with Deever, traceable via subpoenaed bank records. Although Spotwood continued to maintain that Deever had been legitimately employed doing yard work and carpentry in the boathouse, the sums involved—sufficient to buy that spiffy new truck and to rent a comfortable studio apartment—caused general disbelief. It seemed pretty obvious that Spotwood had hired Deever for something important-like, maybe, eliminating Alf Rene.

The real excitement, however, was the involvement of Orlando's favorite mover and shaker, Bennett Dowling. Any number of communities were horrified and fascinated, and speculation about his precise knowledge and culpability soon put even T-Rex's notoriety in the shade.

The key to all this was the sensationalism that soon made even truth irrelevant. That's the trouble with investigations involving big money and powerful interests: sooner or later detection takes second place to public relations—not my forte. I saw the way the business was going, and in watching Dowling and Spotwood and their lawyers stonewall and maneuver, and the Showmen crank up the PR machine, I had a pretty clear picture of what Executive Security would look like if we seriously went big-time. I wasn't sure I was interested; at the same time, to lose Baby and Skipper would be to discard a good part of the firm's value. Between these business concerns, the machinations of the various interests in Horizon Investments, and my continuing interviews with the Tampa and Orlando police, I had plenty to think about during my hours at Suntime Physical Therapy getting my back rehabilitated.

In fact, it was at the physio's one afternoon that Skipper broached the question that had been in the air almost since the day he'd arrived as a sort of glorified intern at Executive Security. I had just finished up my stretches under one of the resident taskmasters when I heard him pedaling for his life on the exercise bicycle.

"How's it going?" he asked, beaming despite the sweat dripping off his forehead. Skipper always looks cheerful at the physio's.

"I'm told I lack application; otherwise, a few more weeks of misery and I can expect improvement."

Skipper clucked in disapproval and pushed the machine into overdrive, his face a mask of determination, his fragile knees small between his muscular calves and thighs. "Golf," he said after a minute. "Golf's my ultimate goal." His smile was rueful.

"It comes to us all," I said. "Or almost all." I had no intention of taking up that expensive, time-consuming, and masochistic pastime.

"Yeah," said Skipper. As he eased up on the machine, the flywheel let out a dry, metallic buzz. "You got a minute? We can get something to drink."

The therapy center had a little courtyard out back with

planters and a couple of umbrella-topped tables where weary clients could relax with healthy fruit drinks and bottled waters. The idea was to sit around avoiding temptation by gossiping about weights lifted, reps done, current diagnoses. It's just the kind of pretty, trendy, oh-so-good-for-you place that I find demoralizing. I think Skipper knew that.

We parked under one of the pink-and-white umbrellas, and Skipper studied the elephant-size horticultural specimens. Gardening appears to be another of his vices. Finally he said, "Remember what I told you when I first came to work for Executive Security?"

"You wanted to learn a business from the ground up."

"Right. And I feel I have. I'll be candid: I can't do everything. This case has taught me that I'd be a lousy investigator; I don't have the touch. Everything else I've got down cold."

"Well, everyone specializes to some extent—even in football, I guess."

"I actually think I'm more versatile than I was on the field. So I don't worry about that. For investigations, I'll have to hire. You could perhaps help me on that."

"Sounds like you're going off on your own," I said.

"I could," he said, "but I'd rather stick with Executive Security—if I had a free hand with it."

It's odd how you make decisions. This had been in the background for weeks if not months, but I hadn't known what I'd decide until that moment when I heard myself say, "I'm too old to change how I run my business, Skipper. The only way to have a free hand is to buy me out."

"I would like to make you an offer," he said.

So there it was: I could retire early and comfortably

with no more for my sins than a cranky back. Harry would be delighted, my accountant, in ecstasy. I could say good-bye to paperwork.

"With Baby as partner," Skipper continued. "I would put in most of the cash, but she'd contribute expertise. I know she's interested."

"Baby's a brilliant analyst. The best around. For leg-work, though, you'll need a couple investigators. Keep Mike Garrett if at all possible. He's as old as I am but awfully good. And Solly in New Jersey is very reliable."

I understood I was taking the offer seriously. If I wasn't careful, I'd commit myself before I left Leisure Land.

"That's why I want to buy the firm," Skipper said. "You have good people, a recognized name, a fine reputation."

"I've got to think about it, though, Skipper. I've got to talk to Harry and the staff."

"When we get back," Skipper said, untroubled. "When we get back, we'll let the lawyers get together."

I had the unpleasant feeling he already knew what I was going to decide. "When we get to D.C.," I agreed, suddenly anxious to escape this depressing retirement paradise with its fitness centers, golfers, and leisure communities.

Skipper smiled. Our stock was up at the moment, and he was contemplating a premium product.

EXECUTIVE SECURITY was in everyone's good graces. We'd decided, in consultation with Sammy Allert, that Skipper was to be the "front man"—a revealing phrase—with the press.

"An irresistible story," Sammy had said as he scribbled notes on his legal pad. We were up in his fancy hotel suite, loafing on rattan furniture in a sea of pastels.

Beyond the metallic tinted window walls came squeals and splashes from the hotel pool. "You've got to like it. Skipper's a story in himself—great athlete making good in a new glamour business."

I raised my eyebrows as I thought of all the boring and unglamorous work that lay behind each little piece of information.

"Bear with me, Anna," Sammy said. "We're not doing a documentary here." Skipper beamed. I could see that he had missed being center stage. His new role as liaison to the media and quarterback of a high-profile case suited him down to the ground, and I had to admit that he was quite brilliant with the press.

There'd been some dangerous moments. At least one of the seamier tabloids had raised questions about Parkes's precise relationship to Alf Rene, but that line of inquiry hadn't gotten too far. Although T-Rex was important in his own world, the sensation junkies really prefer royals and media celebrities. Besides, Richie Parkes took an adorable photo, and the scandal mongers seemed to be opting for miracle cures and fuzzy emotions. Skipper encouraged this strenuously.

"Skipper's work is everything one could wish," I said.

"Then we have Richie," Sammy continued. "The kid idolizes his dad and sees Skipper as the one to clear him. The big guy, knowing he's innocent, is set to tough it out, but he agrees for his son's sake. And what does the investigation turn up? Malfeasance in an investment company that could have taken hundreds, if not thousands, of investors for a ride. It's a dream scenario."

"Alf Rene has almost gotten lost in the shuffle," I observed. True, the police were putting plenty of heat on Dowling and Spotwood, but their respective legal teams were putting on a stalwart slowdown. A criminal trial looked far in the future.

"Remember, your task was to clear T-Rex," Sammy said complacently. "Thanks to your efforts, we now know T should never have been a suspect. Poor Alfie was killed for trying to blackmail the Horizon Investments partners. I don't think anyone doubts that. We can leave further investigations to the Orlando police, who are equipped for the time-consuming forensic work that needs to be done."

That was the official party line.

"We've already done the public a service," Sammy said, "and that's the other angle we need to play up. Whether Dowling knew anything about the dark side of his partner or not, a lot of people would have gotten burned financially if we hadn't started asking questions."

"And if Parkes hadn't snagged those papers," I added, knowing this was a sore topic.

"We'll go easy on that," Sammy said, and Skipper nodded vigorously. "Anything that suggests bodily violence is out, though the papers were important. I think what we'll do is to refer all questions about business to you, Anna, and let Skipper handle the human interest aspects. I think our line is to focus on what your office turned up—the electronic trail, so to speak—and then make clear that the police have various Horizon Investments papers, which had been in Alf Rene's possession. That's how we'll handle that."

I nodded. Of course, this made sense, and Sammy was a master, but all of this getting our story straight was distasteful; it suggested we didn't entirely trust our conclusions. When I mentioned that to Sammy privately, though, he seemed surprised.

"I never had any doubts about T," Sammy exclaimed, looking vaguely uncomfortable. "It's just that he doesn't want to talk about Alfie. So we're saying Alfie presumed on their old friendship, that's all. That T had loaned him money in the past and bought into Horizon at Alfie's urging. But when Alfie started pressing him to buy more, T lost his temper. His famous temper," Sammy added slyly, pleased to be able to spin such an obvious liability.

So that was the story. As for Alf Rene's death, I was convinced Spotwood had hired Deever to eliminate his troublesome employee. Although the police were working away along the same lines, rain, bad luck, and the early focus on T-Rex Parkes had lost crucial time and crucial physical evidence. The upshot was that T-Rex was in the clear, but some questions were bound to linger. I found that unsatisfactory. I'd wanted to go out on a nice, neat case, with no loose ends and no ambiguities. Maybe that was not to be.

Everyone else was elated. Sammy was fulsome in his praises. The Showmen owners, lawyers, manager, and players were touchingly grateful. Skipper even got a charming, laboriously printed letter from Richie. Only T-Rex was silent, and, curiously, I thought better of him for it. Perhaps, like me, he was secretly dissatisfied; perhaps he had other reasons. In any case, I didn't hear from him until months later, when the Showmen were in the initial stages of their Stanley Cup drive.

That was just after news of the sale of Executive Security appeared in the business sections of the Washington papers:

Anna Peters, founder and longtime president of Executive Security Inc., has agreed to sell the company to Malcolm "Skipper" Norris, head of the firm's security services, and to June Quigley, vice president of the corporation. The new owners intend to take the company public and plan to establish a series of branch offices. "The time is right for expansion," said Norris, who is credited with greatly increasing the security and investigation service's business, particularly within the minority community. Peters will no longer have any part in the day-to-day running of Executive Security, but the well-respected investigator has agreed to serve in a consultant's role as needed.

A surprising number of reporters—all remarkably young looking—wanted to know more about this story. They rehashed old cases, interviewed former clients, and asked an assortment of nosy questions. Coached by Skipper, I gave a series of bland and unrevealing answers, until someone asked if I was writing my memoirs.

"Whatever for?" I asked.

"At least six figures," said the reporter, who obviously kept up with the publishing business. Dressed in a trim red suit with an expensive scarf, she looked chic enough to work the Weather Channel or the evening news. Reporters, like detectives, I realized, have gone upscale in recent years to become presentable, franchisable, interchangeable.

"I don't think you understand the concept," I said. "Discretion is our business. If clients want the world to know, they can go on television."

Skipper thought I was less tactful than I might have been; June said it made a nice motto. I sensed I was being indulged and said I thought I'd start cleaning out my desk. I was into the second day of stripping my office and sorting my files when an envelope came bearing the

Showmen logo in one corner. Inside were four hard-to-get tickets to the opening game of their second-round series with the Caps. T-Rex had attached a note: "I'd like you to meet Richie. He and Trish will be at the game."

So the week I officially left Executive Security, I celebrated by taking my husband and the new owners to see the Showmen. We sat directly behind the Orlando bench. Trish Parkes was there, too. The younger children had come for the preskate, then returned to the hotel with the au pair. Richie was to be allowed to stay up to see the whole game. He was dressed in a little Showmen jersey and, although still thin and delicate, he looked remarkably well. His fine blond hair had grown in and darkened, the bluish smudges were gone from under his eyes, and, flushed with the excitement of the stadium and the game, he had the color and vitality of a healthy child.

"I knew he would be all right," Trish Parkes said quietly while her son was talking to Skipper. "As soon as he stopped worrying about his dad."

So she believed in magic, too, just like her husband, but it seemed to have worked. And maybe there was something to her idea, because all through the game, Richie stood up with his hands on the glass, his eyes glued to his father. During the intervals, he chatted with Skipper or examined Harry's sketches, but as soon as the action began, he focused on the game with an almost unnatural concentration for so young a child.

There was between father and son an extraordinary rapport, and I began to see how painful Parkes's situation would have been if he'd been guilty and how difficult it had been even to be innocent. The mess at Horizon Investments and the mass of circumstantial evidence against Deever and Spotwood had already convinced me, but Richie's faith was still impressive. Watching the child's unclouded face, radiant with adoration and joy, gave me the curious feeling that I was seeing the other side of Parkes's soul, the unspoiled, spontaneous part, which, perhaps unwisely, he had suppressed in favor of a conventional masculinity, tinged, given his profession, with brutality.

Certainly his play had an edge to it, and the Caps collected an assortment of bumps and bruises as T-Rex powered up and down the ice, back checking on every play, and going into the corners like a psychotic dinosaur. His play carried the Showmen through a bad patch in the second period, and he set up a late goal in the third that iced the game.

The horn sounded, and, while the sprinkling of Showmen fans danced and cheered, disconsolate Capitols supporters made their way to the exits. Parkes picked up the puck and swept down the ice toward where we stood applauding. With a soft, deft move, he dropped the puck over the glass to Richie, who held it for an instant pressed against his heart, then offered it to me. Beyond the glass, Parkes nodded that I was to take it, and I held out my hand.

"Thank you," I said to Richie.

"To remember us by," he said.

GOING HOME on the Metro, I told Harry that I thought it was the most extraordinary gesture for a child. "It's as if he and Parkes are in some other kind of communication. Even the way he watches his dad the whole game is a bit uncanny."

"It may make for an interesting adolescence," my husband said.

"Maybe they'll lose it before then. Whatever 'it' is that gives them that extraordinary rapport. Maybe if Richie stays well—or if T-Rex"—but then I stopped. I knew that T-Rex had made decisions about his life with just that in mind. He had dedicated himself to his family and to Richie with an almost frightening intensity.

"Or if he did it?" my husband asked.

"Did what? Kill Rene, you mean?"

"He certainly looks capable of it on the ice," Harry observed.

"I think he's capable of quite a bit, but there was never any evidence that he killed Rene and quite a bit to suggest he wouldn't have wanted to—whatever he said in anger. The one he killed was Deever—indirectly. My guess is that Billy would have been spared if he could have turned over those incriminating financial papers. When T-Rex beat him up and took the evidence, Billy couldn't deliver the goods to Spotwood."

"Do you suppose Parkes knows that?" Harry asked.

That was a question I hadn't asked, and I suddenly thought it was a good one. T-Rex had strong, mixed feelings about Alfie Rene, including a lot of old affection and old loyalty. "An even better question is what he thought at the time. I'd like to know just what he thought he was doing. I'd like to know that very much."

"But you're still finished with the case?" Harry asked cautiously.

After having pushed the idea of selling Executive Security enthusiastically, my husband has had a curiously subdued reaction to the actual sale. I'm uncertain whether he hasn't quite trusted me to go through with it or whether he's wondering what I'll do around the house all day. I'm wondering about that myself, but something will turn up. I'm thinking of getting an education, taking up a musical instrument, going to seed in a pleasant way.

"You're never going to get certainty with motivation," I said, feeling philosophical. "But as of now I'm officially retired."

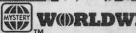

DOWN FOR THE COUNT

Maxine O'Callaghan

A DELILAH WEST MYSTERY

A trip to the mall turns deadly, and only
Delilah West's razor-sharp instincts put an
end to a shooting spree. A dead security
guard is the apparent hero, and Delilah
hopes to keep it that way.

But only when Delilah and her lover's
daughter are abducted, does she begin to
understand the strange twist of events that
have landed both Nicki and herself in a
desperate fight for their lives....

Available December 1998, where books are sold.

MYSTERY WORLDWIDE LIBRARY ®

Brings you the best in Yuletide slayings from

BARBARA BURNETT SMITH
FRED HUNTER
WALTER SATTERTHWAIT

'TIS THE SEASON FOR MURDER

Silent Night

Nothing quite lights up a Christmas party like finding a corpse in the ladies' room in Barbara Burnett Smith's "Mistletoe from Purple Sage."

DEADLY NIGHT

Fred Hunter's Chicago detective, Jeremy Ransom, and his unofficial partner, the seventy-something Emily Charters, discover that a cozy bed-and-breakfast harbors an unsolved murder in "Ransom for a Holiday."

—— Holiday Bonus ——

An original short story, featuring the popular detective Joshua Croft, by Walter Satterthwait.

Available November 1998, where books are sold.

If you enjoyed the many plot twists of popular author

JANICE LAW

then act now to receive these other
Anna Peters Mysteries!

#26179	A SAFE PLACE TO DIE	$3.99 U.S. ☐	$4.50 CAN. ☐
#26201	BACKFIRE	$4.99 U.S. ☐	$5.99 CAN. ☐
#26267	TIME LAPSE	$4.99 U.S. ☐	$5.99 CAN. ☐

(limited quantities available)

TOTAL AMOUNT	$
POSTAGE & HANDLING	$
($1.00 for one book, 50¢ for each additional)	
APPLICABLE TAXES*	$ _____
TOTAL PAYABLE	$ _____
(check or money order—please do not send cash)	

To order, complete this form and send it, along with a check or money order for the total above, payable to Worldwide Mystery, to: **In the U.S.:** 3010 Walden Avenue, P.O. Box 9077, Buffalo, NY 14269-9077; **In Canada:** P.O. Box 636, Fort Erie, Ontario, L2A 5X3.

Name: _____

Address: _____ City: _____

State/Prov.: _____ Zip/Postal Code: _____

Account #: _____ (if applicable)   075 CSAS

*New York residents remit applicable sales taxes.
 Canadian residents remit applicable GST and provincial taxes.

⬡ W◯RLDWIDE LIBRARY ®

WJLBL1